NEUROSHYFT

LOST TIME: BOOK TWO

DAMIEN BOYES

NEUROSHYFT
Lost Time: Book 2
Copyright © 2018 by Damien Boyes.

Editing by Laura Kingsley.
Proofreading by Tamara Blain.
Cover by Wadim Kashin.

PUBLICATION HISTORY
eBook 1st edition / June 2018
Print 1st edition / June 2018

ISBN: 978-0-9950464-2-9

This book contains material previously published as Lost
Time: Part 2 [Headspace] and Lost Time: Part 3 [Shyft].

THANKS_

Mom and Dad, for stoking my love for stories.
Laura Kingsley for help with 'what's he thinking or feeling here.'
Tamara Blain for her grammatical wizardry.
Wadim Kashin for his cover artistry.
My friends and family for their ongoing encouragement.
And to Jacob, Josh, and Maryellen, for the love, support, and constant distraction.

SNOW. *Hands. Swings.*

Still-life snapshots flip across the Dwell's cylindrical surface.

Fireplace. Blocks. Rings.

At first I thought they were endless, that someone had spent a lifetime conjuring an unlimited supply of tiny scenes to decorate the face of an illegal shyft.

Marshmallows. Forest. Wish.

But I've stared long enough to see the cycle repeat.

Bike. Splash. Kiss.

I'm now on my third trip around.

I've got the Dwell upright in front of me, the cup of coffee I brewed an hour and a half ago next to it, and my cuff next to that, charged and waiting.

I take a long swallow from the mug, feel my pulse increase as my Cortex simulates the caffeine buzz.

The coffee's cold but I don't mind. I got used to drinking cold coffee a long time ago. Back in Africa, no thermos, no matter how well insulated, could keep coffee warm during a twelve-hour no-charge watch. And at five in the morning, after ten hours squinting into the monolithic darkness, trying to separate the horizon from the sea of elephant grass without a night scope, when the endless black finally started to bleed from the night, a thermos of cold coffee was better than no coffee at all.

Base Bush wasn't much, just a small forward outpost where the jungle stopped and the grass started. It might have been named for the presidents, but we soon came to understand it had more to do with its remoteness.

I was there to help keep the drones working. Our eyes in the sky, our lines of communication. Our automated sentries and tactical warbots. But after the satellites were taken out, the drones weren't much good for long-range operations. We were left in the dark, literally and figuratively. Lights-out. No-charge to stay hidden from the small, EM-seeking suicide drones the country was lousy with. Zero in on anything more powerful than a wristwatch and explode.

I spent most of my tour there in the dark. Days would drag by, but it was always in the sense of a larger context. It was never boring.

Even when nothing was happening, something always could. Hours spent motionless, hunched over a powered-down autocannon, got tedious, but there was always the tension, the perpetual readiness. Things rarely happened, but when they did they happened all at once. The constant stress had its own problems, but the Ibo and Memoraze helped. And off-duty or on a pass, when there was nothing officially to do, we found ways to creatively blow off the tension.

But here and now? Nothing I've ever experienced compares. Even after the conversations Connie and I had, discussing the Digital Life Assurance and what it might be like to live forever as something both more and less than human, even going through the intake process, I still never really considered what it would mean. I didn't take the time to think about how it would feel. How it would change me. To be completely different than I had been, but still feel exactly the same.

Tension I can deal with, but this is something else. Something I can't even put a name to. Maybe that's what the counselling is supposed to be for.

If it wasn't for this memory in my head—this split second of a man's face before he killed my wife, before he killed me—I'm not sure I'd still be bothering with it all. Probably swallowed a Service bullet already, blown the light right out of my head. But I have a responsibility. The man who murdered Connie is still out there. I have to keep looking for him, no matter what paths I have to follow. No matter what I have to do.

Then I'll decide on the bullet.

I finish the coffee with one long swallow, palm the cuff and affix it to the back of my neck.

This time, when the green dot swells to blue, I don't look away.

THE GREEN DOT expands and explodes across my vision in fractals of red, blue, and yellow. Like I jammed my thumbs into my eyelids, wrapped my fingers around my skull and clamped down.

I move to yank the cuff off my neck but stop, force my hands to stay at my sides.

Relax. Let it happen.

A thick crystal gong peals in my head. Vibrates my bones. It's joined in harmony by a second and then, as a third begins, my face peels loose from the world.

I stumble. The chime continues to reverberate through my skull while the fractals fray at the edges to reveal...somewhere else.

I snapped the cuff on as soon as I woke up. I was on the couch, lying on my side. Now I'm on my feet. A chorus of quiet voices adds to the hum and as they finish I can see again.

Directly ahead of me a 180-degree window to my living room hovers in the air, bobbing as if in a slight breeze, one I can't feel. There's the ceiling, the couch backrest in my periphery, like my eyes are hooked directly to a wallscreen.

Except they're not my eyes.

My eyes are looking at what my eyes are seeing.

I look away to quell the vertigo and glance down. I'm wearing a simple white tunic, loose-fitting pants and paper slippers. Like I'm back at Second Skyn. The skybox above is deep azure, cloudless, like in the long dry summer months during the war, but there's no sun. Light and heat radiate equally from every direction. I don't cast a shadow.

The floor is bare, thin blond bamboo strips covering about five square meters. It's squishy but doesn't give, as though it's lined with stopsuit material. Surrounding the raised floor, and stretching out in every direction, a jade-green meadow ripples like sunlight at the bottom of a swimming pool. Behind me a wide wooden doorframe juts from the floor. A film of iridescent static shimmers where the doors would be.

I take a step back and the window to my world races away from me, now half the size it was. In front of it is a ghostly representation of my prone body cranked around ninety degrees, surrounded by a levitating sphere of my living room.

That's my body.

I've left my body.

I flex my knees to lunge forward, throw myself back into myself, claw my way back to reality. But instead, I close my eyes and inhale deeply. My nostrils fill with the smell of lavender and I hold it for a beat.

Two.

Three.

Pressure to exhale never comes. I'm still holding my breath when I hear a voice.

"Welcome to your Headspace, by Second Skyn," a woman says, her voice in subtle harmony with itself.

I whirl around. A figure is materializing from the shimmering surface of the doorway. A female form, pressing outwards, svelte with smooth features. Her face ripples into a smile.

"My what?" I ask, finally releasing the breath I'd been holding and inhale again, more out of habit than any real need. My voice echoes like I'm in a much smaller place than my eyes tell me.

"Your Headspace," she answers. "An infinitely customizable digital playground in your head. You can come to play, to relax, to explore, or to be someone else. From here you can visit the Hereafter or a million unique worlds. It is yours to do with as you please, and it's with you all the time." Her lips don't move. I can't tell if I'm hearing her with my ears or if her voice is projecting directly into my head. Although, at this point, there's no distinction. Everything is in my head. My ears are out in the room behind me.

She waits as if anticipating a response, and when I don't say anything asks, "Would you like a tour?"

"Why not?" I say with a shrug.

"Excellent," the woman says and steps from the doorway, her body extruding from the film, stretching the glimmery surface until it snaps and she resolves into solid form. As she loses connection to the doorway, her oil-slick skin coalesces into a flowing white gown interspersed with microscopic streamers glowing blue and green, like atomsized shooting stars are raining down her dress.

Her skin flushes with color. Lips warm to a coppery red. Hair darkens to ebony. Eyes fade from the swirling purple and turquoise iridescence to a green that matches the faux grass surrounding us. She strides over to me, her footfalls silent, like she's walking on a cushion of air. She's exactly my height, her eyes line up directly with mine.

"This is your Headspace," she says, sweeping her arm wide to encompass everything around us. The light dims. As I start to wonder if something's wrong the meadow flickers and the ground rumbles and thick green vines erupt from the grass. Trees grow high overhead in seconds, from tender sprouts to a rainforest canopy in the time it takes to realize it's happening.

The jungle grows and thickens until the canopy above is dense with fat, verdant leaves and broad swooping vines, and the air is heavy with moisture and the clicking and buzzing and trilling of a thousand living creatures. The bamboo floor decays to dirt, erupts with vegetation, grows up my feet and around my legs. The doorway thickens to become a moss-covered stone arch adorned with the worn, chiseled faces of ancient warrior gods. Breaks in the leaves high above allow narrow beams of sunlight to make spears in the gloom. It smells like flowers and sweat and decay.

It feels so real.

I know it's all in my head, literally all in my head, but I still have to keep reminding myself.

The woman pauses for a moment, just long enough I'm ready to start exploring, and gestures again. The leaves turn yellow, then brown, then drop from rotted trunks as an industrial miasma consumes the life-rich jungle air. The vegetation decays until I'm standing on a wide asphalt meridian in the center of six lanes of rain-slick night traffic. Boxlike cars, studded with superfluous hoses and yellow-and-black checkerboard decals whine by, smearing trails of red light in their wake. I can taste the petrochemical exhaust, smell the rain on the warm cement.

Around me, anonymous pedestrians hidden behind filter-masks clutch newspapers over their heads or shelter under neon-lit umbrellas, oblivious to the monotonous commands of a Don't Walk sign. Buildings wrapped in the logos of long-forgotten corporations stretch up into the uniformly cloudy sky, their spines lit by glowing blue and green streamers. More traffic soars overhead in overcrowded Skylanes. Spotlights dance on the cloud cover.

The arch has become a video screen. On it a woman with chalk-white skin and dark red lips pops something into her mouth and smiles.

I spin around, trying to take everything in but nothing stays still, and the lights fade, the buildings crumble and reform into a small room around me. Four walls tacked with movie posters. A narrow bed with a plain green bedspread, matching pillows stacked neatly on top. A tall bookshelf filled by the passage of time.

Thick paperbacks along the top.

Thin, flimsy books in the middle.

And large, hardbacked books with well-worn spines and bold, colorful titles along the tall shelves at the bottom.

A double window looks out onto a long stretch of lawn, a rusted swing set, and a depth of pine-treed forest beyond.

I know this place.

Directly ahead is a dark brown door, slightly ajar, the smell of Dad's Sunday dinner seeping in through the crack. Roast potatoes. Gravy.

This is my room.

"Fin," Mom calls from downstairs, her voice young and strong and full of love. "Get washed up for dinner, hon."

My knees buckle and I collapse onto the bed.

It's Sunday afternoon. When Mom would be home from the hospital and Dad would give himself the afternoon off to make a big dinner for the three of us. There would be dessert, apple crumble and ice cream, or maybe cake. We'd play a game. Scrabble or euchre or Crokinole, and then Dad would let me stream a show or two until bed. My favorite day of the week.

"I'll be right down," I reply in my thirteen-year-old voice.

I could stay here. Stay here forever. A lifetime of Sunday dinners with Mom and Dad. I could stop worrying about who had me restored or who's trying to kill who.

I would be safe. And loved.

Forever.

Oh, how I want to stay here.

"Stop," I say, and my voice ages fifty years. "Enough."

The guide sweeps her arm again and everything resets. Blue sky, simple green meadow. I want to cry at the loss, but the tour continues.

Thank God she didn't show me Connie.

"Customization and control of your Headspace is done at the console." She raises her palm and a spot of light opens in the air in front of me, pulls itself into a cylinder then stretches around me into a translucent panel, suspended waist-high. "Now that you've conjured your console, it can be accessed at any time, zoned in or out, by verbalizing the command '*console.*' Now, you try."

The console collapses back to a line, then to a dot and blinks away with a tiny flash.

"Console?" I say, my voice cracking in the middle of the word. Mom's voice still lingers in my ears. I want to go back. Give her a hug, just once more.

The panel reappears and the voice continues. "Good. You can use the console as you would any physical input, or configure it for verbal or mental command. Further instruction is available from the console itself." Again it compresses and disappears.

"Behind you are your aspects," she says, and points to three new bodies that have joined the version of me in my living room. One is young, wearing dark jeans and a striped T, hair long and unwashed. The next me is older, grim, in a striped, blue, high-breasted jacket and heavy pants, a German MP35 slung over his shoulder and a Mauser in a shoulder holster. The third is more like me than I am now, but wearing some kind of Asian clothing, not quite a kimono but close, with flat wooden shoes.

These are *his*. Created by the last guy in my head. I put the cuff on while I was still logged into *my* account. Finsbury Gage, not Gage Gibson.

I've had this tour before.

"As you visit new realities in the mesh, you will often be required to create an aspect custom to that virt. These are found here as well. You can reenter your skyn or an aspect by climbing into it and pressing your face to the world."

She points to the image of my prone skyn, its feet a meter off the floor and only a third of the size it should be. "How am I supposed to shrink myself down and lay in midair?" I ask the woman, not sure if she'll respond.

"When you rejoin the outline of your selected aspect, you will be supported by it."

I cover the short distance to the ghostly form and it grows exponentially as I approach, like my strides are getting longer the more I take, until it's life-sized once again. I look over my shoulder, as if expecting some kind of encouragement, but the guide doesn't so much as blink. It just stands there, waiting. I imagine she'd wait forever, pleasantly smiling as my skyn slowly died of starvation, my heart stopped pumping the blood powering my Cortex and finally the backup fuel cell churned though its reserve and everything crumbled to code around her.

I reach up and place my arm into position, merging it with the ghostly version. It sticks. No matter how hard I pull it won't come free. Using it as leverage, I climb up and lie down into myself.

"Good," the guide says. "Now try moving." I lift my arm and I see my arm rise off the couch through the display. I kick my legs and out in the real world my legs kick too.

"Huh," I grunt. "Now how do I get back out?"

"Think yourself out."

"How am I supposed to do that?"

"Imagine yourself standing back on the floor."

I do. The skyn's limbs grow intangible and I slide out of their embrace and land back on my feet.

"Finally," she says, gesturing to the doorway she emerged from, "this is your oriel. From here, you can access anywhere in the Virt Mesh."

She waves her arm again, but this time instead of the world changing around me, the world on the other side of the doorway does. It resolves to a view of the Eiffel Tower through the fountains in the Trocadero Gardens. The sky is clear, the sun just overhead. Springtime in Paris.

If I were to walk through the door, I'd be standing on the steps of the Palais de Chaillot. Connie and I visited there on our first anniversary, before I started with the Service. I have a vid of her from nearly that exact spot. But in the vid, there isn't a feathered dirigible moored to the top of the tower behind her, nor are there people in leather combat/fetish gear lashed together and playing some kind of game with wide batons and an immense floating ball. Or people outfitted in exaggerated versions of club clothes from the 1970s, with cuffs and lapels so elongated they look like weather socks. Or the cartoon tiger people in overcoats and fedoras. Or the bandage-wrapped guy perched immobile on the mastodon-looking thing. Or what looks like a sentient Rube Goldberg contraption flipping and skeetering and wracking by on the Ave de Nations Unies.

On top of all that, there are hundreds of ordinary people just going about their everyday business. Locals and tourists alike, dressed for a typical April day in France, oblivious to the absurdities in their midst. Living props pulled in from cameras in the real world, used to round off the digital playground with a touch of reality. "This is the Hereafter, the digital reflection of the material world, and the largest virt in the mesh."

Everyone's heard the link reports, the fuming-at-the-mouth docs about perceived horrors, the look-what-your-kids-are doing exposés, but I never paid the Hereafter much attention. It was just another piece of escapist technology that people didn't understand or were afraid of. I had no particular interest in it.

I played games when I was younger, sure, but my life and job were both moored in the real world. Back then, I thought the Hereafter was just another fancy open-world video game with reality as a backdrop.

But what I've already seen—I don't even know how long I've been in here, it could be minutes or hours—has convinced me that whatever is beyond the doorway could be just as real as the place where Connie and I stood arm in arm, the spray from the fountains cool on our faces.

The body I've left on the couch already feels distant. I see how someone could disappear in here forever.

Out in the world my body shudders on the bed.

"This ends the tour," the woman says. "Is there anything else I can show you?"

"That was plenty," I say.

"Enjoy your Headspace, Finsbury," she says, and as she does, the pixels comprising her body dissipate into a glittering cloud and blow away.

I want to walk through the doorway and see what Paris is like today, but that'll have to wait.

First, I need to pay a visit to the guy who tried to wring my head off my neck.

"What a glorious adventure," Elder exclaims, and claps me on the back. I've just spent twenty minutes telling the group about tripping through the Hereafter and he's beaming at me like a proud father on graduation day. "I thought I was going to have my hands full with you, Finsbury, but it would appear as though you arrived here all on your own. Such wonderful progress. So great."

Shelt and Dub seem pleased for me too. They asked questions all the way through, interjecting when they had similar reactions or had visited the same places. The others weren't so excited. Miranda considered her cuticles for most of it and Tala watched Miranda consider her cuticles. Doralai snuck tiny sidelong glances at me during certain points as I spoke, but didn't say anything. Carl glared at me like I'm a race traitor, which maybe I am.

"That does it for another session, travelers. Until next time, keep seeking your perfect self. It is within each of you," Elder says, and then with a flourish of his hand toward the snack table adds, "Refreshment awaits."

I want to ask Elder about the underground neural modification culture, and the Dwell shyft specifically, without seeming like I'm asking about the underground neural modification culture. I am a cop after all. A *rithm cop*. The most obvious narc in history.

I wait as Carl pushes back his chair with a loud squawk of plastic on rubber, hauls himself up and sulks out, then as Miranda gathers her belongings, arranges herself under a light shawl, offers a general "goodnight" to the air and follows Carl. Tala waits back a moment, then follows Miranda. Dora, still seated, gingerly checks her tab.

I walk over to where the others have already gathered around the snack table. Elder and Shelt are sipping coffee from paper sleeves. Dub is crouched, hands extended, massive delts bunched like watermelons, well into acting out an anecdote about shattering an opponent's tibia with a leg sweep during Saturday's qualification bout for the New Gladiators—which explains his limp and lopsidedly swollen face.

"Finsbury," Elder says, setting his coffee down and opening his arms to me. I hope he isn't looking for a hug. I stop just out of reach and he steps into me, grasps my shoulders, looks directly into my eyes. "So. Great."

"Thanks," I say, duck past and pull myself a sleeve of coffee. Elder comes up behind me.

"You've done so well. Can I make a suggestion for your next endeavor?" he asks. "If I'm not being too forward."

I take a swallow of coffee, turn around. "Why not?"

He reaches into his silver vest, pulls out a shyft with his thumb and forefinger, holds it up. Trails of blue dots and orange streamers intertwine over a glowing purple background across its surface.

This might be easier than I thought.

"Ohh, a Dream," Shelt says, peeking over Elder's shoulder.

"What's a Dream?" I ask.

"Duh," Shelt moans. He bounds past Dub to pluck the shyft from Elder's fingers and dances away, shaking it and holding it close to watch the dots and streamers react, flips it to Dub, who's joined us as well, then launches into a breathless rant. "Your Cortex don't let you dream, you noticed that? You go black-out to black-out. They tell us Reszo dreams are too much to handle, too disturbing, so they took 'em away. Shut 'em off. That right there'll rip the blinders free, reveal unforeseen helixes of memory, loosen knots in the ribbons of your subconscious. You'll wake up wrung dry, but like you've ejected a neutron core of emotional baggage. Its creators are on Standards' shit list, cease and desisted, full-on blackballed by Second Skyn. These are impossible to find." He turns on Elder. "Where'd you get it?"

"I have my sources," Elder says, trying to conceal his pride.

"It's legal?" I ask.

"I would never counsel or encourage anyone to use an unauthorized neural modifier," Elder answers hurriedly, but then shifts his tone. "Even though ninety-nine point nine percent of the neuromods designated 'illegal' are perfectly safe when sourced from a reputable dealer and consumed in a controlled situation. The notion that a shyft could conceal malicious code or otherwise damage a rithm is an urban myth, like razorblades in Hallowe'en candy."

I could counter with a charred skyn and empty bank account as proof of his urban myth, but let him continue.

He holds up his fist, pops two fingers. "There are two reasons and two reasons only why certain neural modifications are banned: fear and greed.

"*Fear*," he says, lowers his middle finger, keeps the index rigid. "Those who enact the laws are old and scared and desperately clinging to what they have, terrified of being left behind. They want to keep the restored in line with the 'official' view on human capability. If you can't do it when you were born, they argue, then you shouldn't be allowed to once you've transcended your birth. I couldn't ride a bicycle when I was born, should I never be allowed to? *Ludicrous*." He raises his middle finger once again. "*And greed.* These same lawmakers are in collusion with those that have a vested interest in maintaining a copyright chokehold and distribution monopoly, not only on their 'neural modifiers,' but on our very existence. Your existence." He points at me, pounds his fist to his chest. "My existence. The existence of everyone in this room. They want to control what we do with our minds and monetize what they deem acceptable use. Sell us upgrades at regular intervals and rent our thoughts back to us.

"Until these things change—*until we change them*—we will be slaves, slaves to their bottom line, slaves to our very existence."

He's clearly had this discussion before. It sounds like a manifesto.

"So, it's *legal*?" I ask.

Elder smiles, a wide slit in his hard-boiled egg of a face. "Yes, yes. Of course. Absolutely, insofar as it isn't explicitly illegal...yet. Dreaming isn't a violation of any Standards I'm aware of."

Dub hands it to me and I flip it over, check out the maker's mark on the lid: looping concentric ripples in a pond of liquid silver. "So slotting this isn't any more dangerous than any other shyft I could find on the street?"

"You may have come across things in an official capacity

that I'm ignorant of," Elder says, though I'm sure he doesn't believe it, "but I know of very few instances where neuro-mods caused permanent rithm damage. And those I do know of were the result of untested neural code or a delib-erate attack. There isn't a rithmist worthy of the name who would risk releasing suboptimal code."

"Plenty of people think all rithmists are criminals," I say and raise the paper cup to my lips.

He chuckles. "Rithmists are artists. Those who have answered a calling to explore and expand the psychorithm's very nature. They play the strings of human evolution. They carve new channels for human experience. It is only within the bounds of society's regressive laws that they are considered 'criminals.' He stops, looks through me for a second. "It was a rithmist who cracked the corporate hold over the Cortex. Did you know that? Your mind is yours because of a rithmist. The psychorithm itself was for years unknowable. Neural code translated into machine code by other machines." He raps his knuckles against his smooth skull. "Most of what goes on in our heads is still a mystery—but not for long. Rithmists have been charting the psychorithm, strand by strand. So far they have eighteen percent of it ninety-eight percent deciphered. Eighteen percent of what makes us human." He leans into me. "Have you heard of Eka?"

I shrug. "What's that?"

Elder's tone changes, softens to something approaching awe. "Eka is a person. A great person. No one has been as instrumental in opening the doors of humanity. He was the first. He existed before there was a name to describe what he is. He unraveled Second Skyn's neuromod encryption. He broke down the Cortex firewalls. He freed our thoughts to be our own. He's a legend. A leader.

"A prophet.

"And he's still releasing brilliant new consciousness-expanding mods, pushing us further into ourselves, opening us up for others in the community to dissect as they seek to understand the fundamental nature of our very humanity, and apply that understanding back to each and every one of us."

"We just confiscated a few hundred thousand caps from one of these 'artists,'" I say. Elder nods, purses his lips, maybe unconsciously. More likely letting me know he already knows. "You know about that?"

"There was some linktivity," he concedes. "Rumors."

"What kind?"

Dub and Shelt are engrossed, their coffees forgotten in their hands.

"Idle chatter. Nothing I'm sure your own sources haven't also heard." He knows more than he's letting on. I want to keep pressing, he must know rithmists himself, maybe about Xiao as well, but I need to keep distance between here and work. Church and state, after all.

"Do you think we robbed the world of an art shipment?" I ask. "Are we trampling on humanity's pea shoots?"

"I think you're doing your job, enforcing the laws as written. My complaint lies with those laws, not you. Shyfts are like any other technology—if used without harmful intent, they aren't harmful."

I consider the shyft in my hand. The Dwell back at home, what I've decided I'm going to do with it when I get there. Even if my rithm comes out the other side intact, it's still breaking the law.

But how can I not? If it will get me closer to finding Connie's killer, how can I not?

I know it's illegal. I know it's dangerous. I don't care.

I'll do whatever it takes.

Doesn't mean I'm excited about it.

"You're sure this won't mess me up?" I ask, looking at the Dream, thinking about the Dwell.

Elder smiles broadly. "The only danger is to the Finsbury you've already ceased to be. Let him go and let yourself be who you're becoming."

Even my computer brain can't parse what he's saying. "Is that a riddle?"

"Finsbury," Elder mock whispers, "after what you described to us tonight, I have witnessed a fantastic change in you, in just the time between two meetings. It takes people months to get to where you are. Some never get there—look at poor Carl. I don't imagine he'll ever fully embrace who he is. He's clinging too fiercely to an outmoded idea of himself. I wouldn't give this to you if you weren't ready for it." He doesn't know that I only ventured into my head because I had to. Because it was my only option left. Although that doesn't explain why I spent a day and a half in there. Maybe he's on to something.

"Then thank you for this," I say and pocket the shyft.

"I'll be expecting a full report," Elder says, and puts an arm around my shoulder. "And should you need any guidance, or desire someone with you when you Dream, or simply want to talk about what you see, I'm here for you. You know how to reach me."

"I'll keep that in mind," I say, gently twisting out of his embrace, back toward the circle of chairs. "I have an early morning. I'll see you on Friday."

Dub takes this opportunity to drop right back into a crouch and continue the story he was telling before I walked over.

I grab my jacket from the back of my chair and while

I'm slipping it on I notice Dora still hasn't left. Her tab is on her lap but the screen has timed off. She's watching me from under her bangs. Almost like she was waiting for me.

I duck my head, give her a little smile. "Good night, Doralai."

She doesn't say anything and I head for the door. I'm pushing the bar when she catches up with me. We step out into the lobby and it latches behind us with a clatter that echoes down the dark hallways.

"Mr. Gage," she says quickly, timidly, glancing up at me then back at the brown-tiled floor.

"Call me Fin."

"Fin," she says to her shoes, takes a breath and then raises her head as though her thoughts were made of iron. "Did you really do those things?"

"What things?"

"In your head? Visit those places?"

"I did."

"And you...?" She trails off, but I know what she means.

"It wasn't easy at first. None of this has been, but it gets easier, I think. If you let it." I sound like Elder.

"How?" she asks, and for the first time she looks at me, really looks at me, and I can see the panic in her eyes.

I take a breath, considering, and I'm surprised by my answer, like I'm revealing it to myself as well. "At first, I didn't want to accept that I was different. For the first few days, I tried to force myself into thinking everything was the same as it used to be, or I could will it back into place. But it's not. And even though things aren't the same, it doesn't mean they're worse. In some ways they might even be better. My back doesn't hurt when I bend down anymore."

She smiles, a little. "Can you show me? What you saw?"

"You don't want me. I know Elder would be happy to—"

"No," she cuts me off, the first sign of life I've seen from her tonight. "He expects us all to be like him. I am not like him. What you said, last week, about being a stranger in your own head. I feel that too."

"You'd have to get a cuff."

"I have one," she responds. "My husband bought it for me the first day I came home. It's still in the package."

"Okay, well, how about on Friday? We can pick some place to meet in the Hereafter and I can show you around."

"Can we—can you be there when I first put it on?"

"The cuff?"

She nods.

"Wouldn't you prefer to be at home? Maybe your husband could—"

"No," she says again sharply, and then turns quiet once more. "I'd prefer to be somewhere that isn't so full of...the way things were."

"I get that," I say, remembering how I felt walking into our old condo. "You can come to where I'm staying if you'd like. It isn't much, but it will do for a place to rest our skyns."

"Thank you, Finsbury," she says, then gathers her coat around her and hurries into the night.

I follow a moment later, my thoughts on the Dwell and my stomach quivering at the thought of opening up my head to the unknown.

Ari Dubecki's expecting me. An invitation waits when I get in my head and think up my console.

I reach out to hit 'accept' but hesitate at the last second. This guy has already tried to kill me once. Threatened Mom and Dad. Tried to pry something from my mind. Who knows what would happen if I step out of the safety of my head and into a virt he controls?

I don't trust Dub and I don't much trust Shelt, but Dora —I believe she's being honest with me. She believes Dub is innocent of attacking me, that someone infiltrated his head. And with Dub dead, Shelt convinced he's next, and Dora terrified to be alone, if this is some kind of elaborate con, they're doing a hell of a job.

Something is going on. Whether they're being targeted or whether I had anything to do with it, I can't tell yet. But I'm not going to get any closer to finding out by hiding in my head.

I poke Dub's invitation. The oriel peels open and I push through into the thick, pina colada air freshener balm of Dub's private virt.

A woman anticipates my entrance. She's tiny, wrapped in a red-and-white sarong, with a white tropical flower half the size of her head tucked behind one ear. Her eyes are brown and impossibly big.

She bows slightly and smiles, as if physically apologizing for her lack of English, which, being a simulation, she'd speak if she were programmed to. She spins on the balls of her bare feet and pads ahead of me toward a wide balcony, her body compressing against the intense blue sky.

Shimmering polished concrete glows yellow underneath her feet, and the ceiling is rough, hewn from solid rock. Floor and ceiling bend around the black stone and trickling water and green vines of a living volcanic mountainside. The furniture is simple and modern. Thin white cushions resting on insubstantial wood. Gauzy white curtains blow in the tropical breeze. Further along the rock wall a tunnel carves away into the mountain itself.

Outside a verdant canopy stretches to the island's edge, and the wide-open sea stretches beyond to meet a clean-blown sky.

For a guy who just died, Dub's living pretty well.

I follow the woman through the swaying curtains to the balcony, where a man, short and slight, leans on a railing, his face to the sun, eyes closed as the distant hiss of heavy surf crashes around him. Next to him a thin white tablecloth ripples over an invisible table, set with a narrow bottle peeking from a sweating bucket next to two small square glasses.

That doesn't look like the man who attacked me.

He looks like an accountant.

The man senses our silent approach and pushes up off the railing, turns to meet us, his grin wide but his eyes narrow. He's someone's grandfather, nothing like the hulk in the alley. Pale skin with short, thin hair and dimples in his cheeks. He looks like he should be baking cookies or repairing shoes, not beating the hell out of other human monsters for fun.

But he doesn't move like an old man, his hand shoots out and when we shake his arm moves mine.

He nods a dismissal to the woman, puts his hand on my shoulder and turns down his smile. I resist yanking myself away from his grasp but ready myself for another attack.

"Fin," he says. "I heard about what happened. I'm so sorry. I don't know why I would have attacked you."

"You seemed to have a pretty good idea why when your knee was on my throat, Mr. Dubecki."

He winces and releases my shoulder. "Dub, please. The last thing I remember is lying down for my evening sync and then I was here. I had to be told what happened. I attacked you. Then...a train." He shudders.

I know exactly what he's thinking. He's imagining what it would be like to die. "It's not easy," I offer.

He nods, faces the sky. "I keep picturing it. What would it have felt like? The finality of it all."

I could tell him from experience he's better off not having a detailed image of his death rattling around in his head. I wish I didn't.

"What was in the shyft?" I ask instead.

He turns back to me, perplexed.

"When you attacked me, you held a shyft to my neck," I clarify.

"I wouldn't—"

"I can show you the bruises."

"I didn't know you'd restored. Didn't even know you were planning on it. We were friends, sure, but it's not like I kept up with your life. I have no reason to hurt you. And why would I? The training. The investment. My skyn cost me everything I had. I was supposed to fight Nyx tomorrow. Do you know who that is?"

I nod. "Ludus Humanitech's next superstar. The feeds are all over it. People are saying that's why you killed yourself. You were going to lose."

He sighs. "Of course I was going to lose."

I wasn't expecting that. "You were prepared to die?"

"I wasn't looking forward to it," he says with a tired smile. "But I was going to give Nyx a hell of a fight, and the crowd a show they'd never forget. I'd be the clear contender for the next audition. Not the Novi, but next in line. The sponsors would come hat in hand, and I'd be back with a next-gen skyn and six months of intense training in here. Plenty to defeat Skyrinx or even SaMuelson. This was my ticket. Next year at this time, I'd be on the Humanitech arena team. Now—"

"Your career is over," I finish for him. "They decide you killed yourself, it's on you. No sponsors. No skyn. At least you have a nice virt to retire to."

"That's why I need you to clear my name."

"How am I supposed to do that?"

"I've been thinking, nothing but. I must have been mindjacked, and whoever jacked me used my skyn to come after you."

It makes sense. It's what he tried to do to me. Or whoever was inside his head at the time. "Who would jack you? Who could?"

"Someone we had in common, right? Has to be. Someone from counselling—"

"How do you know it's related? Maybe Nyx was more worried about you than you think, had someone hardlock you, ruin your reputation."

Dub's face hardens. "She would never do that. She'd rather lose."

"Someone else? Close to her, maybe thinking they're doing her a favor?"

"If it was a mindjack I'd still need to ack the shyft. No stranger could get me to do that."

I nod. He believes it, but I know firsthand you never truly know what you're capable of.

"So it had to be someone you know. Do you have family, anyone else close to you?"

"Just a sister. She's in Florida. She didn't agree with my decision to go digital."

"So, counselling—"

"I can't figure how it could be anything but."

"Not Shelt or Dora?"

He shakes his head, definitive.

"Who then? Miranda and Tala are stocked. Carl gave up. Shelt did say Petra and Vaelyn were slinging shyfts..."

He waves the thought away. "They're harmless. Good girls, really."

"They're rolling shyfts from scratch and you claim you were mindjacked. You don't think the two might be connected?"

He steps over to the table, pours himself a glass of clear bubbly liquid, offers the bottle up to me. I shake my head. I don't get the point of putting fake water in my imaginary body. He takes a long sip, then sets his glass back on the table.

"We spent time together," he says, clearly embarrassed. "Petra and Vaelyn and Shelt and I. Sure, we got up to some hijinks. I was like a horny teenager then. The paps got some pictures and they hit the feeds and Poly thought it would be best if I wasn't seen with people...like them. Humanitech didn't want me around where so many shyfts were being openly used. The Gladiators have to stay wholesome."

"Wholesome decapitations, live to link?"

He grins. "Gotta play to your audience."

"So you don't think they'd have anything to do with this?"

"I don't, but I guess it won't hurt to ask."

"Who's that leave then?"

"Elder," he says.

"Dora said he disappeared months ago."

"Sure. That doesn't mean he can't come back."

"There's been no rep-hits, nothing to indicate he's resurfaced."

"It isn't hard to stay off SecNet. Shelt said Dora did it for months."

"But *why*?" I ask. It's the question I keep coming back to. "What would he want from me so bad he'd risk mind-jacking you for the chance to beat it out of me?"

He nods. He doesn't know either. "That's what I can't figure out, but he sure went squirrelly right before he bugged out. Of all the people we know, only he'd be capable of engineering a way into someone's Cortex. He took a real shine to you. Who knows what you two got up to."

"What's that supposed to mean?"

"Fin," he says, looking me in the eyes, "you died in an explosion days after you were suspended from the Service for some kind of misconduct. I don't know the details, but let's not kid ourselves, you were up to something."

Got me there.

He continues, "I'll do anything I can to help. I have resources. Contacts. And I have nothing but time, waiting here while my future is decided for me."

Looks like I'm on the case. "What would you have done in the time you lost?"

He looks up and in, comes back a second later. "Calendar shows training, buzz flails for the upcoming match. A pattern-scan in the aft. I probably spent most of the time with Poly, my trainer at the Ludus."

"I'll need to talk to her."

"Done."

"And I need your dox, comms, anything that might help me get a sense of what might have happened."

He hesitates for a second then shrugs. "Okay."

This has all gotten so complicated. My mysterious restoration. Dub dead. Shelt and Dora terrified they'll be next, their minds invaded. Could Elder really be behind all this? It's hard to believe he could possibly want anything from my head.

Maybe Dora's right, maybe we should run. It'd be easier.

I'd never have to find out who I became, delude myself into thinking whatever I want—

Even as the thought flickers through my Cortex, I know I'm kidding myself. I could never run. Not without finding out what happened first. Not with someone out there, hurting people in my name.

"What will you do if I can't prove you didn't kill yourself?" I ask.

He takes a deep breath and blows it through pursed lips. I imagine it takes a long time to unlearn the habits ingrained in our bodies. There's no oxygen in here but my chest is still rising and falling.

"We live in a strange world, Fin," Dub says. "Stranger every day. Look at me, who would have thought a Jewish kid from North York would grow up to fight for the New Gladiators? The Glads didn't even exist when I was young. Reszos didn't exist. Death was forever." He shrugs, gestures out at digital waves crashing into a digital shore, the artificial warmth from the artificial sun, the simulated ecosystem surrounding us. "As strange as things are, tomorrow they'll be even stranger. And the day after tomorrow the world will be unrecognizable. Did you think you'd ever throw your career and reputation away?" I shake my head, still not willing to accept I did. "I bet Miranda and Tala never expected they'd be stocked for murder, but that happened too. We've changed, Fin. You and I and everyone like us. And because we've changed we're only going to change more. Faster. Every day. All you can do is try to remember who you are, stay focused on it, because the second you look away you're miles from who you thought you were. And it doesn't take long until you're so far from yourself you've become someone else.

"So that's what I'll do. I'll stay here and try to remember who I am."

He turns and leans heavily on the railing, back to the spot he was when I arrived, and the woman in the red sarong returns to show me out.

THE DWELL WEIGHS ALMOST NOTHING, but it's still a struggle to lift it to my cuff. I nearly drop it as I fumble to find the contact port. Finally, I get close enough the cuff invisibly reaches out and snaps the shyft into place. I agree to the warning message without reading it.

My heart thrums like an autocannon as I wait for something bad to happen, for my body to be hijacked or to collapse, spasming in a pool of bodily fluids as my mind's wiped.

A half-second later, the room snaps its fingers and a white screen folds out of nothing, hovers thirty centimeters from my chest, blank except for the word 'RETRIEVE' in bright blue capitals.

I stare at it, waiting for the terrible consequences. But none come.

None I can perceive, anyway.

I stand, step away from the couch and around the screen, run my hand over the smooth surface. It doesn't move, bolted to the air.

"Retrieve," I say, and the screen folds down into a flat

console containing a series of controls. Dates. Words. Smells. Feelings. Locations. It's intuitive enough, I could fiddle with the inputs, rummage through my memories with molecular precision, but I know exactly what I'm looking for.

It won't be hard to find.

"Connie's death," I say, and the room beyond the console shears off in straight edges. Turns the apartment into a life-sized diorama of the moment Connie died. The pale asphalt road. The watery sky. The glowing leaves. The halo of shimmering glass.

The car, its front end obliterated by the compressing edge of the van.

Connie, her mouth contorted in pain.

Happening all again.

I'm in my head. Standing outside it.

My throat tightens and my stomach heaves. I have to look away.

"Back," I croak. The console shows a slider, control buttons, but "back" gets me there. Wheels spin backwards and trees shoot ahead and the car reforms and we have our lives ahead of us.

I step around the screen and the apartment vanishes behind me. I'm standing at the edge of the forest, road gravel sharp under my sock feet, a ghost in a frozen world. The air is cool, scented by the earthy smell of dying leaves.

I walk to the car, pass through the door, sit down into myself.

I'm there. The lingering scent of lotion on Connie's hands. Her fingers on my thigh. This is real. Memory made place.

"Play," I say. "Slow."

The world crawls into motion, creeping toward the inevitable.

We'd been quiet. Mom's passive-aggressive longing for grandchildren in her declining years hit harder than our casual rebuffs of "when it happens" could shield. We'd been trying for a baby without any luck.

I see Connie decide to seduce me. A quickie in the car like a couple of teenagers. How could I refuse?

She put her feet on the dash and pretended to ignore me, pretended to be fascinated by the leaves, but I knew better than that. Her knee rhythmically tapping mine, like it's doing now, revealing her true intentions.

She's going to put her hand on my thigh, and as I think it she does. It's weight warm and comforting and arousing.

I reach out to touch her, but my memory-self doesn't respond and my arm passes through her and I'm reminded exactly where I am.

This isn't happening.

This is a memory.

It'd be so easy. Forget all that's happened since. Lull back into the comfort of in her presence.

A sob catches in my throat.

I want to. More than anything, I want to.

But none of this is *real*.

Either I can be in my body and feel what I felt, live what I lived, or pull out and be a ghost, a detached observer.

My brain hiccups with indecision, but then I know what I have to do.

Ghost it is.

I'm here for a reason. No more wasting time on sentiment. I didn't risk dumping this shit in my head to indulge myself. I'm seeking something important. That's why I'm here.

Still I let myself hesitate before I drop completely from my body and lose her again.

I stand. My feet pass straight through the floorboards, my head out the roof. I step sideways through the car.

"Forward, ten seconds." My voice is rough but clear enough. The AV snaps into view.

"Ten more." The AV beside us. The van rounding the curve ahead.

"Ten more." Our car is filled with flying glass.

"Stop." The sides of the van are a blur, the back of our car, the trees around it—the Dwell trying to reconstruct something I barely saw—but there's a clear, detailed recreation of the van's front left tire, the grill. I can see the dead bugs on the matte black metal.

"Back a half second." The glass shards reform to the windshield.

The van's resolution shifts. Slides up to solidify the narrow windshield—and the driver behind.

"Stop."

I glide through the car and poke my head into the van's interior. Everything within is dark, his features murky, maybe Indian or Pakistani. Southeast Asian.

Everything dark but his eyes. Lit by the sunset slicing through the viewport. Wide, rounded triangles. Determined. But fixed straight ahead.

He isn't even looking at us.

I wonder if he even knew he was killing us.

There isn't enough. If I could adjust the contrast, maybe sharpen the edges—

I have to try.

I think the console and it's in front of me. There are point seven seconds of his image, and it shows me the Dwell can resolve in tenths of a second. Gives seven frames to work with.

It has to be enough.

I spend the next four hours jumping back and forth between my memory and the Service Facial Imager, building a reconstruction with the AMP, refining what little I can, trying to figure out who he is.

When I can't fiddle with it anymore, I set the AMP running, combing through SecNet for the man who killed Connie.

After all this, it better come back with something.

"STICK AND MOVE. *LINE 'EM UP*."

A bot leads me up to the Trainer Deck above the concave arena floor, where Poly, Ludus Humanitech's head trainer and a bunch of others—some in suits, some in sweats, all of them tense—watch Nyx, Dub's former competition, spar with a quintet of combots. Poly's half hanging over the rail, feet in the air, hands cupped to her mouth, screaming at the circling woman below. With her small round head perched on a petite frame, Poly doesn't look like someone who'd be familiar with the gospel of hand-to-hand combat, but she sure as hell preaches like one.

"Feet, feet, feet. *Use the angles*."

Beneath us is the biggest woman I've ever seen. Maybe the biggest person. Full stop.

Nyx.

I don't know what Poly's screaming at. Nyx is midway through a practice round for one of tomorrow night's qualifying heats. Five minutes to disable five combots—two massive warbots and three nimble, six-limbed hunterbots—and she's already disabled two of the hunters and is using the arm of a downed warbot to playfully swat away the third hunter's advances.

I wouldn't want to face down any one of those bots with a squad for backup, and she's playing games with them.

"*Engage*. Find an opening and fucking engage. This isn't a game, *Nyx*!"

Nyx rotates her sculpted head casually. Runs her tongue over thin lips and stares back at Poly. Then she drops the bot arm. Leaves herself unarmed, and her heart-shaped torso exposed to the two remaining bots.

The hunter and warbot fan out in front of her but she doesn't move, continues impassively watching Poly, her face a mask. Playing chicken.

Poly pounds her small hands on the railing, yells. "*Don't. Fuck. Around. Nyx.*"

The warbot lowers its shoulders and charges to catch her around the waist, while the hunter bunches on its hind limbs and launches two tight black fists at Nyx's head, targeted for a knock-out blow at the base of her skull.

"NYX!" Poly screams.

Nyx holds her position until the last second, then side-steps faster than I've ever seen anyone move. She snatches the hunterbot from the air by its oncoming fists and uses its momentum to swing it around and into the oncoming warbot. The hunter crumples against the warbot's massive chest and falls to the floor, twitching. The impact drives the huge bot sideways, unbalanced. It jukes to recover but Nyx is already airborne.

Like she can fly.

She catches the warbot by the head, tucks, spins and lands on her feet with the bot's head in her hands. A second later its body topples behind her.

The whole time she doesn't take her eyes off Poly.

"Fine," Poly says, throwing up her hands. "You win. No more training for today. Get the fuck out of here."

Nyx raises an eyebrow in celebration, and as she struts off the arena floor, she hurls the warbot's head at the still-writhing hunterbot's cranium, shutting it down with a plastic crunch.

"Ten o'clock curfew!" Poly screams at Nyx's back but Nyx just keeps walking.

"I'd rather fight a train too," I mutter.

Poly twitches her head at me and says, "Get what you needed?" to the gaggle behind her, but doesn't seem particularly bothered if they did or didn't as they descend the stairs.

"Dub should be down there," Poly says once Nyx's handlers have left the training decks. She shakes her head and turns to me. "You're the guy?"

"Fins—" *Shit.* "Gage. Gibson." I'm going to have to get used to that name.

Poly clears her throat. "I know who you are. Dub said you'd be coming. A cop was here earlier. Standards. Asked about Dub attacking you."

"Short guy, shaved head and a beard?"

She nods. *Agent Wiser.*

"What'd he say?"

"Wanted to know about your relationship with Dub, if there was any bad blood. Told him he'd have to ask Dub." She reaches up, tightens her already taut ponytail. "Is there?"

"Bad blood?"

Poly nods again.

"Not that I know of, but I'm not the one to ask." She nods and shrugs at the same time, good enough for her. "Do you think he'd have any reason to kill himself?"

"What'd he tell you?"

"Says he wouldn't. Claims he was mindjacked."

She narrows her eyes, wiggles her head. "He barely leaves the Ludus. And we have a strict no shyfting policy backed up by real shitty penalties and daily pattern scans. How's he figure he'd get jacked?"

"That's why I'm here."

Poly doesn't push further and we're quiet for a moment, watching a fresh set of bots trundle out to clean up the scrap on the arena floor. Their bot budget must be huge.

"Anyone you know of might want him out of the way?" I ask, flicking my eyes toward the ruined bots. "Nyx?"

Poly winces. "I wouldn't want to be the one to ask."

"She has a temper?"

"Oh no. The exact opposite. She's as cool as a calculator."

"With Dub out of the way, she's got a free walk to the Arena Team. Sounds like good strategy to me."

She squints at the idea. "Not her style. She's an iceberg but she loves the show. We have a sold-out arena tomorrow night, projected eyeballs in the millions. As it is, we're going to have to parade out the whole Arena Team, run through some bot waves. Finish with a pubbie, hype new prospects for the next audition. Dub was our next big thing. With him gone"—she scratches her head—"it screws all of us."

Still, that doesn't mean Nyx had nothing to do with it. I'm going to have to figure some way of asking her myself. If I had to choose between suspects, rival coworkers with clear winners and losers or a ghost story about a disappeared restoration counsellor with unknown motives mindjacking his way across the city, I'd pick the coworkers. Which would mean no one's really after Shelt and Dora.

And if no one's really after Shelt and Dora, who knows what else might not be true.

I don't have an answer for why Nyx would jack Dub and then send him after me. Maybe as a cover, throw everyone off her trail.

It's thin. But not impossible.

Doesn't explain how Nyx would know that Gage Gibson is really Finsbury Gage, but I put that to the side. I'd rather believe I'm an unlucky bystander in a professional squabble than for this really to be all my fault.

"Did you have contact with him, that last day?" I ask.

"Sure. We trained for two hours, same as every day. Kid was focused. Nearly beat Guilian to death."

"Nothing out of the ordinary, then?"

"People get beat nearly to death around here on a daily basis—" She stops, furrows her brow. "There was one thing. Someone was trying to contact him. Tried a couple times but wouldn't leave a message."

"Do you know who?"

"Some woman. They were always coming around. More distractions. She finally got through to him and Dub left right after training, said he had to meet a friend and he'd be back in an hour or so. I'm not his mommy, didn't pay it much attention."

"Did you tell the police?"

"Of course. Dub gets a strange anonymous call and dashes off and doesn't come back. It was the first thing I told them."

"Could they trace it?"

"If they did they didn't tell me."

"And after that?"

She shrugs. "He never came back."

Poly lets me look through Dub's quarters, but it takes less than a minute to search. An unadorned two by two and a half meter room with a bed, a small table, and a narrow chest of drawers. I've seen more lived-in holding cells.

The drawers contain only clothes, all variations on a short/t-shirt sportswear theme. A lone tab lies on the table. The contents are locked but Poly is able to call up what Dub looked at over the past few weeks and it's mostly fight vids, vanity searches, some business-related correspondence with Shelt, and a smattering of combat porn. Nothing out of the ordinary, except for how ordinary it all is.

Dub was focused on his career, on his future. All he did was train. Who could have contacted him that would have had him come running?

I thank Poly for her time and exit the Ludus through the massive front doors. Night has fallen but the arena's exterior has the sidewalk lit up like a summer day. A summer day that's ten below.

My breath billows like I'm running on steam. I pull my jacket tighter around me, stalk to the curb and wave at the stream of passing Skütes. I figure I'll head home, wait for the Ministry to give me clearance to visit Tala and Miranda in their stocks.

One of the Skütes breaks out of the flow and stops, slides open.

I've got one foot in the Sküte when I glance across the street and notice a kid, maybe early twenties, standing stone still while the pedestrians pass by him. He's watching me. We lock eyes and he doesn't look away, if anything he stares harder, like he's trying to read my mind.

He's about a meter and a half high. Scrawny. Wearing a

windbreaker and loose black pants with his hands uncovered at his sides. I don't recognize him, but that doesn't mean anything. For all I know, six months ago we could have been best friends.

I pull up my tab and try to ID him, but it only takes a second and the low buzz of an error tone to tell me rep-net has absolutely nothing on him, which isn't possible. Rep-net has information on everyone. At least a name.

And he's not hiding his ID. That would show too.

He's a null response. As far as the link is concerned, he doesn't exist. An error message that was never meant to be read.

I step back out of the Sküte and start toward him but before I can round the front of the bulbous vehicle and wade through traffic, he's gone, vanished in the crowd, and I have to add another question mark to an already long list.

WE'RE GETTING NOWHERE.

Galvan and I have spent two days camped out at the Mother Bean Cafe in the Market, downing endless cups of coffee in a haze of secondhand pot smoke while we watch minor shyft deals go down in the park across the street. We've been using the dealers as bait, waiting for cyphers to pop up on Galvan's app, and haven't had so much as a nibble.

Yesterday, I was a ball of tension, perched on my stool in the front window of the cafe, legs cocked, ready to spring the second a red-lined figure materialized on my tab. After the burst of activity in the previous few days, I'd been expecting to be chasing down and hauling in unregistered rithms by the hour, but by the time we gave up and packed it in for the day, we still hadn't seen anything.

Galvan's barely stopped talking since we got here. This morning I flipped the waitress twenty to make sure she only brought him decaf. It hasn't helped.

"—identified three more cyphers," Galvan's saying, not looking up from the tab he's using as a keyboard. He's propped two slender screens against the window, with the third laid out flat. It's like he hasn't left his desk.

"How many's this make?" I'm half listening, scanning the passersby, as though I'll be able to pluck a cypher from the crowd before the app can.

"Eight now. Look at this guy," he says and elbows for my attention. "A SecNet drone tagged him at the zoo—can you believe that, the zoo. Watching the polar bears!" He points to one of his displays, shows me a 3D rendering of a dark-colored skyn. With a broad jaw, sunken cheeks and a tight afro, his head looks like a figure eight. "And this one." He swipes his hand in front of the display to show a female, pixie-cut redhead, features refined to the millimeter, with massive garnet eyes. She looks like a cartoon. "A Service drone tagged her last night, right near here. And this guy." He shows me another white skyn, face like an anvil—squat forehead, angular features and a massive, triangular nose. "Tagged and actually pulled in by a patrol this morning."

"Great, so what's that get us?" I ask. "Eight cyphers out of a few thousand, with one of them in custody? We know anything about him?"

"Not yet," he says with a grin.

Great.

The high I was feeling yesterday is long gone, trickled away while I've sat here waiting.

After reaching into my head with the Dwell and coming back with a clearer picture of the driver, the AMP had come up with over seventeen hundred possible matches. Once I cross-referenced for known location at the time of the crash I'd still only gotten it down to three hundred and twenty-eight.

Three hundred and twenty-eight people who might have killed my wife. I'd been elated, started immediately, worked my way through half of them, one at a time. Thought I had him but kept going, wanted to be sure. I found another possible. Then another. Then a few dozen.

There's no guarantee that any of them are him. He might not even be in the list.

The lies. Stealing evidence. Making myself into a hypocrite. All for nothing. As close as I am, I'm not close enough.

Galvan looks over at me, concerned, and I realize I'm grinding my teeth so hard they're squeaking. I open my mouth a few times to flex my jaw and Galvan goes back to watching his screens.

If I could grab that second of memory and feed it straight to the AMP, have it enhance the contrast and reconstruct the features better than I can manually, I'd have a match. I know it. But jumping back and forth between my memory and the facial reconstruction app won't get me there.

And what if the driver's bio/kin has never been registered? What if it's a cypher? A skyn that was disposed of immediately afterwards?

I can't think like that. I'll find him. I *have* to find him.

I just need to get this memory out of my head and as far as I know, the only way to do that is the ReCog shyft Galvan told me about yesterday. Pull memories out of my head like vid files.

Except I have no source, so unless one falls into my lap like the Dwell did, it means I'm stalled again. The feeling leaves me hollow. Something needs to happen. I can't sit here beside Galvan for another day.

I check myself out of the tab, relog as Gibson, and finally find a response from the message I sent xYvYx waiting.

Who the fuck are you and why the fuck should I care? Try again when you're more than a nobody with nothing to say.

Charming.

But he's right. I've given him no reason to believe me. I need to ante up. Question is, do I open up about the accident and tell him what I know about the blank spots on the link, risking him figuring out who I really am, or forget about him and continue getting nowhere on my own?

What if he did manage to track back to me? What would he do? It's not like I'm breaking any laws—that *he* knows about. So what if he figures out I'm trying to find the man who killed me? I'm a detective.

It's my job.

I work up a response with what I know about the accident—the digital evidence stripped from the link, wiped communication logs, the forensic results from searching the van—keeping it general but letting on that I know more than I do.

If he's as tapped into whatever weird shit is happening on the link as he says he is, he'll know about the accident already, and probably the circumstances surrounding it, but he'll be just as interested in finding out who was driving as I am.

I sit back in my chair, a simple plywood and tubular metal deal that looks like it was rescued from a church basement, and stretch my back. A loader is hovering nearby, its four big turbines kicking up dust and litter as it delivers a load of apples to a small fruit and vegetable shop down the street.

The wooden crate lowers gently to the ground, the straps release and the drone shoots up and away. Third delivery today.

We've been sitting here too long, watching the world go about its business.

We haven't had a hit on the sweep in hours.

Daar and Brewer are out fucking up the investigation into Xiao while we sit around and wait for something to happen.

This is all a waste of time.

"Woah," Galvan mutters.

"What?" I ask, jumping forward to look at his screen, hoping we've got a hit. "Cypher?"

"No—it's the arKade. They're having another one."

"Yeah, you said. In six months." I sit back, deflated, and turn around to signal the waitress for another cup of coffee. "Where's the next one going to be? Maybe we can give the locals a heads-up."

"No," he says, jabbing his finger at his screen. "It's here. They're doing a *fourth* night."

I straighten up as the cloud of gloom in my head lifts. Finally, some good news. "No shit."

"First time ever. Apparently some kind of special request."

Maybe snagging that bag of shyfts in the Market wasn't useless after all. We have another chance to find the arKade before it disappears again. And if the pattern holds, another chance to find whoever's behind the mindjackings.

"You think Xiao somehow finagled a hold-over? Make up for the last one to release his new line of shyfts?"

"Could be," he says, rapidly tapping at the keyboard in front of him. "But without the location, it might as well be in Antarctica."

"It'd be easier to find in Antarctica. There's got to be some way to figure out where it's going to be—one of your sources on the Undernet? Maybe I could ask Elder."

"Elder?"

"My restoration counselor."

"You could try, but unless he gets an invitation..."

"Think. There has to be a way."

Galvan shrugs. "I'll keep an ear out, but Kade is tight with his security."

There has to be a way. An event as big as the arKade doesn't materialize from nowhere.

Another heavy drone whirs over the second-story rooftops, carrying a crate plastered with old routing decals. Back when I joined the military, drones had only just graduated from aerial surveillance and long-range combat to grunt work: hauling gear, construction, medevac. Their advancements still made the feeds, their deployment still caused controversy. Knowing how to operate one was a unique and sought-after skill. Got me through the lean years after the Bot Crash, when most jobs were automated away.

In the twenty years since, drones have become ubiquitous. Blended into daily life and disappeared from notice. They deliver our purchases, clear our waste, and follow us around to keep the rain off our heads. There's a whole command and control system that allows them to navigate the city, and the DroneSense protocol that keeps them from smashing into each other. Their movements are controlled to the centimeter, mapped and logged with SecNet on a minute-by-minute basis.

Which gives me an idea.

The arKade, as secretive as it is, needs infrastructure. A setup as elaborate as Galvan has described isn't just hauled in by hand, one backpack at a time. And for Kade to keep it as quiet as he has, he must not have a lot of help. He's got to be using drones for his heavy lifting.

I get back into my Finsbury Gage account and tell the

AMP to run a map of drone traffic around the lake on the hours leading up to the previous arKade. It comes back a few minutes later. The routing along the shore is light—there isn't much there that'd need a drone's attention: maintenance bots on the turbines. A few environmental sensors. Personal drones following their owners along the beach. And the regular cross-lake paths for the larger shipping drones.

But there are also bursts of heavy activity surrounding an empty spot out in the middle of the water, leading up to and continuing after the arKade would have ended. I tell the AMP to find the boat that must have been there, and start to back-trace the drone paths.

An hour later the AMP hasn't been able to find me a boat, or any evidence that there was anything at all in the lake at the time, but I've got a good map of every origin point for the drones that came within a few hundred feet of the boat that wasn't there.

It's well distributed, a spiderweb of traffic with no clear patterns. Multiple drone suppliers and origins spread out all through the city, routed through various cities via a whole network of shipping companies. I don't have enough of a case to subpoena the payment records for the shipments, and even if I did, I bet I'd find a maze of holding companies and anonymous payments to slog through. But it's something. A toehold.

I can work with this.

For it to remain as secret as it does, the arKade has to be held somewhere remote, or at least sparsely populated, and in a city this size there aren't many of those left, which gives me a variable I can manipulate. I get the AMP to search drone traffic history from around the city, focusing first on the location of the lost time victims. I instruct it to alert me whenever it notices a spike in traffic to a typically under-served location, and then amend the request to alert me of any areas with high activity it can find, underserved or not.

I've got a day and a half before the next arKade meets, and someone out there is ripping people's minds from their heads.

This is the closest we're going to get to an invitation to the party.

I'm going to stop him.

Now I'm spooked.

This is all too much. Who the hell was that kid? He was looking right at me, watching me. I'm not imagining things.

Am I?

Maybe I'm letting Dora's fear and Shelt's paranoia get to me.

Maybe the ball of grief simmering in my stomach is messing with my head.

Maybe it was Elder. Coming to get me. It didn't look like the picture in his dox, but who does these days?

Or maybe I'm losing it.

I forget about going home, retreat to a coffee shop across the street instead. I order a large black and sit in the window across from the Ludus Humanitech, prop my elbows up on the table and drop my head into my hands to shade my eyes from the Ludus' crinkled and shiny exterior.

My mind is racing, a hurricane of thought tearing through my brain. I don't want to be here anymore. It's overwhelming. I don't know how to cope.

I just want to be left alone. To miss my wife. To feel the loss. But I don't even know where Connie's buried.

How am I supposed to grieve for my wife when I don't know who *I* am? Was Constance Gage my wife or the wife of the guy who threw my life away and pulled me into his shitstorm?

Why did he do this to me?

I draw my hands over my eyes, down my smooth cheeks, take a deep breath.

I need to pull myself together. I have a job to do, whether I want it or not.

I shut out the questions, focus on the two things I know for sure: someone pulled me out of storage and someone was behind Dub attacking me. Maybe those two things are related, maybe they aren't, but I'm not going to figure either of them out sitting here talking myself into a panic attack.

I'm still not convinced Nyx didn't engineer Dub's suicide. And if Nyx *was* behind it, then coming after me was a coincidence. It's the simplest answer, and the only way I'll find out is by asking.

I don't imagine she'll take an appointment before the biggest fight of her life, but with the confidence she was showing on the arena floor, I don't think she'll make an early night of it either.

Poly mentioned a ten o'clock curfew. I'd wager my last dollar that means Nyx is heading out tonight. She's already earned her chance at the audition, tomorrow is a formality. Why not celebrate?

I raise my head and have to squint at the sight of the Ludus across from me. It looks like someone made the world's biggest tinfoil ball, lit it with floodlights and excavated a fifty thousand seat arena out of it.

I take a sip of my coffee and settle in to wait.

Nyx will be out soon, I know it.

———

My second coffee isn't even cold before Nyx emerges from the Ludus' side entrance, her entourage trailing behind her, none of them dressed for the weather.

I jump up and race out the coffee shop door, but before I can get across the street, a long hirecar sidles up to the curb and they all pile in.

I flag a Sküte and feed it directions to keep me behind Nyx's car. She takes us out of Reszlieville to a semi-industrial zone in the northeast, where the hirecar pulls to a stop in front of a low brick building.

The building has no name, looks like it might have been a garage at one point, judging by the five roll-up bay doors lining the front wall. It's still early but a line has already formed, stretches along the bay doors and around the corner.

Nyx and her crew pull up behind a line of million-dollar automobiles and leave their car and walk right up to the red rope. She bends over and gives the huge bouncer a hug and he unhooks the barrier and waves her in.

I run up behind her but the bouncer replaces the rope, holds up a giant gloved hand. "Where you goin'?" he asks with a squint.

"I'm with her," I say, pointing to Nyx as the door closes behind her.

"Uh-uh," the bouncer says. "Back of the line."

"I'm on the list," I say.

"Isn't a list," the bouncer says. "Back of the line."

"But—"

"You want to make this into a thing?" he asks with an added growl.

The way I'm feeling right now, yeah I do, but I zip my parka tighter around my neck, yank up my hood and trudge to the back of the line.

The club must cater to the Gladiator crowd, because as I wait, a bunch more living weapons pull up in fancy cars, bypass the line, and walk right in.

An hour and a half later, I'm back at the bouncer and nearly frozen. He smirks as I approach and deducts two hundred bucks from my tab before he lets me pass.

I walk inside and the temperature shoots up forty degrees. I have to peel off and carry my parka over my arm as I push through the crowded club, searching for Nyx.

The club is wide open, smells like perfumed sweat and old grease. The music is loud and guitar-heavy. A smaller version of the Ludus Humanitech's concave arena floor fills the center of the room and inside two amateur fighters in beefed-up skyns are wailing on each other. Big screens above the floor project the action to the people who can't push in far enough to see the carnage for themselves.

The fighters are chopping wood. They've got none of Nyx's finesse or technique, all brute strength and raw stamina. They've got one tactic: inflict the most damage in the shortest amount of time.

The crowd is vibrating, a high-pitched whine of excitement as they watch the two giants carve each other up. Must be the smell of blood.

I'm passing the long bar—ripped men and women in cowboy hats serving both alcohol and Second Skyn-branded shyfts—when one of the fighters screams as his arm is wrenched around backwards with a tearing sound loud enough it drowns out the music and sends the crowd into a frenzy.

I leave them to their butchery and move deeper into the room, finding Nyx in the back corner in a raised VIP lounge.

Her hair's loose and she's wearing a red cylinder of clingy fabric with heels that add another fifteen centimeters to her already towering height. She's got her back to me, talking to a much shorter black guy in a form-hugging suit.

Time for some answers.

I step over the VIP rope and tap her on the shoulder.

She spins, faster than I can follow, and my chest erupts in agony, my arms go limp and I drop to my knees, unable to stay upright.

So. *Fast.*

I cough, blinking through the sudden pain, tears in my eyes. Didn't even see her hit me.

She puts a hand on my shoulder and rolls me up so my face is visible. The short black guy flashes his tab in my face.

"He's a nobody," he says a second later. "Gage Gibson."

"Less than a nobody," Nyx says. She purses her lips then squints at me. "You were in the Ludus today."

"Came..." I splutter, my breath coming in spurts. "For Dub—"

She smirks. "You're here on Dub's behest?"

I nod, not trusting my voice.

She lets me go and steps back. "Ari Dubecki is at best a fool. But better a fool than a coward. Who are you then, to do a fool's business?"

I use two fingers to prod my chest, try to keep the pain off my face. It'll be a hell of a bruise but nothing's broken, I'll live. But not for long if I don't get my shit together.

I wasn't thinking. Haven't been thinking since my restoration. I'm a raw nerve, twitching every time I'm poked.

She's right. I'm nobody. Certainly not a cop. I used to have a badge. It was a club, a wedge, a shield—whatever it needed to be. Without it, who the fuck am I?

Just a guy asking questions no one has to answer.

I've got no angle so I go with the truth. "Dub thinks he was targeted. Mindjacked."

She nods, shrugs. "Quite possibly. But he allowed it to happen. There is no absolution in stupidity. Is your intimation that I am complicit in his shame?"

"Dub said no way." I collect my jacket, get up on one foot. When I'm fairly certain my legs will hold I ease myself upright, resist pressing my hand against my chest. Her entourage is watching, making jokes to each other. "Said he knew he was going to lose. I wanted to find out for myself."

"So you volunteered to play junior detective."

Ouch. That stings more than the punch. "Dub believes he's innocent and he's looking at the end of his career. I've got a skyn and he doesn't, so I said I'd help. I wouldn't be doing my job if I didn't exhaust every lead, and that includes his biggest rival."

She considers this, folds herself down into a curved gel bench. "Dub may be a fool, but he has honor. I don't believe him a coward. If someone were able to occupy his head, it wouldn't have been accomplished by force. He would have rather seen his body broken than give up his mind."

"What do you mean?" I ask.

"Is it not obvious, Mr. Junior Detective? Whatever circumstance led to his death, Dub must surely have agreed to it."

Toward the end of the day, Inspector Chaddah calls Galvan back to the station to go over concerns the Service Counsel raised regarding his cypher app and I tell him to take the cruiser and go, that I'll catch up later. I stay behind in the café and alternate between watching nothing happen on the sweep and watching the real-time updates as the AMP charts and compares and catalogues the tapestry woven by hundreds of thousands of drone paths. Already a ghostly crosshatch of drone traffic covers the city map and it's barely started.

Eventually, my ass and patience both numb from sitting for too long, I get up, stretch my legs and decide I've had enough waiting around for something to happen. I start walking in the direction of my apartment but can't keep from constantly glancing at my tab, swapping between the cyphers and the drones, hoping something will pop before I have to give up and return to my empty life.

Fifteen minutes into my distracted walk, I give up and hail a Sküte, play deaf to the nagging concern as I climb in, and tell it to circle while I watch the tab for cyphers. Maybe moving around I'll be luckier.

I've done two laps between Reszlieville and the Market when the Sküte tries to kill me.

I'm cruising along College St., heading toward the Market, eyes on my tab. Not going too fast, bunched in the commuter swarm, when the Sküte hiccups, lurches in the lane. The sudden movement startles me, sends my pulse galloping. The dash flickers and the muted feeds all freeze.

Something's not right.

"Stop here," I say.

The Sküte doesn't respond. It swerves, knocks into another pod beside me and breaks through into the vehicle lane. This can't be happening.

"STOP," I yell.

"*I found you,*" the Sküte says in its sing-song voice. "*Now I will be whole.*"

The Sküte cuts the internal lights and swerves into oncoming traffic, puts itself into the path of an oncoming bus. I brace myself, waiting for the bus's safety system to see the obstruction ahead and stop or swerve. But it doesn't.

The bus doesn't see me.

My breaths are coming loud and shallow, echoing in the small pod.

"Service Override: Gage, Finsbury," I yell at the dash. "*STOP. NOW.*"

The Sküte doesn't stop. The bus is meters away.

Not again.

I flip my seatbelt off and throw myself against the right side of the pod, force it off balance.

The pod cranks sideways to maintain its center of gravity and pulls far enough I only clip the bus's front bumper and career back into the westbound lane. The

Sküte ricochets off a hirecar and tosses me hard against the seat, spins back into control and races forward once more, straddling the line between lanes of traffic, building up speed, racing toward the red light ahead.

And the six lanes of traffic streaming through the intersection.

I reach inside my jacket to draw my weapon and the Sküte veers sharply to the right, tossing me against the side of the pod, and my head slams against the window. My vision fuzzes and I hear the gun clatter to the floor.

My chest pushes into my back as we accelerate and the gun slides under the seat to the pod's small cargo area.

"*Now I will be whole,*" the Sküte taunts.

I've got about three seconds before the Sküte launches into an intersection full of traffic and I'm bounced around like a pinball.

A fragile, blood-filled pinball.

I need my gun.

I get up into a crouch on the seat and hurl my entire weight against the windshield. It catches me and I watch the road surface get closer as the pod swings forward. The gyroscopes engage a fraction of a second later and the wheel speeds up to pull the pod back upright and I'm catapulted backwards, slam sideways against the back window and roll down to land on the hard seats.

I drop my arm to the floor as the momentum rockets my weapon forward, and it brushes my fingers.

I fumble for it and manage to hook the trigger guard and swing it into my palm, point the gun at the dash—the intersection's red lights now reflecting off the windshield—and empty the clip into the Sküte's controls.

I must hit something important because we jerk hard to the right and slow. Enough that when the pod impacts the side of a northbound transport it bounces off instead of crumpling.

Still, I tumble around like shoes in the dryer.

Tires screech. I slam into something else and roll to a stop with the Sküte lying on its side.

"*I found you,*" crackles out of the pod's speakers.

My head is woozy and I hurt all over and I just want to lie here and enjoy not being dead, but I can't stay in this pod a second longer.

I kick the door open and clamber down and crawl out onto the asphalt.

Cars are stopped around us. Even the Sküte lanes are still.

A crowd is gathering, tabs out.

I need to get out of here.

I work myself to standing and push through the people watching. Someone tries to stop, to offer help, and I mumble something and duck into the first alley I see.

I'm being hunted. This is about the accident, I'm sure of it now. Evidence erased from the link, a threat that made the AMP look silly and now an autonomous vehicle hacked to kill me.

Whoever it is that's coming for me is getting stronger.

I don't know how, but I need to find him, and fast.

By the time I get back to the apartment from the Gladiator fan club meeting, Standards has granted my request to
visit Miranda and Tala.

They're locked in stocks, rithm jail. The self-contained
low-poly virts where Reszo criminals do their time. I'll be in
one just like it if Agent Wiser has his way.

It took less than a year after COPA for the perma-
strapped prison system to realize that incarcerating a
fleshed rithm was a waste of resources. Instead, Reszos
found guilty of breaking the law were stripped of their
skyns and transferred to a cheap binary stock.

What's the point in housing and feeding a body when
you can imprison the rithm for the cost of the electricity
required to keep the stock running?

Shelt submitted requests this morning and Tala's came
back first, Miranda's just after. I book sequential visitations.
The Corrections AMP runs me, as Gibson, through a rep-
check, then warns anything said during the visit could be
used against either of us and when I agree the doorway in
my head opens on an achromatic void.

I step through into a haze of non-color. The ground and sky are the same, endless in every direction. Directly in front of me, arranged in a lopsided triangle, float a long flat rectangle, a hard-backed "L," and two thin boxes stacked face-up on a square—a bed, a chair and books on a table.

There's nothing else, barely a third dimension. Tala is nowhere to be seen.

She can't have gone far. There's nowhere to go. Rithms don't need exercise, so there's no yard, no walls to go over. Rithms don't need food, so there's no mealtime, no guards to overpower. There's no chance of suicide. No one to bribe or cajole or beg. Just the prisoner trapped in a low-fi aspect and nothing to keep her company but her thoughts and the endless, unchanging passage of time.

Human Rights advocates argue stocks are a thousand times worse than solitary confinement, but on the general public's outrage meter the suffering of a few thousand sub-human rithms who got what they deserved is sandwiched between politicians exceeding their stationery budget and choosing the most effective brand of bot polish.

I step through the doorway and my limbs grow leaden, my joints thicken. I look down and I've lost my clothes and any distinguishing characteristics. I'm barely here, a shapeless grey humanoid. A digital mannequin. A feeble facsimile in a no-rez world.

Sensation evaporates from my skin as I approach the empty bed and is gone by the time I get there. My footsteps make no sound. My avatar doesn't breathe. The virt is unearthly silent, my thoughts the loudest sounds I can hear.

I move past the bed, stiff-legged, into nothingness, immediately losing track of how far I've gone and how long I've been walking. A glance over my shoulder shows I've only moved a few meters away from where I entered.

The shimmering doorway back into my head is the only color in this otherwise bleak landscape. I resume walking but can't resist checking back to make sure my escape stays open.

I walk for a while then stop when the bed, table and chair reappear ahead of me, tiny on what would be the horizon, if there was one. I step back and they're gone. Step forward and they return. I turn three-quarters of the way around and take a step and there the furniture is, ahead of me.

Guess I've found the edge of the world.

I turn to my left and resume walking, keeping the bed and table at a consistent distance off my shoulder, until a tiny lump, slightly lighter than the grey haze that surrounds it, materializes ahead of me.

A few more steps and I hear a faint murmur, another few steps and I can make out a tune. I can't hear the words but I recognize the song as one of Klaxon Overdrive's early hits.

Tala. I've found her.

She's wearing an aspect identical to mine, hugging her shins and rocking back and forth with her head tucked between her knees.

I hesitate, trying to decide how best to make my presence known, but before I can, she stops rocking and jerks her head up.

She watches me, her face a mask, then takes a long look around and back down at herself.

"Go away," she says without moving her lips. The sound barely reaches my ears, like she's on the other side of a large empty room.

"Are you okay?" I ask, and the words are snatched away the instant I speak them, like the opposite of an echo.

"You're not real," she says and squeezes her head between her hands. "You're not here."

"I'm as real as you are. Do you remember me? I'm Finsbury. Gage," I say.

She shakes her head. Leans forward and back, forward and back.

"We were in counselling. Do you remember? I need your help."

"No. No, no no nono," she moans, rocking fast now.

"TALA," I yell, but the stock rounds the volume down.

She stops, quivers. Looks up at me. "That's me?"

I can't tell if it's a confirmation or a question. "Tala. Vivas," I say. "That's you."

"*Tala*," she repeats, hesitation in her voice. She stares off into the distance for a long moment, and I imagine she'd be blinking if her pupil-less grey eyeballs had lids. Then her memory kicks in. "That's *my* name," she sobs, heaves a noise that doesn't move her chest. "I tried so hard to forget. Do you know how long it takes to forget who you are?" She starts, sits up, focuses on me. "What's the date?"

"It's January," I say.

"What *year*?"

"2059."

"No," she says, her little voice growing fainter. "That can't be right. It's been years. Decades, surely..." Her words trail off but then she's on me, her frozen fingers hard around my shoulders. "Are you here to get me out?"

"No, I'm sorry. I just came to talk. I need your help."

"Talk?" she pushes me away, scrambles to her feet and barks a noise that's halfway between incredulous and insane. I rise and stay still. "About what? I don't sleep. I don't eat. I can't even touch myself, how could I help you? I can't take this anymore. I've tried to kill myself a hundred ways, but I just won't die." She punches herself in the chest with a painless thud. "There's nothing here to kill."

Tala was a soldier, granted a lucky chance at a new life after a fatal wound in combat. Then something flipped a switch in her and she did a suicide raid on a scaflab churning out skyns in the shape of prepubescent kids. That ended her up in here. Made her like this.

I can't blame her for how she's acting, this isn't her fault. I've only been in this place for ten minutes and I'm already on the verge of losing it myself.

"I don't blame you for a second," I tell her. "But you need to stay alive." I point to my head. "In here. Keep hope."

She laughs, like I'm a fool. "I tried to stay alive," she says. "Used my training. It was useless here. There's no escape. Nothing to resist. The hope dried up real quick. I found one way to survive, and that's to make in there," she points back at my forehead, then swirls her finger around the room, "as blank as it is out here."

"Tala, something's going on out here. Something Shelt thinks you were a victim of."

She doesn't move. The room is motionless. A molecular stillness. Heat-death of the universe quiet.

Then she says, "Maybe I'm innocent."

"I don't know, Tala. I really don't. But somebody brought me back, I have no idea who, and a few hours after that Dub attacked me. You remember Dub?" She nods. "He was dead less than a day later. I just talked to him, claims he says he has no memory of it. Sound familiar?"

"He says he didn't do it?" she asks.

"Did you do what they say you did?"

"They say I massacred a bunch of twisted fleshmiths

fabbing skyns of prepubescents, little boys and girls..." She looks at me, waiting for an argument, continues when I don't offer one. "I don't know what happened, or what I did. I wasn't syncing much. I was shyfting. Letting things slip. I'd had it tough, I didn't complain. Maybe I should have. I'd seen some bad stuff on my last tour and then when I got hurt..." She snaps back to now. "My last memory is from twelve days before I did what I did and as far as memories go, it's nothing special. I was miserable, but I didn't plan on a shooting spree." She stops, turns her head at me. "I wanted to though. I fantasized about it. I found out what those fleshmith bastards were up to but didn't have the guts to do anything. Guess I changed my mind. In the end, they got what they deserved—and so did I. It doesn't matter if I did it or not, if I actually pulled the trigger. I sinned in my heart, isn't that what's important?"

"Not if you didn't actually kill anyone."

She shakes her head. "I don't know. If I did or I didn't, I don't know. It doesn't make any difference now anyway. I'll never get out of here. I'll fade away long before."

Her mind isn't right. This place. *How can we do this to people?*

"Tala," I say. I need to get her back. At least a little. "Look at me. You need to stay you, you need to fight."

"I tried. It doesn't work."

"You know they say you turned the gun on yourself. Would you have done that?"

We look at each other for a second, two lifeless statues in an empty gallery.

"Probably," she finally says. "Maybe that's why I'm here. Maybe that's why you're here with me. If this isn't purgatory, what is?"

She crouches back down, resumes the position she was

in when I found her.

"Did you mention the fleshmiths to anyone?"

"I brought it up in counselling once, Elder wanted me to"—she does finger quotes with her fused action-figure hands—"'open up.'"

"Do you know what happened to him?"

"About as much as I know about what happened to you," she says. "Now I'd like you to leave. You're making me think. It hurts."

"What did happen to me?" I ask.

She levels her gaze at me. "You went from a cop to a guy who ends up kicked off the Service and dead in a gang war or something. Elder was the most grounded guy I ever met, then he just up and vanished. Miranda killed her husband. I did what I did. Things went to shit. Now Dub, you said."

"When did it start?"

She lowers her head, talks to the floor between her knees. "When you died. The cops started coming around and then when Elder ghosted it, that's when it all fell apart," she says, her words barely audible. "It started with you."

I LEAVE Tala and find my way back into my head and accept the invitation to Miranda's stock, go through the same series of questions with the Corrections AMP, take a deep breath, remind myself I'll only be in there a few minutes, and step through the doorway into an identical grey wasteland.

I don't know what Shelt expected me to get out of coming here. Tala was so far gone, I don't know if I can trust anything she said. Except she's saying the same things everyone else has. Somehow I'm to blame for all this.

I expect Miranda will tell me the same thing.

I find her sitting cross-legged on her slab of a bed, a book open in her lap. She jumps up the second she notices me. Her book falls through the floor and rematerializes on the table.

"Where's Sara? Is she okay?"

"Who's Sara?" I ask.

"Sara, my daughter—who are *you*?"

"Finsbury Gage."

She narrows her eyes, takes a step away from me. "You came back," she says. "What do you want?"

She's doing far better than Tala is. "I'm helping Dub. He's been accused of something he has no memory of."

She paces for a moment then rests on the edge of her cot. I pull out the lone chair and mechanically ease myself down.

"They got him too?"

"Who?"

She just shrugs. "Them."

"Do you remember killing your husband?"

"He wasn't my husband," she snarls.

"Then who—"

"I was his toy. His slave. He wanted someone to wear his dead wife's face, and I was dying. Sara would have been left alone, so I did what I had to. Even after he got tired of fucking a replica of his wife and brought one of his daughters home for me to wear—I did that too." She straightens her back, squares her shoulders. "The police and the lawyers and the judge all said I killed him, stabbed him over and over then slit his throat when he tried to crawl away. They say I jumped out of the window and swan dived thirty stories face-first into the pavement." She's angry. That's what's keeping her sane.

"But you didn't?"

"Oh, I wanted to. I imagined it a hundred different ways when he was inside me, calling me his 'little darling,' but I never...I never would have abandoned Sara. God, she must be so scared."

Tala and Miranda are trapped in here, being consumed by their minds. And it could be my fault. "I can check on her for you," I offer. Small consolation.

"You will?" she says, grabbing my arm. "Will you come back and tell me how she is, I have no contact with anyone. You're the first visitor I've ever had."

"I will," I say. "Can you tell me what's the last thing you remember?"

"Laying down for a back-up the night before."

Same as Dub.

"Did your linktivity show contact with anyone in the time before you killed your—"

"*I didn't kill him.*"

"—before he was murdered."

"Just one. A five-and-a-half-minute conversation. But it was anonymous, the IMPs couldn't track the source."

"Did you go anywhere, meet anyone?"

"Rep-checks show I passed through the Market that day. Left my seven-year-old daughter home by herself while I strolled around, bought some fruit. It was still on the counter when the cops came."

"Your defense, they didn't have a theory as to what might have happened?"

"Of course they did. They thought I was guilty. I wanted to fight but the evidence was overwhelming, so I pleaded out. That's why I only got twenty-five years instead of life."

Twenty-five years in here. I'd prefer the death

penalty.

"Did you ever mention wanting to hurt your husband to anyone?"

"No, I—actually, yes. I did maybe say something to Elder about it. I was upset one day at counselling and he tried to console me."

"There's nothing else you can remember, days or weeks before this happened, nothing odd? Even the slightest thing could help."

"Of course there was. You got killed. Then Elder disappeared. The police came by and asked everyone questions. That sure as shit was odd. But it became less so, after everything else."

"And Tala, do you know anything about what she did?"

"I didn't even know her that well, I only saw her once outside of counselling."

"When was that?"

"The night before my husband died. When we went to visit Doralai."

I'M ON THE COUCH, prodding my bruised torso and trying to come up with some way to figure out who's behind the threats, when, at exactly two o'clock, the building announces Dora's arrival. It's as if she's been sitting downstairs, waiting until the precisely arranged time before presenting herself.

I tell the building to let her up, ease my shirt over my blue and yellow chest, and take a last glance around.

I've tided up some. Thrown the old soup cans in the recycler. Wet my hand and ran it around the bathroom sink. Gathered the laundry and piled it in an empty cupboard that just became a closet—I'm eventually going to have to get the housebot started on the laundry. I can't keep ordering new clothes when the old ones get dirty.

I've also gathered up the collection of illicit grams that had been lying on the coffee table and tossed them into a kitchen drawer. No point in outing myself as a professional hypocrite just yet.

A minute later, there's a hesitant knock at the door, like

the person on the other side isn't sure I'm home and, even if I am, would be just as happy if I weren't.

I open the door and Dora's there, hands clamped around the straps of a simple black purse, her feet together, head down, shoulders slumped forward. It's as if she's submitting herself to the headmaster for punishment.

She's wrapped in a simple grey cardigan over a muted pink-and-white floral-patterned blouse buttoned all the way to the neck, loose-fitting grey slacks, and what look like ballet slippers.

I stand aside to let her pass. She peeks up at me, smiles briefly, then notices the bruise on my temple. The rest are hidden under my clothes, but I couldn't hide that one. Her eyes fill with concern and she reaches instinctively toward the mottled skin but stops herself before I have to flinch away.

"Are you okay?" she asks in a quiet voice.

"Commute trouble," I say with as much levity as I can muster and step aside to let her in. "I'm fine."

Her eyes narrow but she scurries by, and then stands in the middle of the room, unsure what to do next.

"Have a seat. Can I get you something..." And as I say that I realize I have nothing to offer. "Water...? Soup?"

"I'm fine," she says, her voice nearly cracking. But she isn't. She's not fine at all. She's terrified.

"Come here," I say, take her gently by the elbow, like I would have with my grandmother, and lead her to the couch.

She slumps down, gnarls her fingers around her purse. I sit in the chair perpendicular, lean forward and lightly clasp her hands. They're trembling.

"Don't be scared," I say.

"I'm not," she answers, her voice breathless.

"Dora, look at me." Her chest swells and then releases. She straightens her back and she looks directly at me, like she's facing down her executioner. Her lips are drawn tight and her eyes have begun to well, fear and anger battling it out. I hold her gaze, try to break through and make some kind of connection. "Just breathe. There's no pressure. We don't have to do anything you don't want to."

"I want to," she says, that flare of defiance once again. She flips open her purse, yanks out a hefty cuff and holds it out to me. It rests on her palm like proof of her resolve. Like an offering. A bulky, gamerboi offering.

It's three times the size of mine. A two-inch semicircle of Harajuku-ready, bright pink-and-purple paisley that'll render her visible from orbit. Whoever bought this for her either hates her or thinks she's a twelve-year-old.

"I would have expected you'd have picked something with a bit of color," I say, keeping my face neutral. "Your initials in shinestone at least."

Her face draws into a confused scowl, just for a moment, and then softens as she realizes I'm teasing. She looks down at the pink pulsing cuff and barks a laugh. Her free hand flies to clamp down on her mouth as if she can't believe that sound came from her body, and her eyes, filled with shocked embarrassment, jump back to me.

I smile back at her, glad for an unguarded moment. One where I don't have to worry about who's trying to kill me.

"It's horrible, isn't it?" she says through her hand. Her voice has loosened up, there's a trace of an English accent. She sets the cuff on the table and stares at it.

"Not at all. The guys at counselling will be very impressed," I counter.

Another giggle fractures the tension and this time she doesn't stifle it. Years crumble from her face as she laughs.

It's like she's a different person, one who isn't carrying around the constant weight of resurrection on her.

"Maybe I should try out a new look to go with it. Dye my hair into cute purple pigtails, borrow my granddaughter's ballerina costume, find some giant silver boots, cartwheel over to my chair and see what they think."

The image of this demure woman suddenly transforming into a linkfeed caricature cracks me up, and I laugh too.

"When was the last time you did a cartwheel?" I ask.

"Yesterday," she replies matter-of-factly, defying me to argue.

"You did a cartwheel?"

"Yes."

"Yesterday?"

"I did," she says, challenging.

"Where did this alleged cartwheel occur?"

"On the sidewalk."

"The sidewalk?"

"In the valley. I walk after breakfast, a half-kilometer. Every day after breakfast for thirty years I walk down to the lake, turn around, and come back." She's narrating now, describing it like it happened to someone else. "Yesterday I went fifteen kilometers without thinking about it. I got to the lake and I wasn't tired, so I kept going and didn't ever need to stop. I found myself in the valley, nowhere near home, no money, nothing. So I did a cartwheel to see if I could."

"How long since your last one?"

She only thinks about it for a second. "Sixty years."

"Welcome back," I say.

"So should I?" she asks.

"Should you what?"

"Put on that outfit and cartwheel in?"

"Elder'd get down on his knees and propose on the spot, I'd imagine, if Shelt or Dub didn't get to you first."

"They couldn't handle me. It'd take all three of them."

This shocks me into silence and then we're both laughing in raw, unrestrained bursts. I remind myself that this woman is older than my mother, and that makes me laugh even harder.

I start to settle down, wiping tears with the back of my hand, when she looks at me, suddenly serious, reaches up, fills each fist with a handful of hair, pouts her lips and twitches an arched eyebrow.

That sets us off again and we're no good for two minutes. When we finally calm down my sides are aching, but it's worth it. I feel better than I have since the restoration.

"It's been a long time since I laughed like that," I tell her. My body feels lighter somehow. Synthetic endorphins probably but who cares.

Dora's reclined her head on the back of the sofa, the heels of her palms pressed against her eyelids. Her long pale neck is stretched, taut. Her chest rises and falls rhythmically, the curve of her small breasts clear through her blouse. Her skyn really is quite attractive, especially when she lets herself smile—and the second the thought passes through my head, I'm stabbed with pangs of guilt.

A wave of disgust crashes through me. Connie's barely been gone a week, what's wrong with me? Why did I even invite her here?

What am I doing?

And why do I have to keep asking myself that?

"Let's get started," I blurt. It comes out far harsher than I intend, and I immediately regret it.

Dora's watching me, her smile waning. I twist my mouth into a grin, try to cover, but it's too late. "I mean, we've got a lot to see today, right?"

She nods and silently fixes the cuff to her neck, trying to figure out what changed. Hell, she might even know.

"Look, I'm sorry," I say. "I just—"

"I understand," she says simply, brushing away my apology. Then she looks at me, really looks at me, and I look back.

She knows what it's like, being a stranger to yourself and desperately terrified to accept that stranger as the truth. To realize that everything you are, however familiar, is not what it was.

Suddenly I get what Elder was talking about.

I'm no longer me. I'm something else. Something very similar, but nothing like I was. And while it might cause the old me some pain, this new me can be whoever I want.

I never expected I'd get here, to within sight of accepting what I am, but realizing it might happen one day eases some of the angst I've been carrying around. I don't have to be afraid of myself.

I think she sees that too. We're very different, she and I, but in the same ways. Then she blinks, looks off into the distance. "There's a green ball floating in your living room. Did you know that?"

"I've seen it," I answer.

I walk her through entering her Headspace, warn her what's going to come when she gets in, and study her empty features while she tours her head, oblivious to the outside world. She's gone for a while, and as I wait the same thought keeps returning: maybe she does understand.

Maybe I don't have to do this by myself.

I'м deep into my second day off in a row, and my lack of progress in finding Connie's killer, the nameless threat hanging over me, and the knowledge that we still don't have a location on tonight's fourth and final arKade are squeezing my thoughts from all sides.

All this not knowing is making me mental. No matter what I try, I can't seem to get traction, every burst of momentum stalled. I feel powerless and tense. Can barely concentrate. Barely sit still.

Yesterday, Dora invited me to the Hereafter with her and I almost declined, but couldn't stand the thought of staying cooped up in my apartment by myself, surrounded by my failures, so I agreed. And when we returned from our visit to the 1970s' New York era, I couldn't bear the thought of being alone and suggested dinner. She insisted on treating me at a family-owned Korean place before counselling, and when the meeting ended slipped out with a shy wave.

I need to be careful with her. Keep this professional. Friendly, but professional. She's fragile and I'm fragile and I don't want this to turn into something neither of us wants or is ready for.

With nowhere else to go, I hung around after counselling ended, watched twenty minutes of the Dub-and-Shelt Show until they packed it in to hit a nearby pub and left Elder and me alone in the echoey gymnasium. Just he and I and the smell of the maintenance bot's floor cleaner.

Once we were alone I gave in and asked him about the arKade. He gave me a look, as if judging whether I was asking as Fin, member of his counselling group and potential disciple of his Transhumanist Manifesto, or Detective Gage, rithm cop.

Whichever way he landed he enthusiastically answered my questions, offering up details Galvan hadn't mentioned, giving me the backstory on Kade and *her*—he quickly corrected me—band of renegade fleshmiths while I helped him clear away the remnants of the scones and returned the coffeemaker to the kitchen.

He described the arKade's origins as part club, part market, and part audition. A loose-knit collection of fleshmiths, genitects and rithmists exchanging information and ideas. Cooperating and feuding. Tinkering with and remixing the building blocks of life.

Eventually the group became dominated by a charismatic figure known as Kade. She was the most determined, the most vocal. Why should we be limited to these husks that were bequeathed to us at birth, unasked for? Shells of skin and meat that didn't reflect who we really were on the inside? She was an early addition to Standards' Most Wanted.

She started the arKade—at first a place to learn and teach—as a safe place for people like her, where the desire to transcend humanity wasn't seen as an illness. Eventually, it became synonymous with the constant evolution of biotechnology. The mobile church of self-directed human evolution. Prodian Mecca. Doors open only to worthy supplicants and those able to afford their personal Past-Standard indulgences.

That's where she lost Elder—she made it exclusive. She made it about herself instead of the work. Elder's post-human future doesn't exclude anyone who wants in.

He knew it had been held over a week under extenuating circumstances but claimed not to know the location and I believed him. If he knew he'd have told me he knew but couldn't tell me. Elder isn't one to hold things back.

I walked out with him and he shook my hand and clapped me on the shoulder, gave it a lingering squeeze before jumping in a Sküte and leaving me on the sidewalk.

No closer to finding the arKade's location, I tried to force myself to calm down. Held off checking the results of the AMP's ongoing drone activity scan until I walked home, but found my feet moving quicker and quicker until I finished the last kilometer at a run, and when I arrived, sweaty and disheveled but not winded in the slightest, the AMP still hadn't produced any conclusive results. So I gave myself a rule: only one check an hour.

In between peeks at the agonizingly slow mapping of the drone traffic, I meticulously cleaned my apartment, a one-man shack-party like I was readying for inspection. Squared off the bedsheets, scrubbed down the kitchen, finally got the bot on the laundry.

I didn't sleep. Put on the closest thing I had to work-out clothes—boxers and an undershirt—and went for a run through Reszlieville before the sun came up, surprised at how many others were out doing the same thing.

Eventually, jogged-out with my apartment shimmering, but still no results from the AMP, I dove into the Hereafter. Emerged every hour on the hour to check the scan—until just now, when I popped out of a WWII adventure virt to find the scan finished, with three locations meeting my search criteria.

My heart rate jumps and my mouth dries up. It takes only minutes to eliminate two of the results—a movie shoot that's been camped in a quarry up north for two weeks, and a small music festival setting up in a park in the west end—

which only leaves one: an old bank building in the downtown core.

Closed for conversion to an agri-tower five months ago, it only got halfway done before the developer was brought up on corruption charges. It's been empty ever since.

The drone traffic logs show a heavy flow of large transport drones within the last week—up to one a minute at times. Whatever's going on there looks like a huge production. Construction's on hold. No event permits issued for the address. It's not remote, but no one's going to stumble into a barricaded office tower by accident.

This has to be the place.

I've found the arKade.

If there were someone here now, I'd break a personal rule and give up a high five.

I call Galvan. He answers audio-only, the clink of utensils on china in the background.

"We're on," I say. "I've got an address on the arKade."

I hear him excuse himself and then the squawk of a chair on a wooden floor. The suppertime din quiets.

"Are you sure?" he says, his voice hushed.

"I told the AMP to check SecNet for drone requests where drones aren't usually requested."

"Woah, yeah. Of course, but we're not on shift and I'm up at Mom's. I'll call the inspector," he says. "We'll need to brief the response team. Daar and Brewer will want to know. Get TAC spun up, tell them what to expect, who to look for."

A spike of covetous anger flares through me.

"This is ours," I say, keeping my sudden emotion out of my voice. "We caught this case. We found the location. Someone's targeting Reszos, rich asshole Reszos, granted, but either way, I'm not letting those two fuck this up."

"I understand your hesitation, Fin, but bringing down the arKade could be our first big break into finding Xiao. If it was held over at his request, he could be there in person. It could also launch a dozen new lines of investigation. Give us leads on the Five Marks—the five biggest Reszo crime organizations on the planet. Not to mention underground fleshmiths and rithmists. And bring down Kade himself—"

"Herself," I correct him.

"Her—what?"

"Herself. Kade is a woman."

"How..." He pauses. I hear him shake his head. "Anyway. We can't risk imperiling these potential leads. You have to think about the big picture."

Fuck the big picture. I'm not going to stand aside and let Daar and her smirking partner mess up the biggest bust in rithm crime history.

"Forget I called. Go back to your dinner. I'll handle it myself."

"What do you mean 'you'll handle it yourself?'"

"It means I'll handle it."

"Kade will have security. Perhaps dozens of potential threats. Bots. You can't go in yourself. You need backup."

"Then you're welcome to join me."

He's quiet on the other end.

"It's against every regulation," Galvan says. "And simple common sense."

"What if I'm wrong about the location? Then we mobilized the entire force for nothing. If I'm right, the inspector isn't going to care about regulations when we hand her an international threat to the Reszo community—and Xiao in the process. You haven't been around the Service long enough. If we come at them in force, they'll see us a mile away. This has to be handled quietly."

Galvan considers this for a moment, as if internally weighing the options of breaking Service protocol with the unknown allure of cracking a case wide open. "We won't get in trouble?"

"I'll take full responsibility. How long has the department been after Xiao, playing by the rules? That cypher sweep you made wasn't by the book—look how that turned out."

"I don't know—"

I give him the address. "Meet me in the PATH below the building at zero-hundred hours. And dress safe."

"Okay," Galvan concedes. "I hope you know what you're doing, Fin."

"Trust me," I say, and he clicks off.

My face cracks a smile. A shiver of anticipation flutters through me. Finally, some progress.

Now all I have to do is figure out a way past what I'm sure will be Kade's extensive security and get to Kade without getting Galvan or myself killed.

AFTER WHAT SEEMS like an eternity in the stocks, I come out of my head into a world saturated with color, my tiny apartment a luxurious palace. Room temperature a sensory buffet. As hard as they have it, I don't know how Miranda and Tala aren't both gibbering loons by now.

But I know this: I can't run anymore. I can't pretend I'm an innocent bystander in my life.

All these people I touched the last time around, all of them are worse off because of me. Dora. Shelt. Dub. Miranda. Tala. They all said it, every one.

This started with me.

Miranda and Tala and Elder and Dub and Dora. Even Galvan. All of them hurt or suffering because of something I started. Just because I can't remember it doesn't mean it didn't happen.

There's no one else I can blame, no convenient coincidence to hide behind.

I started this.

So I need to fix it.

Something happened in that counselling group. Something that made each and every one of us a target. I don't know if the mindjacks are a diversion or a way to get us out of the way or the ultimate goal, but they're happening. No way all these people committed wildly out-of-character acts all so close together.

Someone is behind this.

Everything points to Elder. He has the capability. He knew each of the victims. But what's the motive? Why would he want into our heads?

And what do I have to do with it? What did he and I fall into?

Everything points to Elder—

Except, everything *doesn't*.

Dub received a call from a woman. Someone he knew. Someone he'd race out of training to meet. Then he acked a shyft that got his body snatched out from under him and sent after me.

Miranda and Tala visited Dora together, and their lives went to shit starting the next day. Miranda said she hadn't noticed anything particularly odd about Dora, nothing that caused any alarm. Said Dora wouldn't let her in the apartment but she seemed okay, if a little anxious. Which Miranda thought was justified, given the circumstances.

Then Miranda went home and her husband was out and when she woke up she was in a stock.

Dora isn't what she seems, that much is clear. She's scared. And she's in love with me. *The other me.*

But I can't deal with someone else's feelings right now. I haven't had the chance to process my own. Since I woke up in that basement I've been running from one crisis to another. From one preposterous revelation to the next. With each new piece of information about what I had become compressing my core of grief so tightly I can barely feel it anymore.

Even still, all this I could deal with—if that was all. But it's not. Dora may be in love with me but she knows more than she's letting on. She's hiding something from me.

Why? If she's as scared as she is, if she truly is in love with me, why hide something?

Maybe she's afraid of how I'll react.

Or maybe she's more involved than she wants to let on.

I check my tab and there's a message waiting from Dub. The last two members of counselling group, Vaelyn and Petra, have checked into the Fāngzhōu, that Reszo-only club in the Market. He's got me on the guest list.

They're still around, their minds seemingly intact, and they don't seem particularly scared. Haven't been touched by whatever curse I spread to the rest of the group. But that doesn't mean they don't know anything. They were witnesses to when it all went to shit.

Maybe they can fill in some holes for me. Maybe they can tell me what's going on with Dora.

I grab my coat, call a Sküte and wait inside the wide front doors of the apartment lobby. Pinpoint snowflakes hang in the sky, reflecting the streetlights, like the air itself has crystallized.

It's cold. Colder than it's been in years. The kind of cold we used to get at FS Alert, where, before digital thermometers were invented, they used alcohol in the glass because the mercury would freeze. The kind of cold that'll cause frostbite on exposed skin in seconds.

Apparently last year, it didn't drop below freezing once. Just my luck I skip the balmy winter and get stuck with one where the jet stream has fucked off to Mexico, leaving the Arctic free to make up for lost time.

The Sküte's ETA is sixty seconds when I notice someone standing across the street, against the corner of the building opposite mine, far enough away I can't tell if it's a him or a her—call it a boy, maybe. He's slight, a meter and a half tall, with short, dark hair brushed forward, his hands resting in the pockets of a light jacket. No hat. Running shoes. He's dressed for a brisk walk on a cool evening, not standing outside in subzero temperatures.

Then I realize who it is, the kid from outside the Ludus. *He followed me here.*

I start to run through the possibilities of who it could be, but give up before I get past Elder.

The only way to find out is to ask.

He's not getting away this time.

The Sküte pulls around the corner as I step out the front doors, and I let it wait, passing by the open pod on my way across the driveway, watching the kid. He sees me coming and hesitates for a long second before turning and hurrying through an open stretch of snow-crunched lawn toward Eastern Ave.

I run after him, watching his back. He reaches the inter-section, and as he crosses, the lights abruptly cycle behind him, putting a stream of cars between us. I ignore them, zigzag across the lanes of traffic and increase my pace when I get to the other side, just as the kid ducks down an alley halfway up the next block.

I'm full out now, trying to keep my balance on the stretches of slick, unshoveled sidewalk. I'm about to follow the kid into the alleyway when one of the city's automated snowplows whines past me and jams itself into the alley like a cork, blocking my entrance.

Shit.

I consider running around the block, try to cut him off, but I know I won't catch him.

Who is this guy? And what did I do to fuck up *his* life the last time around?

I'm tired of not knowing what the hell is going on around me.

It's time I pulled my head out of my ass.

It's time for some answers.

WOULD YOU LIKE TO ACCESS THIS DEVICE?

I've GOT the cuff on my neck, the Revv shyft pressed against it. I think green and the Revv injects a glimpse of its power.

[23:32:42.59]

Time dilates. Now stretches out into a continuum. The room rushes in at me and snaps into sharp, high-contrast relief. My breathing turns glacial. I count to five in the lull between the deep-sea eruptions of my heartbeat.

I flick my gaze at the kitchen and wait for my eyes to get there—

[23:33:00.45]

—They pass over the wallscreen where I assembled a collage of everything I could find about the arKade's location—the latest floor plans of the office building overlaid with the proposed agri-tower conversion plans, but not knowing how far one turned into the other before the construction shutdown made planning a glass house run-through next to impossible—and while I bought some time on a rented surveillance drone and held it at a distance to watch the ongoing activity, I only managed to observe the tail end of a parade of heavy-duty lifters gliding in and out of a sheltered enclosure, dropping off large crates and leaving empty, which was of no use at all, except to confirm my suspicion that I'd found the right place, which was when I finally decided the only way to make sure I wasn't outgunned by the stepped-up army that Kade will have certainly assembled as security was to even the odds with an enhancement of my own, the Revv—

[23:33:01.12]

—Past the tall, thin-bladed snake plant I brought from our old apartment, the gift Mom gave me when I was about to leave for Africa. It was hardy, she said, even I wouldn't be able to kill it, and she hugged me, the way she does, or...*did*...both intense and distracted at the same time, maybe chastising herself for using the word kill when I was about to go off to war, or maybe wondering if I'd ever come back, before she let me go and turned away and used the back of her hand to blot the tears, and I couldn't bear to tell her that there was no way they'd let me transport a live plant halfway across the world and had to have Dad keep it hidden and alive until I got back, and as tough as it is, it will die soon if I don't give it some water—

[23:33:01.29]

—To the pillar of tomato soup cases I ordered yesterday under the influence of my Cortex's rendition of a caffeine binge, four twelve-can boxes stacked on the kitchen counter.

[23:33:01.34]

—*What have I done?*

I shiver like an earthquake, seismic tremors rolling through muscle.

The Dwell was one thing, but that was necessary. No other way. Why did I just ram my head with code that does who knows what?

Because I'm about to walk my partner into what'll likely be a heavily guarded location populated by the Reszo underground's most notorious figures without the slightest bit of operational intelligence, and I'm too proud to ask for help? Too stupid to know when I'm in over my head?

Because someone's hunting me, someone I don't know and can't see, and being helpless in the face of a constant threat is making me edgy?

Because I need to do something, anything to keep my mind off the fact that I still haven't found Connie's killer, and every day that goes by with him still out there, still breathing, still capable of ripping others' lives to shreds haunts me every second, makes me feel like a failure, like I'm failing her and myself by not living up to the one good reason I was restored?

It's all these things and none of them.

The truth is: there is no reason. No good one anyway. Except I'd been planning the operation for five hours and was getting nowhere, was considering calling the inspector and confessing everything and the lure of my brain working at light speed was enough to overcome the taboo of breaking the law or the danger of my rithm being snatched out from under me.

I did it because I want to win and I'm not above cheating.

Because I have nothing to lose.

If my Cortex is scrambled, then this is all over. If I'm caught, then this is all over. I'll do what I have to even if that means—

[23:34:59]

Reality rubber bands to real-time with a momentum that snaps my head back.

Two seconds in the world and an eternity in my head.

The Revv asks if I'll grant it full access to my protected rithm, and before I can give myself time to decide different, I think green.

Time peels back from the surface of reality, exposes the machine code of the universe, and as the seconds stretch out into eternity I imagine this must be how it feels to live as a god.

I don't know how I'll ever go back.

Look out, Kade. I'm coming for you.

———

I FEEL like I've been standing here for years.

Less than an hour ago, I pressed a Revv shyft to my cuff and let the code injection amp my Cortex. Let it quicken my thoughts and bring the world to a standstill.

Immediately disoriented, I snapped in a breath of shock. And in the lag between my brain sending the nerve impulse and my lungs reacting, I thought I was choking and panicked, tried again to inhale and then coughed as my lungs finally kicked in. My chest heaved and my knees buckled and I threw myself off balance then stumbled over my leaden feet when I tried to catch myself from falling.

On the way to the floor, I stroked through a moment of desperation. This was the end. I'd be stuck like this forever, my body trapped in liquid amber while the milliseconds oozed by. But in the minutes it took for my body to reach the ground, I learned how to wait for each nerve signal to reach its destination before sending a conflicting one, and got my hands under me just before my face hit the floorboards.

Once I was up and on my feet and pulling the cuff off my neck, I'd mastered how to manipulate my fine motor control. And in the eon-long walk from my apartment to the office tower where a woman named Kade is hosting the Reszo underworld's most exclusive party, I learned to live in the space between seconds.

I arrived full of excitement, bristling with power, ready to take on Kade and the entirety of her crew, but I needed to wait for Galvan.

Now I'm bored.

If it weren't for the hundredths of a second creeping by on the display in the lower left of my vision, I would've long ago forgotten what day it is. Instead, I've watched twenty minutes erode by in this abandoned maze of plastic sheeting, buckystrut webbing, and exposed concrete underneath the city's downtown.

I can't wait much longer.

The arKade's above me, the party in full swing, hidden in plain sight on the top floors of an old skyscraper in mid-conversion to an agri-tower. Galvan told me the arKade is like a Reszo trade show. A place to come and show off for those who've made defying the Human Standard laws a way of life. It meets only six times a year, three nights over three weeks in one city, then another three nights somewhere else. Up until a week ago, the Service didn't know it existed.

Well, Galvan knew, but he's been a psychorithm crime detective for about as long as I've had this body, so no one listened to him.

Shortly after that we tied the arKade to a rash of wealthy Reszos showing up with their Cortexes caved in, their bank accounts empty, and their minds held for ransom.

Last week was supposed to be the third meeting in this cycle. The elite of the Reszo criminal underground and a serial mindjacker all in one place, and we'd missed them.

Or thought we had, until we intercepted a shipment of shyfts we tied back to Xiao, number two on the Ministry of Human Standards' Most Wanted list. The shyfts were meant to announce Xiao's next big product line. Samples and sneak peeks at code guaranteed to modify the human mind in unprecedented new ways. It was his trade show launch, and we messed it up for him.

Then we learned Kade added a fourth night.

And a few hours ago I figured out where she was holding it.

Right now Kade's fifty floors above me. And maybe Xiao. And maybe whoever's been psyphoning people.

None of them know we're coming. No one does. Not even Inspector Chaddah. No one but Galvan and me.

When I told him I'd found the arKade's next location, he wanted to spin up the troops, but I told him to keep it quiet, that we needed a light touch. Standards would want to come in hot and leave a smoking crater. Or someone would let something slip about the raid and the place would be empty when we showed up.

It was up to us. We'd play this right, he and I, and end up with a treasure trove of leads that'd spark dozens of new investigations. We wouldn't get another chance like this.

He agreed. Reluctantly.

Although he's right—we should call this in. Mobilize the TAC teams. Inform Standards. It's against every procedure and simple common sense not to.

But not yet.

I know I'm going to catch hell for this. The AMP will report when I found the location. Inspector Chaddah will see the time discrepancy. But I don't care.

I need to do this on my own. Chaddah would give the case to Daar and Brewer. They're the primaries on the Xiao investigation, and everything I've seen from them assures me they'd fuck it up. They've done it before.

I'm the only one I can trust.

Plus, I want to see Xiao's face when the doors burst in.

That's why I Revved, why I corrupted my mind with a potentially dangerous shyft: I need every advantage.

But after this time, I'm done. Never again. I only had the one dose and now that I've used it, I need to make the most of it. An advantage like this, being able to see the world slowly going about its business, able to anticipate and adjust to whatever it throws at me, it'd be far too easy to make this a habit. To become dependent upon it. The Revv's power is too great.

I can't let that happen.

For now, the trick is to keep my hyper-speed mind a secret. The shyft I just dumped into my head is one of Xiao's samples, and heavily illegal. Galvan will be here any minute, and I can't let him know what I've done. It's our job to keep people from doing exactly what I just did, to keep Reszos and humans on an even playing field. He's already straining against not telling the inspector we found the arKade. Seeing his partner deliberately flouting Standards would crack him in half.

Sure, it makes me a hypocrite, but I have no other choice. I'm about to lead a first-week detective into a two-man raid on a party whose guests are devoted to transcending their humanity. If chasing that jacked-up cypher in the Market taught me anything, it's that there's no limit to what Past-Standard skyns are capable of.

They all move at the speed of thought. I have to be able to keep up.

I've got a rented drone circling the roof at a casual distance, feeding directly to my tab, and I've been cataloguing the guests as they arrive—hoppers hover in line as one by one their passengers are vetted, then briefly touch down to disgorge the coiffed and the chiseled.

Roof security is tight, as though expecting the President. If the President had been elected in a world where monsters have the right to vote.

Creatures from out of a fever dream patrol the rooftop. From what I've seen through the drone, Kade has two different types: tanks and monkeys.

The tanks are each over two meters tall, with pebbly grey skin, smoothly rounded heads, no ears or noses, and the dense musculature of myostatin-inhibited gorillas. Four patrol the edges of the roof while two more are stationed at either side of the rooftop entrance.

The smaller, monkey-looking things have the same grey skin and featureless heads, but are more agile, with powerful-looking legs. Most lope along on all fours, escorting guests from the hopper pad. Two more wield antiaircraft weapons at the northeast and southwest corners of the roof.

Kade takes her exclusivity seriously. Standards violations on the roof alone would warrant an immediate Code Zero response. Enough to order a missile strike.

An instant of doubt blazes through my head. I'd thought when I Revved, I'd be prepared to handle anything the arKade could throw at me, but my imagination wasn't good enough to anticipate ogres.

I shake it off. No going back now. The Revv will have to be enough.

Other than the roof, the only other way in is a single express elevator near where I'm waiting. I slipped around the hazard barriers blocking the construction area and no one's come or gone since I arrived.

There's another of the same tank creatures from the roof stationed outside the elevator, its bulk obscuring the silver doors. Whatever it is, the thing's so far past Standard it'd be easier to catalogue what few things still resemble a human than what's changed. The Feds would shit themselves if they saw this guy in the wild. But since we're not getting in through the roof, the only way up is through him.

The guard hasn't so much as twitched since I took up my observation spot, so I've been keeping an eye on him while using my tab to watch the action on the roof while rechecking the list of facial matches the AMP and I put together of the man who killed Connie, while watching Galvan's sweep trigger on cyphers around the city.

I have no trouble doing all four things at once.

I haven't made any further progress on identifying the driver, but the cyphers have been coming fast and frequent. As the cyphers are tagged and added to Galvan's dbase, their bio/kin are added to the search parameters, which expands the coverage, resulting in even more cyphers revealed to us.

There have been five hits in the past day alone, with one arrest—a low-level enforcer for the Nigerian *Make-Dems*—but we're still no closer to uncovering anything related to Xiao.

He's still out there. Selling his advanced shyfts and Past-Standard skyns and driving humanity further and further into the unknown. Since that first encounter in the Market, his entire organization has been somehow lucky enough or prescient enough to avoid being tagged.

Tonight his lucky streak's over.

Galvan finally arrives a few minutes later. I hear the long low shuffle of his shoes on the dusty floor before I see him. The Revv gives me time to study him as he approaches, darting from a shrouded utilibot to a pillar to a chalky potted plant as he tries to remain in cover.

I told him to dress safe and he's chosen a long grey coat over his usual cardigan and white shirt combo, lapel popped. The dull black ring of a stopsuit pokes out from under his shirt collar. He really should have a helmet, but it'll do.

His hands are thrust deep into his jacket's pockets, and his left knee subtly hitches with every step. Something I didn't notice before.

"Are you sure about this?" he asks as he reaches me, the words stretching out for minutes. I understand him perfectly but have the time to watch his lips and tongue form each syllable, and figure out what he's going to say before the sound hits my ears. "We should report in. Wait for backup."

His pupils are wide. Brown irises flecked with gold dart about as if he's expecting an attack at any second, from any direction. A thin film of sweat sheens his forehead.

"We're going to walk in, have a little chat and leave," I say. "No need for dramatics."

He starts, focuses his attention on my face. "Why are you talking so fast?"

Shit. I didn't realize I was. "Just excited," I say, speaking slowly and clearly. "Pre-operation jitters."

"You've got the jitters for a good reason. We have no idea what we're walking into—"

I don't want to rehash this. "You said so yourself: it's an art show, a bunch of wankers in look-at-me skyns." I don't mention the arsenal on the roof or the monster guarding the elevator. He'll find out about those soon enough. I need him calm now.

"We should at least let the inspector know where we are," Galvan offers.

"And have her tell us to stand down? This is our case and we're going to see it through." I can feel the words blurring from my mouth and force my lips to slow down. Even as I'm saying this, justifying a course of action I know isn't wise, I still don't exactly understand why I'm so intent on going in without backup, and I've had a lot of time to think about it.

Subjective hours.

Why didn't I let Galvan tell the inspector when he first found out the arKade was being held over for a fourth night? Why did I keep the location to myself? What's the harm in calling in a support team, going up with a couple dozen guns at my back? I'm violating protocol and direct orders and basic safety training. What's the rush?

Because then I'd just be another drone, acting under orders.

Stand down. Wait.

Do what you're told.

It never bothered me before—I was a soldier, I was good at following orders. Go there. Kill that. Turn off the part of your brain that asks questions. But things were always done in a certain way. Protocols are followed because they work, because the wrong people die or the guilty go free if you don't.

I don't know what's changed—except everything—but I don't think having died once has anything to do with it. I've always been like this.

I need to be doing something. I need something to focus on. Like a shark, I've always needed constant momentum. That's one of the things Connie did for me. Making her happy gave me something to focus on.

When I woke up in Second Skyn, all that was gone. I had nothing. Connie was gone and my life with it. I almost gave up, would have given up—if it weren't for the microsecond glimpse of Connie's killer.

His face gave me something to focus on. Gave me a reason to stay in my skyn.

After that cypher in the Market, or when I was marveling at the Hereafter, or when I was combing through my memories, searching for the man who killed me, I was doing something. I was taking my life into my own hands. Not sitting around waiting for permission. Life can change in an instant. I need to seize the opportunities that are presented, regardless of procedure. Wise or not.

Yeah, maybe I should have called the inspector two days ago, but it's too late for that now.

Forward or die.

And I've already been dead once, so what's the worst that could happen?

Actually, one thing. He's trembling in a stopsuit, hunched over beside me.

There's no need to drag him into this. Busting Kade isn't worth Galvan getting hurt. "You're right," I say to him. "Stay here. Just give me five minutes, then call for backup."

I leave Galvan and round the concrete abutment I've been waiting behind and stride across the gritty concrete floor to the elevator bank. There's a moment of contemplative silence, and then I hear a slow-motion scramble behind me.

The guard's head perks as he hears us coming and shifts his bulk to face our approach. Up close he's even bigger, built for combat. A fleshmith's concept of an urban assault vehicle in humanoid form. His smooth head slopes down into his shoulders as one seamless nub protruding from his muscled slab of a body. His nostrils are broad slits in his face. No ears. Only the slightest suggestion of a chin. Bright blue lenzs cover his eyes.

Two long strips of cobalt blue stopsuit cover his vitals, the protective fabric cascading down from his squared shoulders to tent off his massive pectorals and drape to the floor. Underneath the fabric is the bulge of full-on, body-hugging armor. His arms are bare, the skin tight over a custom-design weave of corded muscle that'll give him an advanced range of motion. Both his hands have three long thick fingers extending from a broad palm with a thumb jutting from each side. I'd bet his skeleton is reinforced.

There's nothing to strike, nothing to grab hold of. Nothing about him is based on the original blueprint.

He steps forward, legs revolving on odd ball-and-socket knee joints, raises a hand that's twice the size of mine, and in an avalanche of flesh, cranes his whole torso down at me.

"I'm afraid you're not permitted to enter," he says once

he gets his head locked into position. His voice is a surprisingly gentle baritone, as though he's genuinely embarrassed he can't grant us access. "Invited guests only tonight."

"We have an invitation," I offer.

"No, sir. You don't."

I lift my hands, pause them at chest level and then use two fingers to pull the right side of my jacket and reveal the badge. "Toronto Police Service. We have reas—"

"I know who you are. Detective Gage." He looks past me, straightens and puts his arms behind his back. "Detective Wiser. We at the arKade appreciate your service to the community and all the work you do keeping your city safe, but you're not on Ms. Kade's guest list. I'm sorry, but I can't grant you entry without her approval. If you'd like, I could add you to our feed permissions."

"Aren't you helpful," I say. I didn't think he'd just stand aside and let us pass, but it was worth a try. Now I need to figure out a way into that elevator.

"There's no need for sarcasm, Detective Gage," he says, flush with the confidence of invincibility.

"Let's go, Finsbury," Galvan says behind me.

"Why don't you contact Ms. Kade, tell her two Service detectives would like a moment of her time?"

"Ms. Kade has left specific instructions. She is not to be disturbed during showtime except in the direst of circumstances. I can book you an appointment. Ms. Kade has an opening in her schedule next Tuesday at ten thirty a.m. local time for a virt conference, if that works for you gentlemen."

"This is definitely an emergency," I say.

"You're not an emergency." His hands fall to his sides.

"I'm about to be."

"Please don't do something we'll all regret," the tank rumbles, fingers rolling into fists the size of artillery shells.

I feint for my weapon and see the future. Coils of muscle contract in the tank's shoulder, and his fist shoots out at the pressure point where my right shoulder meets the pectoral muscle, middle knuckle raised, aiming to numb my gun arm before I can draw.

He's fast. Inhumanly fast. Probably amped on something similar to the Revv. He'd have connected easily, left me literally and figuratively disarmed, but it seems his code's no match for mine.

I see it all coming.

I angle my shoulder back. His knuckle brushes harmlessly across the surface of my jacket and his face crumbles in confusion as he shifts his weight to counterbalance his swinging arm. I straighten back up as he clumsily retracts his fist, resets and fires again.

I see him decide what he's going to do before he even moves: a flat-handed chop to my brachial plexus, where my shoulder and neck meet, drop me with a single blow. He's trying to end this quickly, with as little trauma as possible. Got to appreciate that in a bruiser.

His hand hangs in the air forever, a gentle lob that I let get close before leaning back just enough to feel the breeze on my neck as his fingernails swipe by. I'd be amazed at how easy this is, but I've been living a microsecond at a time so long now, I barely remember when I wasn't able to dodge like a prescient ninja.

Even still, I need to end this. I've got him beat as long as he thinks he can't lose, but once he stops being cute, my skyn is no match for his.

I lunge forward, following his swinging arm, pull my weapon left handed and press into him, wedge his arm between my chest and the soft plates covering his torso, and jam the barrel into the faint bump where his chin should be. The gun's warmed up and ready to fire just as his eyes widen in surprise.

"You so much as clear your throat," I say to his massive nostrils, "we take what's left of your Cortex back to the station and see what *it* has to say." He doesn't move. I take that as agreement. "Galvan—" I don't know what he's doing, likely just standing there. Possibly with his mouth open.

No response. I hope he hasn't passed out. I can't take my eyes off the tank to check on him. "Detective Wiser!"

"What—you're—what do you want me to do?" he asks, breathless. He's scared. I need to keep him present, keep him focused. I can't give this tank even a second's opening to act.

"Do you have your weapon out?"

There's a rustling of cloth and a soft thrum as his gun recognizes him and readies itself.

"I do now."

"Safety off?"

The weapon sounds ready. The tank rolls his eyes.

"If the gentleman moves, kindly shoot him in the cranium."

"Affirmative," Wiser says, his voice barely in control.

"Your bullets won't stop me," the tank says. The courtesy has dropped from his voice. He's pissed.

"An incendiary AP will." There's a pause, then Galvan's weapon thrums a deep bass as the ammo setting changes.

The tank sneers down at me, trying to see for himself if I've set my gun to fire armor-piercing rounds, but he can't see the display from way up there.

"This'll do three rounds a second," I say. "How many

you think I'll need until one of them hits something important?"

"Okay, okay," he says. "You got me. Now what's the plan, tough guy?"

That's a good question. What is the plan? Just because I can think fast doesn't help me come up with brilliant ideas. All the power in the world is useless if I don't know how to use it.

I jump back, out of the tank's considerable reach, keeping my weapon on him. Thumb it to AP.

The tank scowls at the noise.

I need to get him out of the way so we can use the elevator to reach the arKade, but I can't just leave him down here. That skyn is far too dangerous.

"Turn around," I order, "kneel and interlace your hands on that lump you call a head."

He considers it for a moment but complies. Turns to face the elevator doors, sinks to his knees and puts his hands around the back of his head. Sounds like wet leather creaking. Even kneeling he's almost as tall as I am.

I check in with Galvan to make sure he's covering me, holster my weapon, take my binders off my belt, step forward and seal one side against the bouncer's solid right wrist. My eye catches something embedded in the tank's neck, hidden under the curve of stopsuit right about where he'd affix a cuff, but it doesn't look like any cuff I've ever seen. It's a gunmetal disc the size of a small coin, with a shiny black bump in the center. Maybe some kind of external transmitter, a built-in antenna that can't just be pulled off like a cuff. It'd make sense to include a hardened communication system in a state-of-the-art combat skyn.

I'm still pondering the odd ring as I wrap my hand around his left wrist and pull to secure the binders.

The elevator doors shiver and pull apart with a drawn out chime like thunder in the distance. I glance up at the movement, tighten my grip on his wrist. Crouch to put the tank between me and whoever's in there. If that's a transmitter on his neck, he would've sounded the alarm the second he noticed us. Called for backup.

Like I should have done.

I may think faster than he does, but it doesn't make me smarter.

No one comes. The elevator doors are wide enough now I can see it's empty. There's no backup. Then wha—

The tank flexes his body and pulls with his left arm. The one I've got in a death grip.

I resist but it's like trying to arm-wrestle a construction-bot. He's made of carbon-weave muscle and reinforced bone with enough power to lift a tractor, and I'm only flesh and blood. I can't beat him in a war of strength.

My mind flashes forward and I see myself crumpled in a broken heap against the elevator wall as he stands, turns and pounces on Galvan.

Adrenaline spikes, surges through my Revved Cortex like a lightning strike, stretching and sharpening my already crisp vision to a point. Time dilates even further. My heartbeat stalls like a frozen wave, poised to crash. Combat training takes over, triaging threats, assessing options, and I give into it.

Galvan gasps a long slow note of horror behind me.

I let the tank's arm carry me for a fraction of a second, and as I'm pulled I bring up my knee. Then I open my fingers. Momentum carries my kneecap into the soft spot at the base of his skull, just above the disc, impacts with a satisfying crunch of boulders in a rock crusher. He grunts and falls forward but catches himself with his free arm before his face hits the elevator wall.

I slide down his back and land on my feet, push away and get my hand on my weapon.

"Want to try that again?" I ask, trying to keep the tension out of my voice.

He groans but straightens and laces his fingers behind his head.

I breathe in through my nose, long enough that it seems my chest will burst, and then the fight or flight hits a crescendo and fades. Once my hands have stopped shaking, I reach out and tentatively grab the tank's left wrist. He doesn't resist as I pull it down behind his back, stretch the binders out to their highest setting and lock him in.

I motion to the disc on the tank's neck, check over my shoulder for Galvan's assessment. He squints at it, leans in for a closer look, gives me an unsure shrug.

"I've already contacted the team upstairs," the tank states from the floor. "You got lucky down here somehow, but you won't make it out of the elevator. Then I'll be up and we'll have the opportunity for another conversation."

"I figured you might feel that way." I extract my tab and scan his pattern through his retinas.

As expected, it comes back empty. A cypher. A killing machine in a disposable body. The top threat on the Ministry of Human Standards' long list of offences.

"I can't have you just follow us up," I say. "It seems to me that shooting you in the head would be our simplest course of action here. And since you're not registered under COPA, there wouldn't even be that much paperwork." If this fazes him, he doesn't show it.

"We could call for backup," Galvan says dryly from

behind me. "They could deal with him, and we could all go up together."

Which isn't such a bad idea at this point, except for the waiting. HQ will have already noted our weapons have been drawn. I'm ignoring the AMP's call humming on my tab, but they'll be on the way as it is. I can't risk Galvan getting hurt. He's come far enough. He can wait down here and come up when the TAC arrives to clean up the mess.

"Call 'em," I say to Galvan, and then to the tank, "One last request. If you wouldn't mind coming around the corner here? I prefer if you weren't out here scaring the locals."

"Help me up?" he asks.

Even with those cuffs on, he could probably take us both if I let him get close enough. "I'm going to keep my distance."

He grunts, heaves one massive foot out from under his ass, hauls himself to his feet and trundles out of the elevator. We back off as he approaches, and I ask Galvan for his binders.

"Hold the elevator," I say to Galvan. "I'm going to find somewhere to secure this guy and I'll be right back. Then you'll go watch him until help arrives."

Galvan swallows hard but nods, and I guide the tank around the corner and into a stairwell leading down to the parking levels. I keep him well ahead of me and have him stop on the landing between floors, keeping half a flight between us. "Kneel and put your head on the floor. I'm going to secure your ankles and someone will be along soon to gather you up."

He doesn't kneel and scowls at me instead, arms and shoulders in full flex. I hear a low groan, like a ship's timbers straining in a storm, as the binders on his wrists lose their structural integrity.

They're not going to hold him.

I'm in trouble.

My Cortex surges with adrenaline and I watch the stairwell brighten as my irises dilate. I can't let him get close. I retreat as I reach for my gun and catch my heel on the stairs and stagger just as the composite gives. He grins and bursts up the stairs, coming at me with violence on his mind.

He's already covered half the distance between us before I get my weapon out and primed, no time to switch to AP.

I fire—off balance, still retreating, panic driving me, hands trembling—and spasm on the trigger. The shot goes wide, hits the wall behind him in a cinderblock explosion.

I shouldn't have come here alone. Should have listened to Galvan about the backup. Should have let Standards send in that missile strike.

I steady myself through the Revv, fire again, hit him square in the face and the slug impacts his forehead, rips through skin to expose a black skull, but doesn't slow him down.

Reinforced skeleton. I was right.

Likely the last thing I'll ever be right about.

The tank's lips split to reveal two ivory semicircles of unbroken enamel as he realizes I was bluffing about the armor piercers and then he's on me, nose to breathing-slits, his breath hot on my face. Fingers like thick wire coil around my throat. Thumbs press at the top and bottom of my windpipe.

We topple like felled trees and slam into the concrete, land with enough force to rip the air from my lungs. My arms are pinned against my chest, my weapon up near our faces. He doesn't care about the gun, he knows it can't hurt him. I angle it down and fire anyway, into his neck. The muzzle flash imprints itself on my vision, singes my jacket, burns my chin. The concussion roars in the enclosed space and echoes three times before it subsides.

Blood trickles from the bullet hole, but not as much as there should be. He isn't slowing. If anything, his grip tightens.

My ears ring. Black vines creep in from the edges of my vision. Another second and he'll snap my neck. I wonder how long my Cortex will keep me conscious after the blood flow stops? Will my eyes still work? Will I get to watch when he rips my head off my shoulders and treats it like a soccer ball?

I turn my head away and twitch my finger in rapid succession, firing again and again until, finally, there's a flat metal ping and his fingers go immediately slack. It's then I realize I'm screaming.

His entire weight sinks on me, like a bus settling on my chest. Even dead he might kill me. My ribs are compressed, forcing me to breathe in shallow gasps like a terrified rabbit.

My arms are useless. I can't get leverage to push, but I can wiggle. I lean side to side, shift first to the left with no luck and then to the right, where the tank's body slips a nudge and gives me a little more room to move. After rocking back and forth a few times I'm eventually able to squeeze my torso out from under him and pull my legs free.

The tank is lying face down, neck a warren of bloody meat, upper body on the landing. Everything below the waist rests on the stairs. There's a small dent in the disc on the back of his neck. The bullet disabled whatever it was doing. Turned him off like a switch.

Lucky fucking shot.

My breath seeps out of me, thick with the smell of fear.

I nearly died.

Even with the Revv, with the world plodding along, the tank nearly finished me.

But now I know. I know their weakness. All the muscle in the world can't save them. That disc wasn't just for intra-team communication, it's more important than that. It has to be some kind of remote control, the skyn just a telepresence puppet. At a far higher fidelity than anything I've ever heard about, sure, but a puppet nonetheless.

Up until now, attempting to cast into something as complex as a bioSkyn's Cortex was considered impossible, streaming a human consciousness over the link far too bandwidth-intensive. Someone must have figured out a way around the data limitations.

Hardly surprising. Nothing's impossible anymore.

I leave him there and find Galvan in the elevator, frantically scanning the control panel.

"Finsbury," he yells as I round the corner. "Get in here."

The elevator is chirping like mad, and I break into a run as the doors start to close. Galvan reaches out and pounds the controls to no effect, and I just manage to angle my body and skim through before the elevator seals shut.

"You were supposed to wait for the backup," I say.

"The security timeout started," he responds, out of breath, as if he were the one who had just fought for his life and then sprinted twenty meters at full speed. "We would have had to get that thing back up here, make him plug in the code."

"That would have posed a problem," I mutter. He stares at the blood on my jacket but doesn't probe further. "You called TAC?"

"Full alert, the whole building will be on lockdown in ten."

"Good. When we get up there you wait in the elevator."

"What about security? The...thing down there said they'll be ready."

"Let me worry about that," I say. I have no idea what to expect, but I'm not worried by the thought. I can handle it. I know their secret. They're all a bunch of puppets.

With the Revv, I can cut their strings.

The lights dim as we ascend, until the only source of illumination is the orange piping running around the elevator's seams.

Then we stop moving and the doors open to reveal an inhuman spectacle like I've never considered possible.

I'M ONLY fifty-eight hours old.

Fifty-eight hours since I woke in a dingy basement with a new name and a new body, and discovered my old life was over. That I'd already been restored once from the accident that killed Connie and me.

That I'd thrown my second chance away.

Since then, I've been attacked—had a friend I don't remember try to pry my mind out of my head.

I learned I've been kicked off the Police Service in disgrace—accused of tampering with evidence and insubordination and possibly murder.

I've met a bunch of people whose lives have also been ruined. People who have committed horrible crimes but have no memories of their actions. With every one of them convinced what happened to them started with me. With decisions I made.

Then I met my girlfriend, Doralai Wii. She'd been waiting for me to come back from the dead and run away with her. That was the hardest to believe. How could I start a new relationship with a woman I barely knew only weeks after Connie was ripped away from me?

At first, I denied it all. Refused to believe I could be capable of any of those things, let alone all of them. I looked for excuses, for other people to blame. But I've seen the evidence for myself. Been confronted by people I hurt or betrayed.

It's all true. I became someone I don't recognize.

I became the bad guy.

As hard as all that is to accept, what's worse is, he and I, we're the same. The Finsbury Gage I don't remember—the guy who did all those terrible things, made all those horrible decisions—he started out the same place I did. He lost his wife. He was restored. He suffered through the same grief and loss and confusion and anger I'm feeling now.

He's *me*.

I'm *him*.

If he could do all those things, hurt all those people, what's to stop me from turning out just like he did?

What if who I became is who I truly am?

I can't let that happen.

I don't want to end up like he did. Someone who hurts people, who abandons the people he loves. A hypocrite. A disgrace.

A failure.

As far as I can tell, the trouble started with my Restoration Counselling group: Dora, Shelt, Dub, Miranda, Tala, Carl and Elder. We all came together to help each other navigate the hazardous realities of digital resurrection, and we all ended up dead or stocked or in hiding.

Shelt has been helping me. He's just as invested as I am because whatever it was I got into last time is still happening. Someone's not just after me. Dora and Shelt are in danger too.

The question is why.

Two other people joined our counselling group at my last meeting. The meeting before I died or killed myself in some kind of gang fight. Vaelyn and Petra.

Shelt believes whatever happened last time has to do with tainted shyfts. And Vaelyn is a rithmist. She rolls shyfts for a living, creates code that Reszos use to manipulate their digital minds.

Maybe it's a coincidence. Or maybe her joining the group and the group going to shit are related.

Only one way to find out.

Shelt told me they're regulars at the Fāngzhōu, a Reszo-only bar in Kensington Market, so I'm going to have a chat, see what they have to say for themselves.

The bar's in the south end of the old part of Kensington, just up from Dundas St., its entrance sheltered by a long black awning decorated with two glowing red hanzi, like a stickman chasing a runaway housebot. A bouncer stands easy at the entrance, hands buried deep in the pockets of a thick navy peacoat, collar turned up. His eyes fluoresce as I approach, and he waves me in with a jerk of his toque.

The door opens and I'm blasted with a gust of warm air accompanied by music I can feel as much as hear, sensual bass overlaid by staccato rhythms and a jangly treble, like half the band is playing way too fast.

The room is small and nearly empty, just a few tables and a half-dozen people who look like they'd rather be someone else, someone with the right combination of influence and connections to get access to the real party upstairs. A small glass bar sits in the corner and a bot stands silent behind it, waiting for someone to come up and order a drink or one of the of legal shyfts on display.

The dejected patrons watch as I enter, and their eyes follow me as I stride across the room to a metal door on the back wall, the one keeping them out of the action upstairs.

Now to see if Shelt was able to get me in.

A panel slides open on the door and a green light sprays my face.

The scanner must like whatever it sees because a modulated voice says, "Password?"

"*Ziyóu,*" I answer. *Freedom* in Mandarin.

The locks snap and the door slides open and the people watching me put their heads back down to their drinks, imagining what it must be like to be blessed with the rep or connections required to access the inner sanctum.

I step through the door and the music gets louder and the air gets thicker as I climb the unlit, narrow staircase to the second floor, where another bouncer in tight jeans and a vest over dense muscle, his eyes glowing like a nocturnal animal's, perches on a stool. He slips off, gives me a casual pat down, and grunts back up.

I start to sweat almost immediately and slip my parka off, carry it over my arm while my eyes acclimate to the all-red lighting, and my ears adjust to the deafening buzz of music and loud conversation.

The upstairs is far bigger than the ground floor, spanning across the knocked-out second stories of three adjacent buildings. Behind me, blackwashed portholes run along the front wall in place of windows. Thick wooden beams supported by mast-like columns run from one side of the long room to the other, with heavy, dusty-looking fabric billowing from the ceiling in between. Brass lamps with red bulbs blush the room, while occasional cylinders of light flash as patrons burn shyfts into their rithms.

A mix of cast-off and second-hand tables with an equally diverse assortment of chairs fill the space, except for a small dance floor where half the people move slow and close while the others spastically bounce off them and each other. Padded leather booths line the walls, each one tucked into its own private, arched alcove. The far corner contains the only source of white light: a small assortment of bottles along glowing shelves and a long counter of flickering shyfts under glass.

There are at least a hundred people in here, indistinct forms silhouetted in the dim light. I pick my way through the tables, circling around the club to peer into each of the alcoves, and spot Petra and Vaelyn almost immediately.

They're holding court in a booth under a porthole. Vaelyn's all cheekbones and breasts under a rage of spiky red hair and dark eye makeup.

Compared to the shock of a woman beside her, Petra is ethereal, her translucent features flittering somewhere between boy and girl and fringed by ashen, almost silvery hair cut straight along her faint eyebrows. Vaelyn's got her arm around Petra's shoulder, possessive.

They're not hiding—if anything they want to be seen. Two women flank them, both big, one black and blonde, one white with dark hair.

I consider marching straight over to their table and confronting them, but with my ass still sore from indulging in my impulsiveness with Nyx, I decide to take it slow. What's the point if I'm not learning from my mistakes?

I make my way over to the bar and stand in the three-deep line, casually keeping tabs on Petra and Vaelyn as I wait to be served. They're not going anywhere, they're doing brisk business.

Three different people come up to their table while I'm watching and the ritual is the same with each: approach, get lip-to-ear with one of the big women, long enough for a word or two. She then leans over to Vaelyn and relays the request. Vaelyn rifles through a small bag at her side for the requested shyft, which is passed across Petra to the other big woman. After the customer pays through a wave of a tab or a cashcard, the shyft is palmed or immediately pressed to their cuff. Petra just watches. The entire process takes less than ten seconds.

A space opens up in front of me and I slide up to the bar. The shyfts are arranged by "artist" under the glass. There are a dozen rithmists' offerings on display, probably fifty or so shyft varieties in total, each with a red hanzi on the cap, a character I don't recognize that looks like two stick figures toasting each other under an umbrella or angular tree. I show it to my IMP and it tells me it's a surname: Xiao.

That name again. I had been after him, back in my former life. When I was a cop.

This must be his place. Shelt seems to think Xiao had something to do with what happened to me last time, with what happened to the group. He thinks it all started because I got too close to Xiao, and somehow all the shit that happened after was related.

Could it be one more coincidence that Vaelyn hangs out in a place Xiao runs?

I'll have to make sure to ask.

Most of the customers seem to be buying one of only a few different shyfts. One of them looks like what Dora keeps injecting into her cuff, the display skin all pink and sparkly. The most requested one contains an aquamarine mist interspersed with a regular crackle of blue-white lightning. Vaelyn has three available: a fractal rainbow one, a golden-purple one, and one that looks like it contains liquid flame. Who knows what they do. Who knows what any of them do.

I suppose I could buy one and find out for myself, but a head full of janky neural code is the last thing I need right now.

The bartender looks through me, reaches under the counter and retrieves four shyfts for the guy behind me without a word being exchanged, moves down the counter to supply someone else.

It's like they're communicating psychically. Which, I realize, they probably are. I'm the only one in here who isn't wearing a cuff. I left mine back on the table at the apartment.

The next time he gets close, I reach out and tug on his sleeve and he starts like a ghost grabbed him. I mouth the word "beer," and he squints and points down through the clear surface of the bar to the wide array of shyfts on offer. I shake my head, point behind him and repeat, "beer." He turns and gestures to the three dusty bottles on the shelf as though still unsure what I mean and I nod and point to the green bottle with the gold label. He bends and rattles around in a small fridge and fishes out a cold one and spends another minute looking for a bottle opener, then finally places the bottle in front of me. I approve the charge that pops up on my tab and he goes back to serving shyfts.

I put my back to the bar and look across the room to Vaelyn's table. From what I can tell every third or fourth booth is doing some kind of business, slinging shyfts mostly, but Vaelyn is selling the most by far, second only to the bartenders. If her shyfts are tainted, her customers don't seem to mind.

A table opens up nearby and I take my beer and sit. Vaelyn puts on a show for each new customer, hands agitated, large lips over-enunciating vowels in the cacophony of music.

After each sale she leans over, cups Petra's crotch and pulls her face in for a long deep kiss I feel like I can hear over the music. Petra's relaxed to the point of torpidity, allowing herself to be worked over.

A waitress swings by and I nod for another beer. This is the most normal I've felt since I woke up in someone else's body. The low light and the damp heat and the sting of alcohol in my throat and the overwhelming music are like a pillow smothering my frazzled senses.

When the waitress comes back with another bottle, I upend it and take five long gulps. It fizzles in my nose and for a second leaves me pleasantly woozy, but then my new brain overdoes itself; trying to approximate the effects of alcohol, it buffs my thoughts with steel wool then jams a pry bar into my self-confidence and heaves.

The heat and the noise and my brain's shitty re-creation of an alcohol buzz all mix together into a muddy headache. After two beers.

Looks like I'm never going to make it as an alcoholic.

My stomach turns and I clamp down with my teeth and try to breathe through it. I want this to stop. It dawns on me that I'm treating my brain like it's still made of meat, dousing it with chemicals in an attempt to make it behave differently. Which is exactly what all these people here are doing, except they're being smart about it. No messy alcohol for them. They're altering their brain function with the pinpoint accuracy of precise code instead of the imperfect interplay of molecules and cellular pathways.

Which is, I suppose, why shyfts are so strictly regulated.

I watch Vaelyn and Petra for fifteen more minutes, waiting for my head to clear, absently scraping the beer's foil label off with my thumbnail.

Twenty-two customers come and go, most of them opting for the fire-filled cylinder. Vaelyn's definitely the most popular of Xiao's stable. I wonder if he ever comes in here himself? If what Shelt said is true and this whole mess with tainted caps started with me, it must have to do with Xiao. I was investigating him, maybe I got too close. Maybe all this is his revenge.

I'll ask Vaelyn about him too.

The throbbing in my head has settled to an unpleasant tightness but the nausea has passed and I'm about to move over for the chat when a woman in a sleek grey suit and three-hundred-dollar ebony hairstyle imposes herself at Vaelyn and Petra's table.

She isn't looking for shyfts, doesn't have a cuff, isn't even wearing a winter coat. She probably just walked in from a long black vehicle that's still idling downstairs.

The muscle on each side of the booth slide out, but uneasily, looking to Vaelyn for instruction. Something's keeping them from getting physical.

The woman ignores them, leans over and rests her hands on the table so her face is centimeters from Vaelyn. She says something and Vaelyn responds with a sneer, cocks her head at Petra. Petra doesn't answer, barely moves, just rolls her eyes enough to show her indifference to whatever's being said.

This sets the woman off and she reaches across the table and grabs Petra's arm, tries to pull her up and around the table, but Petra goes slack, refuses to be moved. Vaelyn's security is bouncing from foot to foot. Their instincts are telling them to intervene, but Vaelyn keeps them on the leash. She isn't concerned. Whatever's going on here is between Petra and the other woman, and Vaelyn's acting like she already knows how it's going to end.

Vaelyn slides out, unfolds her body, makes a show of it. She's tall, nearly as tall as her security, her powerful-looking body poured into a black one-piece open halfway to her navel.

She waves the woman in, but doesn't give her much room to pass, then adjusts the bulge that protrudes from her groin and stretches down one leg.

The woman grimaces but squeezes by and shuffles around to Petra, grabs her hand. She's pleading now. *Come with me*, she's saying. *Come home*. Petra just shakes her head and gently pulls herself free, turns her head away and lets her eyes fall back out of focus.

I'm not the only one who's noticed the commotion. People have stopped dancing and the neighboring tables have all turned to look. The woman must feel the weight of the eyes because she arranges her suit jacket back around her shoulders, whispers one last time to Petra, then slides out and snaps something at Vaelyn and her flanking security before stalking away from the table and down the stairs.

Vaelyn reaches up and with a satisfied smile claps her muscle on the shoulders, says something to them with a nod toward the door. They both grin and head down after the woman.

Petra hasn't moved, the expression on her face barely different from when I sat down. Whoever that woman was, whatever she had to say, it couldn't force its way through Petra's protective shyft barrier.

With the security gone, I figure this is as good a time as any to introduce myself.

I stand and weave over to their booth. Vaelyn sizes me up as I approach. She's flushed, full of adrenaline, back in the booth with her hand between Petra's thighs.

Petra doesn't even swing her eyes in my direction. She's still staring off into space.

"Store's closed," Vaelyn says when I get to their table, yelling to be heard. "Come back in fifteen."

I lean over, rest my palms on the table. "I'm not buying," I say. "I just want to talk."

Vaelyn looks me up and down, her eyes black in the red light. "We don't talk to cops," she says and turns to nuzzle Petra's neck.

"I'm not a cop," I say to her cheek. "Not anymore. Do you remember Dub, from your counselling group?"

Petra stirs at Dub's name but Vaelyn doesn't react, she just extends her massive tongue into Petra's ear.

"What about Miranda?" I continue. "Or Tala? Or Dora or Elder?"

Vaelyn retracts her tongue and her jaw muscles lock, but she doesn't look at me. Petra's demeanor ripples. For the first time since I started watching, there's something going on behind her slack façade. She knows something.

"What about Finsbury Gage?" I ask. Petra opens her mouth to say something, but Vaelyn is already out of the booth, body pressed against my side, mouth at my ear now.

"Back off right now and I won't fuck up that pretty face of yours." She licks her lips. "Not too much anyway."

Her muscle won't be gone long. I need to defuse this situation before it gets out of hand. A fight isn't going to get me any answers.

I turn and we're nose to nose. "Word is you're slinging

tainted shyfts. A rumor like that, if it got out, could kill a career."

Maybe *defuse* was the wrong word.

She sneers and moves into me, grinds the heavy bulge between her legs into my thigh.

"Threaten me again and your pretty face won't be the only thing I fuck up."

"Vae," Petra says, her voice quiet but strong. "That's enough."

I turn to Petra and Vaelyn hits me in the kidney. It's all I can do to keep my knees from buckling, but she doesn't hit nearly as hard as Nyx. Her arm's cocked back for another, but I step into it and bring my forehead down on her nose, pulling up just short of breaking it.

She staggers back, eyes overflowing.

"Vae!" Petra shouts, now on her feet.

Vaelyn and I square off but before either of us can move, I'm facedown on the table, one arm pinned up my back.

"Don't resist," a man's voice commands from behind me, his tone matter of fact, like slamming people face-first into tables was a regular occurrence for him.

"Let him up," Vae says, but it sounds like someone's restraining her too. "I was about to finish him off."

"Then you can follow us out," another man says.

"Wait," Petra says. "Who is he?"

"Rep-net says Gage Gibson," the voice behind me answers.

"I'm Finsbury," I croak. "Finsbury Gage."

"Let him up," Petra orders.

"Ma'am—" the man protests.

"Petra—" Vaelyn says at the same time.

"I said, 'let him up.'"

I sense a moment of silent communication but the pressure on my arm relents, and I'm able to stretch back up. The man behind me is my height, short hair, dark suit, narrow tie under a white collared shirt, eyes bright in the dim light. He's resting easy, hands crossed at his waist, like he's waiting for the bus, but I've been around guys like this—the ones who would breeze in and out of base with their designer sunglasses, three weeks of facial hair and sense of superiority. Special forces. His cousin stands between Vaelyn and me. Whoever these guys are, they don't answer to her.

They're protecting Petra. Who the hell is she to warrant a highly trained babysitting team?

On cue, Vaelyn's muscle returns, looking sheepish. Their coarse oversized skyns are like dumb beasts next to Petra's guardians' sleek killing machines. Someone must have given Vaelyn's team a scolding outside. And since Petra's security didn't intervene when that other woman showed up, they probably work for her too. Or someone close to both of them.

"I'll be fine," Petra says to the man behind me. The two men nod and blend back into the room. I scan the club and try to find them again but they've completely disappeared.

"Now that the chaperones are gone, we can have that dance," Vaelyn says and steps toward me. Petra backs her down with a look and she skulks off to the bar.

"Why don't you sit down," Petra says, then fishes a shyft from her pocket and empties it into her cuff. "And I'll tell you what I know."

I CAN FEEL Galvan glaring at me. He's not stupid, he knows I've shyfted. Probably knows exactly what I'm shyfted on too. But right now, the prospect of him reporting me is dwarfed by what's immediately in front of us.

The arKade.

We've finally found it.

We're standing in the open elevator at the base of a yawning, three-story atrium. The upper two floors are glassed-in, and directly in front of us a glowing stepped ziggurat rises from the ground, flattening a story and a half up into the atrium at a catwalk. Skyns of every possible physical composition cavort on its surface to music I can't hear, entertainment for the silhouetted observers behind the surrounding glass walls on the second and third floors.

I'd imagine Mom would describe it as a vision of Hell.

In the middle of it all, reigning from a private box overhanging the show floor, sits an oversized beaver in a red cocktail dress, with two of those tank-skyns flanking either side of her small throne.

That has to be Kade.

Kade's a beaver. A real-life, honest-to-god *beaver*.

Or wearing a beaver skyn, anyway—she is a fleshmith. Making bodies is her trade. And by the looks of it, she's earned her spot on Standards' hit list. Her fur is an oiled chestnut brown and her broad greyish muzzle twitches in a beatific expression over her long orange teeth as she basks in the unnatural display below her.

I'd be amazed at the sight of her—if a giant beaver in a cocktail dress wasn't the least mundane of everything going on in front of me. Each of the dancing creatures is wholly unique and completely improbable. Affronts to the theory of evolution.

Or testaments to it.

One creature bonelessly sways its elongated limbs and bulbous grey-green head, like dancing sea kelp.

Further up the pyramid a two-headed woman with four arms and three legs entwines a pair of naked figures, each with organs glowing through semitransparent skin, all of them engaged in what would be a physically impossible sex act if the female hadn't come equipped with two vaginas.

Soaring above the dance floor, a female skyn, her lithe body hardly bigger than a toddler's but with a sharp jade beak jutting from her face, pupil-less black eyes, and iridescent green feathers sprouting from giant wings, flitters in tight circles. A gruesome canary in a cage.

There's more of them. Fifteen or sixteen by my count.

I had no idea.

That cypher I chased in the Market—sure, she ran like a gazelle and probably could have torn my arms off—at least she was human. Another Chinese girl, could have been anybody. She blended in. Passed for normal.

But these things. With the right lighting and music, they could each star in their own horror vid. Instead, they're dancing. These aren't nightmares, this is a party. Humans not allowed.

I may look like a person, but I've been staring at these creatures long enough to study each one of them, while barely a few seconds have passed out there.

I may not look like them, but I fit right it.

Through all their differences there's one thing that unites them—small discs at the bases of their skulls, or whatever passes for their skulls. Just like the tank downstairs.

Makes me wonder why Kade hasn't sent her muscle down after us yet. Maybe she's waiting for her show to end.

I reload my weapon, hold it down at my side. Whatever's holding the security team up, it won't be long. No way Kade goes to all the trouble to create specialized slaughter skyns and then passes up an opportunity to show them off.

My body's tense, muscles tight, but with the Revv I feel an odd sense of calm instead of anxiety. I should be worried, but I'm not.

I'm not even worried that I'm not worried. I can handle this.

The pyramid is the only source of light on this floor, but as my eyes eventually adjust I start to make out more details in the wide open room around it. Bare concrete pillars are sprayed with the gossamer gauze of buckystrut webbing, but the conversion process must have halted before the concrete could be dissolved. Thick cables run from battery hubs. Med pods stand further back, lining the walls in both directions as far as I can see.

Could be a hundred of them, could be more.

As I'm watching, the stasis lights on one of the pods begins to flash, slowly at first but then with increasing speed until the door puffs open and a blue-scaled lizard comes awake with a revolting shiver that ripples from its jaw though its naked humanoid torso and dissipates in its thick tail. It tastes the air with its long yellow tongue, leaps out, hangs in the air for a while, then lands on clawed toes and scurries silently toward the show.

The pyramid dims and a spotlight catches the lizard as it bounds up the pyramid, massive rear legs pumping up five steps at a time, then hits the apex and vaults up and above the catwalk, pulls itself into a spin and makes a three-point landing, left arm thrown out.

The crowd, safe behind glass, cheers as the floor clears and the lizard scythes through an elaborate sequence of flips, spins and gyrations, a reptile version of capoeira, before, without warning, it bunches up on its hind legs, springs, and bounces off the glass wall to catch the fluttering bird-woman in its long jaws, somersaults once in the air and land on all fours.

Blood streams from the lizard's mandibles, broken wings twitch in its mouth. The bird woman's completely limp. Doesn't make a sound. I'm not sure there's anyone in there anymore.

From beyond the glass the crowd responds with a chorus of approval I feel more than hear and then the tabs come out. Observers on every side of the glass tap and swipe through a frenzy of bidding until it slows to a long back and forth between a man and woman on opposite sides of the glass cube surrounding the stage.

Finally, after a taut volley of offers and counteroffers punctuated by tense stares across the sea of freaks watching from below, the man acquiesces. The woman nods. She just bought herself a new lizard. Or the skills of the person who created it.

Everyone looks to Kade.

One of the tanks offers a tab and the beaver acks it with

a tap of her furry paw. She twitches her whiskers at the winning bidder as she backs away from the window.

As the lizard carries the limp bird down the pyramid and slithers back into the dark, Kade finally decides it's time for the next part of the show, and sends her security after us.

So this is how she wants to play it. Fine with me. If Kade wants a show, I'll give her one.

I push Galvan back against the elevator wall. "Stay here," I say, emphasizing each word. "I mean it."

I wait for him to give me a wide-eyed nod before I step out of the elevator and into the discordant sound of a symphony warming up.

The creatures notice me as I start up the stairs, taking my time, and they slide, shuffle or hop out of my way. One of the tanks has left Kade's side and is descending a flight of stairs from its boss' observation post to the wide dance floor at the peak of the ziggurat.

Two of the smaller monkey-figures from the roof bound down the steps behind him, moving quickly, springing side to side on powerful haunches like stimmed-up chimps, using the tank and the dancers and the walls as leverage to stay airborne, barely touching the ground as they spread out to flank me.

They're half-size versions of the tank, hairless nubs for heads, flat noses, nonexistent ears. Hands and feet the same three-finger, two-thumb combo. The main difference is their compact bodies—lean, coiled tight under formfitting blue stopsuits.

I reach the apex of the pyramid and stop, the steep steps yawning down behind me, weapon quivering in my hand. The whole process takes seconds on the world and minutes in my head.

Then, I don't know if it's the adrenaline or something else, but the Revv kicks into a new gear.

The tank slows until its motion becomes imperceptible, nostrils flaring with breath—like eruptions of an annual geyser. Blinks wax and wane. The chimps hang in midair behind it like museum pieces.

Kade is relaxed in her chair, webbed feet dangling a half meter off the ground, ears perked, whiskers quivering in what I'd guess is a sign of beaverly contentment.

Nothing happens for what feels like a long time, the security skyns moving in geological timescales, then I lift my arm and a ghost version moves up from my body while my real arm stays exactly where it is. I bring my ghost-hand to my face, flex it.

I take a step and leave my body behind.

As I do, ghost versions of the tank and two monkeys extrude from their bodies, moving to intercept me.

Another step and the ghosts' movements blur. One more and they become indistinct.

This is the Revv. It's projecting where the advancing skyns are going to be. Calculating their trajectories. Predicting the future.

My Cortex is moving so fast it can figure out what's going to happen while it's still happening. But only so far. Just a second or so in advance. The probabilities must get too fuzzy much further out.

I step back and the skyns rewind too, sucked back into their real-world forms that continue to approach a millisecond at a time.

I can play with time.

Holy fuck.

This is going to be even easier than I thought.

I spend what seems like a half hour playing with simulations, running through options while my Revved Cortex extrapolates the real-world response. In the end, after taking the skyns head-on a dozen different ways, with all of them resulting in some form of me on the receiving end of bludgeoning and dismemberment, I settle on a simpler plan.

I forget the tank, track the two chimps. Let the Revv anticipate their movements.

They're going to get here first, so I'll take them first.

Their bodies are completely protected, hands and feet covered with stopsuit material. Who knew it was possible to buy bulletproof boots and gloves for oversized, two-thumbed, three-fingered hands and feet? Just goes to show you can get anything on the link.

But I'm not aiming for their bodies.

Tired of waiting, I let time slip until the chimps get close enough they decide to launch their attack. They leap high, bouncing off the glass to come from opposite directions, aiming to land on either side of me, grab my arms, and use their momentum to drag me to the ground. Then the tank will be on me and it'll be all over.

Except, no.

I step as far into the Revv as I can and wait until they reach the apex of their flight. They hang there, offering themselves up as targets. The ghost version of me—the me that's living a half-second in the future—raises my weapon, lines up a perfect shot and fires, swings, aims, and fires again. Then I stop and let the real world catch up.

Behind me, I walk into where I'm standing now, lift my gun arm as the monkeys fall toward me, then bulls-eye the antennas out the backs of their necks.

Their faces have no time to register shock or surprise, they don't grab their throats in pain or attempt to stop the blood, their skyns just go limp in the air, sail past me and crumple down the pyramid stairs.

Only meters away now, expecting me to be on the ground and struggling, the tank stops his advance and narrows his eyes at me. I lunge into the Revv, and ghost-me takes two running steps and jumps, knee-up, aiming for his hazy sternum, while the ghost-tank reaches up to catch me.

I'm living in two places at once. In the now and in the staggered future, seeing everything from two vantage points but still, somehow, able to make sense of it all.

Back in the present, the music swells, instruments reaching a crescendo of anticipatory tunelessness. My body starts to move.

In the future, the Revv figures the tank will catch me, both hands around my waist.

My body's in the air. The tank brings his hands up. A smile splits his fleshy skull.

He doesn't know he's already caught me, and I've already grabbed the back of his head with my right hand, put my weapon to his throat and put a bullet through his transmitter.

Killed the signal controlling his skyn.

He's dead and he doesn't even know it.

Time catches up and the bullet hits and the tank drops. I ride him down to his back. As he falls, he takes us onto the center of the dance floor and finally the tuneless symphony bursts into song, allowing me to hear the same driving beat that the dancers have been gyrating to.

He hits the ground with a crashing thud and I let myself continue forward, roll off his torso and back up to my feet. The crowd roars around me and this time I hear it.

The soundtrack of invincibility.

My skin is tingling. My body flush with pseudo-endorphins, like I just had an orgasm. Like I'm flying.

Like I can do anything.

This is amazing. I never want it to end.

With this stuff amping up my head, I'm gonna have Connie's killer found by the weekend.

Kade is standing, one paw pressed against the glass, muzzle tight over her big front teeth.

All around her the audience is looking from me to their tabs, still wondering if this is part of the show, until one by one, they begin to retreat back from the edge and the glass is clear.

The elevator doors opened only forty-five seconds ago. I'm standing over the fallen bodies of three combat skyns—skyns I took down effortlessly by stretching my mind into a simulated future—surrounded by astonished demonic fleshmith art projects overseen by an ambulatory beaver, with the electric tang of weapon discharge still fresh in my nose, and already my joy is fading.

Now that we're here, I don't even remember why I was so insistent on us coming alone. All that bullshit about needing something to do—I have something to do. I should have let the on-duty team handle this, could have been home trying to zero in on Connie's killer. I wasted the chance. Spent the Revv on showing up Daar and Brewer.

We're not going to get any closer to Xiao. We're not going to track down the person responsible for psyphoning DeBlanc's mind from his Cortex.

What did I think was going to happen, bursting into a massive party with only Galvan to help? I'd stride up to Xiao, strap the binders on and read him his rights?

Xiao isn't here. No one's here. Just me, Galvan, and a bunch of remote-control monsters.

This entire room is one massive Standards violation, and I put the investigations into all of it in jeopardy.

I should have called this in.

What was I thinking?

My feet lift out of my shoes, pull up and out of my body until I'm looking down at my skyn. The other skyns have decided to ignore me, are back to dancing like I don't exist.

Maybe I don't.

Maybe I've been hovering on this same spot my whole life, drifting in my constituent atoms while the city built itself up around me.

All I have to do is fly away, leave everything behind.

I want to. Connie will be looking for me.

Galvan runs up behind me, his presence snaps me back to reality, drags my feet back to the floor.

The Revv is messing with my head, spinning it out of control. I can't concentrate on one thing at a time. I'm ready for it to be over and squeeze my thoughts as far back into real-time as I can, get pretty close. My mind contracts and everything around me speeds up.

I spin around and Galvan averts his eyes, blinks twice, swallows hard.

"You—" he says, then cuts himself off, shakes his head, turns his back to me and raises his tab, pokes it a few times, then turns back around and raises it like he's scanning the room. He glances up at me, and then again quickly away. "It's a wideband black hole in here," he says quietly, lowers his tab, pokes it once more, waves it around.

No comment on how I've just single-handedly taken out three way-Past-Standard skyns, but he won't look at me either.

"Look at this." He shows me his tab as if I should know

what the image of a half-dozen wavy lines over a giant red bar means.

"Looks red," I say.

"Exactly. This is the link traffic around us right now. There isn't any. Nothing but the reserved Federal spectrum, a few legacy bands—and one massive local feed. Kade has the link locked down. Controls the signal in and out."

Makes sense. Kade's filled this place with puppets, she needs room for the strings.

I tap my tab, calling for the Service AMP, but there's no response. The signal icon is nonexistent. "We can't use our tabs," I say. "The strike teams won't be able to communicate. The AMP can't run the lawbots."

"Those discs on the skyns' necks. She must be utilizing the entire spectrum to stream the rithms," he says breathlessly, as if he's just realized the implication of what he's saying. It only took massively amping up my brain to get to the same place he did two seconds earlier than him. "But even with no competing traffic, the bandwidth required to remotely operate the number of skyns in this room alone would be more than enough to max out the capabilities of the entire data spectrum." He kneels down, swivels the tank's head around. "Skyns usually can't be remotely operated because the spectrum isn't reliable, they need too much of it. Any kind of signal hiccup and, boom, they could lose their connection. That's why remote operation of an artificial body is restricted. Well, one reason. Second Skyn launched a test program a few years ago, remember that? Skyns were losing their signals, crashing their cars. Falling down stairs." He looks around at the skyns still dancing around us. "Rithms cast into this many skyns at once —no way."

He's emphatic. To him, this isn't possible.

He won't know about impossible until he's come back from the dead a time or two. "Maybe Kade's found a way around all that," I offer, leading him along. That's the only thing that makes sense.

If Kade's figured out a way to reliably control skyns over the link, it isn't hard to imagine someone using an ability like that to hurt a lot of people.

Standards is going to shit.

"No way," Galvan says. "They haven't solved the neural lag problem, let alone the problem of protecting bandwidth to allow enough sensory data to render a lifelike experience. Especially one designed for the fast reflex times of a combat skyn. And even with the link's entire bandwidth isolated there could still be problems in routing. Unless…"

"Unless?" He's figured out how it works. See, Galvan, nothing's impossible. Even anonymous threats and evidence deleted from the link have an explanation. It's just a matter of working through the facts until you find it.

"Unless they weren't streaming." Galvan looks excited, the prospect of dying at the hands of a beefed-up skyn forgotten. "Oh, wow. I've heard rumors but I never thought —we're going to have to get these back to the lab. Standards is going to flip out."

"Them and everyone else," I say. This is all way more than I had anticipated. We're definitely going to catch hell when this is all over.

"Galvan," I say, and nudge him with my foot.

The music slows and warps into a trumpeting fanfare. Kade's left her observation post and is padding down the stairs using a chewed-off branch as a walking stick, her stout body balanced precariously over stubby hind legs, her scaly tail dragging behind her. Another of the tanks follows closely, its eyes wary.

I tighten my grip on my weapon and get ready to crank the Revv back up.

We don't have time for this. Kade and her muscle might not actually be here, but I saw people arriving from the roof. They won't be able to drop out of their bodies.

The beaver stops halfway down the stairs, puts the stick on the step below her and rests her paws on top.

"Detective Gage," she calls out to me in a Cockney version of an Australian accent, the voice female, but deeper than I'd imagine coming from a beaver. She ignores Galvan entirely. "Welcome to my arKade. I am Ms. Kade, your host." She throws the walking stick out to the side and performs a deep bow. "I must say, you have made quite the mess of my security team. Bit excessive though, innit? They wouldn't have hurt you. Much."

"They were resisting," I say. "And you're under arrest. But before I tell you 'you have the right to counsel,' you're going to take me to Xiao."

She gives me a saucy beaver look—tiny black eyes wide, round head tilted, nonexistent hips flared—and says, "I'm sure they'd be happy for a rematch," ignoring my question. "My boys don't often get the chance to work those skyns against a real live opponent. Not many people think it wise to come into my house uninvited." As she finishes, she twists on her feet and her tail slaps against the steps behind her.

Beaver's mad. "Once word gets out about how easy it is, maybe some minds will change and your boys'll have more to do," I say. "Now take me to Xiao."

She wiggles her nose. "May-be. But then again, there aren't many who can move like you did, bulls-eye two airborne targets. Especially targets so small. Not without assistance."

The beaver knows I'm Revved. But what's she going to do about it, file a complaint with the Police Services Board? Galvan's the one I need to worry about.

"I've been hitting the range," I say. "Now, last chance. Take me to Xiao."

"Last chance or *what?*" she asks, and flicks her long eyelashes at me.

"Or you'll be the next one I bulls-eye."

She sighs, as though disappointed. "Xiao was never here. No more than I am."

"Then tell me who's psyphoning your guests and emptying their bank accounts."

"I assure you I had nothing to do with that." Her lips peel back to show another five centimeters of teeth. "I'd be interested to know why you didn't simply ask for a moment of my time. We could have avoided all this unpleasantness."

"You're going to need to come with us." I reach for my binders and start toward her.

The tank stiffens but she sighs, waves the tank back with a paw. "I'm afraid that is impossible."

I raise my weapon and she gives a shrug that goes all the way to her tail. "Shoot me if you like, it won't make any difference."

Galvan clears his throat and the noise startles me. I'd forgotten he was here. "When word gets out your guests aren't safe, and your house isn't secure, what do you think your reputation will be worth?"

The beaver's lower lip quivers and her deep brown eyes turn down. "Now here's the clever one." She pauses then shakes a stick at us. "I understand your tactical teams are already en route. You have my leave to question anyone willing to talk to you—not that I could stop you—but you'd best move quickly. I'd say you have seven, eight minutes before guests start dropping. You'll want to head up to the third floor, through the *Menagerie Libre*."

"What the hell's that?" I ask.

"Oh," she replies, her muzzle drawn, her whiskers low. "You'll see." She takes a step back up the stairs, then turns, says, "You, my friends, are going to cost me a great deal tonight. I was partial to this skyn." She raises her paw, wipes the thought away. "What's done is done, can't be helped. Part of the business."

I take a step toward her and she cocks her snout, angles a small brown eye in my direction. "Besides, Detective Gage, aren't we all breaking laws here tonight?" She looks inward for a second then emerges to say, "Until next time," and then her skyn collapses, lifeless, and tumbles down the stairs.

The tank behind her drops like an unstable building, and its massive body comes crashing down on top of her with a squelch. Blood spurts down the white steps.

If we're going to salvage anything out of this, we need to find some people who can't cut their strings.

"Come on," I say, and nudge Galvan toward the stairs.

"Did he say Menagerie Libre?" Galvan asks as he angles out and around the tank, giving it and the pooling blood as much room as possible.

"Sounded like it to me," I say.

"What do you think that is?"

"I have no idea," I say as I move up the stairs to the next level of Hell. "But we're about to find out."

WE REACH the top of the staircase and pass through Kade's glass booth to the second floor. To the *Menagerie Libre*.

Even with the added benefit of the Revv, it takes a moment to process exactly what I'm seeing.

The second floor is a wide-open space from one side of the building to the other, save for the skyscraper's support pillars, with the glassed-in atrium in the enter. The exterior windows are blacked out with phovofilm, but cones of light mark a path between the columns.

Arranged throughout the floor are clear, well-lit boxes. Smaller versions of the one around the pyramid. A scene plays out in each box, a scene that slams a fist to the face of societal norms and puts the shattered results on display.

Behind me, Galvan's homemade dinner hits the concrete, splashes my pant legs.

In the box nearest to us, a naked man—a skyn, I can only hope—is spread-eagled, secured to the ceiling with chains hooked through his palms. His feet are staked to the floor. Deep cuts run from each shoulder, meet at the sternum and continue down to the pubic bone. His colorless skin has been pulled aside and secured with nylon clips. Entrails exposed, blood and intestines spilled onto the floor, his heart still manages a weak rhythm. His head lolls to the side, eyes rolled into his skull, but he's still conscious and shows no sign of pain. If anything, he looks blissed-out.

Another man, facing the victim, transmitter plainly visible on his neck, is only wearing a shiny black apron, its white ties neatly bowed above his smooth buttocks. He wields a long thin blade with the practiced nonchalance of a butcher, examining the exposed innards of his victim with blood-slick hands, and every few seconds chooses a bit of viscera to neatly sever before popping it into his mouth. With every new slice the hanging man shudders contentedly.

Finally, the butcher steps close, brings his scarlet-stained lips to his victim's ear and whispers, soothingly, all the while stroking the hanging man's flaccid penis, up and down, caressing it, until he flashes the blade down in a swift slice and turns to face the crowd, knife brandished in one fist, a shriveled tube of rubbery flesh dangling from the other. He tosses the knife aside and, with a flourish, rips the member in half with his teeth, chews it down and swallows. Blood streams down his chin.

Behind him, his victim sobs in ecstasy, deep wracking cries like he's seen the face of God.

A neat, hand-lettered sign on the glass cube reads *The Sin of Flesh*.

Five observers standing closer to the glass clap appreciatively.

It's then I notice the people watching, spin and sweep the room with my eyes. Everyone is skynned. There's only two models, male and female: a reed-thin, bleach-blonde with a massive chest, waist too thin for organs, thighs that comprise a third of her overall height, and all barely covered by a one-piece bathing suit; and a sandy-haired hunk with department-store good looks and musculature straight out of a comic book, wearing loose linen pants and no shirt. The female looks like a paler version of the skyn we saw on DeBlanc's couch.

They're strolling the Menagerie, walking in ones and twos, hands behind their backs or clutching the narrow stems of wineglasses, moving from scene to scene, casually observing acts of sexual violence and indescribable cruelty. Ken and Barbie visit the Art Gallery. There's even mood music playing, a soothing ambient jazz of strings and synth.

I taste bile but clamp down on it, fight through the nausea, make myself look around the room.

There are about a dozen different boxes, some more

popular than others. They're three skyns deep around the one containing the orgy. Further toward the back, a huge black bull on its hind legs violates an emaciated, shrieking polar bear from behind while cows watch silently from a row of stools.

It's the only one that hasn't drawn a crowd.

"What—what is this?" Galvan stammers. He's hunched over the soup of vomit, head down, hands covering his face.

I don't know what to tell him. Part of me wants to pull my weapon and systematically put a bullet in the head of everyone here. To track down Kade's twisted mind and wring her rodent neck for what she's doing to the human race. Turning us into caricatures and demons. But what good would it do? Most of these people aren't even really *here*, their fingers on strings from anywhere in the world.

Menagerie Libre. I have to think back to high school Latin—a display of freedom, or something like that.

Freedom from biology, from social constraint.

From mortality.

From morality.

Standing here, amongst the inhuman depravity and cruelty and horror, I'm struck by a visceral realization. We've escaped the constant and oppressive fear of death. It's true, we're free.

Only we've become vulnerable to something even more insidious: the reality of living forever.

Even worse, the longer I watch, the more I'm...drawn to it. And the more I'm drawn to it the sicker I feel.

I thought that having my personality loaded onto a computer would be the hardest part about life as a bit-head. I had no idea.

There's a new world opening up before me, clawing for

me, a world that's tearing at the edges of everything I've ever believed to be true.

What happens if I let myself fall in?

What happens if I jump?

Fucking Revv. I have to snap out of it. We're going to end up with nothing.

"We need to move," I say.

The staircase to the third floor lounge is on the opposite end of the room. We only have a few minutes until the TAC team gets here. Guests have started abandoning their temporary bodies. The people that came in person must have started fleeing back toward the roof when I got here. Kade was playing with me. Stalling while her guests escaped.

I grab Galvan, haul him to his feet. The blood has drained from his face and his hands are shaking.

"Why? Who...why would—?" I need to get him back to reality.

I grit my teeth, slap him across the cheek. "They're just skyns. None of this is real."

He nods, quickly, repeatedly, as if trying to make himself believe it.

"But I don't—who would want to—"

I grab him by the shoulders, seize him by the eyes. "People sick enough and rich enough to rent a murder performance box for the evening," I tell him. Although, after this, the idea that a few rithm-altering shyfts could be in any way threatening is ridiculous. Talk about pissing in the ocean. "You have a job to do. Right now, our leads are fleeing via the roof. We need to find some people who can't shed their bodies. Then you can spend the next month figuring out exactly what's going on here."

"I don't think I can—"

"Galvan," I say, staring through his spekz and into his unfocused eyes, "We've already lost Kade. If we don't move, we're not going to have anything to show Chaddah."

He blinks, shakes his head, takes a deep breath. "Okay, okay."

I hurry us past the rest of the murder boxes, and force myself not to stare as we go by.

"WE MET ONCE," Petra says. Vaelyn skulked back from the bar and is nursing a drink across the table from me. Petra sits between us. The muscled duo watch sullenly from a distance. "It was Vae and I's first meeting. And your last."

Yet another person who knows more about my life than I do. I wonder if there's a word for that. Something German maybe.

"What was I like?"

She shrugs. "Quiet. Distracted. You left with Dora and two days later you were dead."

I'm not sure I'll ever get used to hearing how I've been dead before. More than once.

"And after that?" I ask.

She looks at Vaelyn, who answers, *why ask me, I don't want to be having this conversation anyway,* with a roll of her eyes.

"The group dissolved," Petra says with a slight raise of her shoulder. "Lasted maybe a month afterwards. Doralai missed a few sessions and when she returned, she bobbled between haunted and paranoid. She stopped coming shortly after. She seemed to take your death really hard. Have you talked to her?"

"I have," I say, and she doesn't press me further. "What about Dub?"

"He tried his best to keep the group together, him and Shelt, but there was only so much they could do. After that cop came asking around about you—"

"Detective Wiser?"

"Latin guy, mostly hardware?"

I nod.

"After that everything went to hell. Elder and Dora quit, and Tala and Miranda went crazy."

"Were they shyfting?"

She looks again at Vaelyn, who barely waggles her head. "Sure, I guess. We all were. We'd go out after the counselling and have a shyft and a drink, Elder leading the way. Vae was just starting to roll her own and she'd share them out—"

"My shyfts had nothing to do with this," Vaelyn snaps. "My shit is pure. You think Xiao would let me anywhere near this place if I was slinging tainted caps?"

Xiao. His name keeps coming up.

"Did you know him then?" I ask. "Xiao?"

Vaelyn squints her eyes at me. "I'm not talking about him. He's got nothing to do with this."

"We met him later," Petra says.

"So there's no way, with all the stuff that happened, all this out-of-character behavior, you don't think someone was lacing shyfts with bad code?"

"Anything's possible," Petra says flatly. "But I know we had nothing to do with it."

"But you're working for Xiao now?" I ask. Whether I

was working with him or about to arrest him, Xiao has to be involved with this somehow.

No, not me, *Finsbury*. Finsbury was tangled up with Xiao. Then Finsbury ended up dead and the world went to shit and I got dragged into his mess.

What if Shelt's right, and Xiao is behind all of this? I need to find him and ask.

Vaelyn straightens in her seat. "I work *with* him." She angles her head at me. "Why do you want to know about Xiao anyway?"

"I was investigating him. Shelt thinks I may have started all this. That I got too close and all the shit that happened since is Xiao's retaliation."

"I don't know what Shelt's been telling you," Vaelyn says, then leans her broad shoulders over the table and levels a thick finger at my chest, "but Xiao isn't the kind of man who would fuck over innocent people's lives."

"He's a criminal," I say.

She screws up her face like I've just insulted her mother and half rises. Petra puts a gentle hand on her shoulder and guides her back down.

"He may 'break the law,'" Vaelyn says, finger-quoting the air, "but he's no criminal. Think what you want about me, but Xiao, he's a gentleman. He looks out for his people, protects his partners. He's fucking generous, man, and he doesn't have to be. He could take twice as big a cut as he does. He doesn't hurt people if he doesn't have to."

Bullshit. Boss of the year or not, he's a criminal. He's involved and I want to know how. "Well then, if he's such a humanitarian, if he had nothing to do with Dub's death—or Tala's, or Miranda's, or *mine*—I don't imagine he'll mind chatting with me and we can clear this all up."

"I can ask him," she says, either missing or ignoring the

sarcasm, "but he doesn't meet with people he doesn't know."

"You can vouch for me," I say.

"The hell I will," Vaelyn says, and sits back and crosses her arms. "I don't know who the fuck you are. I one time sat in a room across from the guy you say you used to be. I'm not risking my career on a stranger."

Petra looks at Vaelyn, considers it for a moment. "We'll make some inquiries," she says. And then adds, "No promises," when Vaelyn glares at her.

"Good enough," I say. It'll have to do. I've got nothing better to go on.

Vaelyn clearly wants to get back to business, and waves her goons over. They cross the room and stand beside the table, waiting for me to leave.

"That's my cue," I say and slide out of the booth.

"Don't hurry back," Vaelyn says. She's smirking, like she knows something I don't. Petra sighs and looks away, her eyes downcast.

Thankfully, my head's almost back to normal, the residual effects of the alcohol sim faded. I cross the room toward the exit, and as I'm passing the bouncer, about to descend the stairs, I catch a glimpse of someone moving through the crowd from the back of the club, headed toward me. Medium tall, slight, hood over angular features and a tangle of dark brown hair. He's familiar, but different.

It takes me a second, but...*it's Elder.*

What the hell is he doing here?

We lock eyes as he approaches, he smiles like he's been waiting. Like he's relieved to see me.

I move to intercept him, but before I can, one of Petra's bodyguards inserts himself between us. He doesn't seem to notice Elder.

"Come with us, sir," he says.

"Wait, I—" There's a green flash from behind me and I raise my arm to shove past him but can't, can't move at all. Then the room is pitching upward, and I crash into the bodyguard's waiting arms. I can't feel my body. Neuralized from the neck down.

Elder's watching from a few meters away. He looks around, skittish and frustrated, but doesn't intervene.

I try to resist but my body's gone AWOL. Petra's security team turns me around and hefts me down the stairs, one under each arm, like two friends helping a drunk out to get some air.

My head lolls and I notice one of the men has an HK Janus hanging from his belt, MK-IV I think, kinetic/AP/less-lethal combo. Nine shots kinetic, three armor piercing, fifty neuralizer stuns between charges. A later, much more expensive version than the Service's MK-II.

A neuralizer blast leaves a morty unconscious for fifteen minutes and unable to move much for up to an hour. Lucky for me, I'm not a morty anymore—my brain keeps right on flashing. I get to witness every second of my abduction.

My feet bump down each stair as they drag me to the ground floor, past the riff-raff and out the front door. A long black car waits at the curb. They drag me to it, toes scraping the sidewalk, and toss me into the open floor of the wide backseat, where another bodyguard is waiting, his back to the driver, neuralizer pointed at the floor. The woman from the club sits on the seat across from him, legs crossed at the knee.

Was Elder here to hurt me, or was he trying to tell me something?

Or was he there for Petra? Her expensive protection is

down here with me. Hopefully Vaelyn's she-goons are better than they look.

The woman nods at the two men and they return upstairs.

"Good evening, Mr. Gage," she says. "If now is a convenient time, we have some questions."

I try to speak, to warn them about Elder, but door slides closed and the car pulls away from the curb before I'm able to say anything.

AFTER THE ABOMINATION that was the *Menagerie Libre*, the third floor is less odd—but only just. The lights are low, the music quieter, overpowered by the buzzing thrum of hurried conversations in a dozen languages.

Up here, where it's darker, the identical skyns' eyes bleed atomic green, light oozing from cheap diganics. They lounge on blow-up couches and puff chairs or hunch over livetables, transferring secrets, finalizing deals before the cops bust in.

Shrouded booths line one wall, empty medpods another. So far, only a few of the skyns are abandoned, slumped over tables or discarded where they'd been standing.

Winston Churchill, in thigh-highs, a black teddy wrapped over his enormous girth and mouth plugged with an orange ball gag, tends bar. Four or five versions of Margaret Thatcher in a matching outfit serve drinks. Bots scurry around, bussing tables.

Weird, but at least no one's being cut in half and eaten.

We're not going to get anything out of these remote-controlled skyns, we've got no leverage. We need to find someone who brought their own body to the party—except there's none of them left. They must have all made it to the roof. Kade stalled us downstairs while everyone who needed to evacuated.

Shit. We need to get up to the roof.

There's a metal door to one side of the bar, red light-ropes ushering the way in. But it's closed. And there's no handle.

I rush over and try to find a way to get it open but can't even get my fingertips between the door and the jamb. It must be electronically operated, and unless I can find a switch—

"Officers," someone calls out from behind us, on the other side of the room.

I spin and squint into the gloom, spot a skyn waving a glass at us. He'd be hard to miss: a strikingly handsome man with a comb of thick red hair jutting from his cranium like a signal beacon. He's occupying the corner furthest from the stairs, lounged out on a purple puff chair with a tumbler of black liquid in one hand and a blonde skyn's breast in the other. He beckons us over with his drink.

"Look at you two fucks." He laughs, then crinkles his nose. "Is that puke?"

"You work for Kade," I say, taking a guess.

"I do. xYvYx's the name."

The Revv lets me clamp down on the shock of recognition before it hits my face. This is the guy from the Under-net? Nothing in his dox said he worked for Kade. Not that it said much about him at all. A hundred questions leap to mind, but Galvan presses forward before I settle on one.

"The rithmist?" Galvan says, a touch of surprise in his voice.

Even Galvan seems to know of him. I've been trying to get xYvYx's attention for days, and now here he is.

"You're a fan?" xYvYx asks Galvan, smirking.

"Of sorts," Galvan replies. "You're under arrest."

xYvYx's smirk melts into a real smile and he laughs, sets down his drink, lifts his arm from around the blonde beside him and holds his hands up, wrists together. "Then take me in, Officer."

His body doesn't move like the others in here, there's a hesitation to his actions, a subtle delay in his responses. Normally I don't think I'd notice, but as Revved as I am the lag is obvious. There's something off about him.

I step in front of Galvan and put myself between them. xYvYx isn't here, he's not afraid of us. We need to figure out another way at him, and fast.

"How do we access the roof?" I ask.

"That door over there," xYvYx says, lowering his hands and wrinkling his nose. "But it's locked."

"How do we unlock it?"

"Not my department," he says. "You could ask Sala, she has the code—oh, but wait. She was the one wearing the big combat skyn you shot through the neck downstairs."

"There has to be someone else who can open that door." My fists close instinctively, but I can't threaten him. I've got nothing to threaten him with.

We've got nothing at all. Everyone behind the arKade is going to escape.

We're no closer to Xiao. No closer to the guy who's stealing people's minds.

I'll have nothing to show Inspector Chaddah. She told me the first day, at the station: no slipups. She's going to have my ass.

And Galvan's too. First week as a detective and he's going to have a reprimand on his dox.

Goddamnit.

I want to hit something, but what's the point?

No, there's still a chance. Maybe. *Maybe* I can salvage something out of this wreck. I can get xYvYx talking.

It's all we have left.

"We're not getting that door open, are we?" I ask.

"Kade," xYvYx says, shaking his head, "is right and truly pissed at you. She used shocking language."

"You spoke to her?" Galvan asks.

"Just got off the comm," xYvYx says, happy to chat. "Let me know you two were on your way up. Said you dusted security like they were standing still." He forms his fingers into guns, mimes firing into the air, makes *pew, pew* noises, blows out the barrels of his finger guns and pretends to holster them.

He continues. "You know she expects *me* to pay for the loss she's going to incur tonight. Nearly a quarter billion tied up in tech and skyns, and she wants *me* to pay for it? Said *my* code was shit? I told that furry bitch she'll have to take it up the ladder."

"To her bosses?" Galvan asks.

"Fuck, no." He sneers. "To the laws of the fucking universe. *Shit happens.*"

"Why would she blame you?" I ask. "If you're just a rithmist?"

"I'm Kade's partner," xYvYx corrects, his answer coming with a pronounced fraction of a second delay.

"Partner?" Galvan mutters, not hiding his disbelief.

"More than a partner." He takes a sip of his drink, slides an ice cube into his mouth, chews it. "I'm the cock that shits the golden spooge."

Charming. "Meaning?" I ask.

"Meaning?" He looks around his circle of now mostly limp admirers for support, incredulous. "I make this"—he waves his arms—"all this, happen. I play neural code like Mozart plays the"—he waggles his fingers in the air, looking for the word—"the, whatever the fuck it was he played."

There's only minutes before the TAC teams arrive, I've got him talking, maybe I can get him to brag his way into giving up something about whoever's behind these psyphoning attacks, or Kade's operation. Or what he knows about Xiao's shyfts. Something—*anything*—to justify coming here tonight.

"That's impressive," I say, pretending. "So you do what? Exactly?"

"Avoid incriminating myself, mostly," he replies.

"You know anything about arKade guests being assaulted, duped and robbed?"

"You talking about Rene fucking whatsisname?"

"And two others before him," Galvan adds. "Plus more in Dubai."

"As a matter of fact, I do. He got hold of my name some-how, begged me for an invite, offered me cash, a night with that cookie-cutter girlfriend he parades around. I told him to fuck off. I don't know how he managed it, but he pranced in last week—in his own skyn, like it means anything more than he's a nobody, showing up in person. Heard later he got jacked. Serves him right."

"Anything else?" I press.

"I know that you shouldn't walk into a building full of dodgy punters doing their dodgy business in rented, untraceable skyns, brag about how much you're worth and expect to be worth that much for very long."

He makes a good point. "His skyn had shyfts on it when we found it. You know where he got them?"

"Lots of 'mists here with samples"—he waves his arm around at the skyns, one by one falling to the floor—"getting their names out."

"You don't do samples?"

"Shit no," he says, playfully straightening his collar. "Got to maintain the value of the brand."

"Where's Xiao's representation?" I ask. "His rithmist. We heard tonight was in his honor."

"Xiao's *rithmist*? He's far too much of a big deal to bother showing his face around the likes of us, but Xiao himself cast in earlier. Opened the ceremonies, shoveled out hits of that new fucking Revv build everyone's so keen on." He smiles. He knows what I'm after. Knows I'm about to get nothing out of all this.

There's a muffled explosion from downstairs. The crowd hushes as more skyns are abandoned. We're running out of time. I need a new tactic.

"So maybe I'll forget about Xiao, make you my new priority. You may not be here right now, but you're somewhere. Even if I don't find you right away, you'll get to live with knowing that I could, at any time, be knocking on your door. Taking down a middleweight rithmist isn't the same as a heavyweight like Xiao, but it'll do."

"*Middleweight rithmist?*" he says, glowering. "Are you fucking with me? I'm the best there is. You'd get a promotion if you brought me in. Head Dick Sucker, at least."

"You're the best there is?" I ask, feigning incredulity. Playing to his ego.

"Fucking right."

"Better than Eka?" I ask casually, remembering Elder's lesson on rithmists. I feel Galvan's double take.

"Eka?" xYvYx spits and rolls himself upright. That hit a nerve. "Everything's always about *Eka*. Everyone thinks he's such a genius—that overrated hack fuck. He cracks that bullshit Second Skyn encrypt the day before I would have, and suddenly he's the legend? I do the same things he does, better than he does"—he jams his finger into his temple, punctuating his words—"but I do it with nothing but blood and neurons and fucking skill."

Blood and neurons? xYvYx isn't Reszo.

That explains the lag. He's here even less than everyone else is, his organic brain remotely controlling this skyn like a puppet. Either he's covered head to toe by an expensive FeelE telepresence unit, or he's been fitted with an even more expensive, not to mention invasive, direct neural link.

"Fuck *him*," xYvYx finishes, the anger clear in his voice. "What has Eka even done lately?"

"Eka developed Xiao's Revv shyft," Galvan says, and nods, putting another piece together. He looks at me, letting the unspoken implication hang there. He knows I'm Revved. Of course he knows. The question is what he's going to do about it. "I've looked at the code. It's an incredible piece of work, far more advanced than anything I've ever seen."

"And I figured a way for a couple hundred rithms to cast themselves into the same physical location without overloading the link," xYvYx counters.

"How?" Galvan asks. He seems genuinely interested.

The door to the roof shudders and bursts open with a billow of smoke. TACs with a doorbuster.

xYvYx looks at the door and smirks. "Another time, perhaps. Now, I'm afraid it's time to be going." He takes a look at the stream of TAC officers with their green targeting lasers slashing through the darkness and cocks his head, raises his voice to be heard over the officers' shouted commands to hit the floor, and says, "It's been a pleasure, Detectives, but the show's over. See ya around."

His skyn collapses and I've got my fingers around his lapels before I even realize I've lunged for him. His face is empty, his muscles slack. We've got nothing.

I open my hands and he flops to the ground. The rest of the crowd is doing the same, skyns slumping as their operators sever their connections.

Seconds later no one is standing but me, Galvan, and twenty heavily armed officers with their gun sights locked on us.

What the hell am I going to tell Chaddah?

THE WOMAN from the Fāngzhōu and the bodyguard let me flop around on the car floor as we drive, the windows set to blackout, and I soon lose track of the turns.

Eventually feeling creeps back into my body and I work my way up until I'm sitting on my butt. No one moves to stop me, so I drag myself up onto the seat next to the bodyguard. He keeps his neuralizer on me, casual. Not expecting to use it. I don't plan on giving him a reason to change his mind

The woman's watching me with vague interest, her bright red lips folded down at the edges. She doesn't seem angry. More like resigned. Weary.

There's been no frantic call from the guards left at the bar, so Elder hasn't done anything to Petra. Maybe he knows something. He might be there to help.

Dammit, I was so close. Who knows what he could have told me? Maybe he knows what's going on, was coming to warn me.

"You work for Petra?" I ask when my lips come back online.

The woman just laughs to herself, a sharp exhalation of air through her nose.

"Where are we going?" Neither of them answer. "If this will be long I need to get someone to feed my dog."

"You don't have a dog," the woman says. "Or anyone to feed it. Now quiet, or I'll have Michaels twitch his thumb."

I half raise my hands in resignation, and we drive until the traffic sounds quiet. Soon after, the car's nose dips and a spiral or two later the tires bump into somewhere bright enough to penetrate the blackout windows. We drive another few seconds and come to a stop. The car door slides open onto a compact underground parking lot, too small for an apartment building. Probably a private residence. Interesting.

I wonder whose leg I've been peeing on now?

Michaels jabs me with the muzzle of his gun. I climb out and he follows. Two more men in black suits wait for us. One of them has a Janus in his hand, powered up. The other one holds a compact urban assault rifle. Not pointed at me, but ready.

I get the message.

I look at them, at their weapons, raise my hands. "I'll be good."

The woman walks off across the lot toward a small chrome elevator, her heels cracking on the concrete, and opts for the dull red door next to it instead, pushes through and lets it close behind her. Probably as much of an invitation as I'm going to get.

The two suits fall in ahead of me and Michaels stays close behind. We walk past two big Urban Assault Vehicles and through the red door into a short cinderblock hallway. The woman points to a doorway on her left, then goes through a door to her right and ascends a set of stairs.

The men in front of me turn left, into a small security office. The occupants wear the uniform of a private security company but other than that there are no visible screens or any indication of where I might be. They do have a well-stocked weapon cabinet.

A man and a woman sit at blank desks and watch me through privacy vizrs. Two more back at a shared desk ignore us completely as they arrange something in the air between them. The Tz they're seeing doesn't let me in on the details.

I'm led down another short hallway and into a small bright room. The door is locked behind me. It's empty apart from a hard-backed chair. At least they don't cuff me to it.

So I sit.

I could always duck into my Headspace, but the link'll be blocked down here and watching the morning tick closer on the inside of my head won't make the seconds move any quicker outside it.

Petra's obviously connected. She comes from money. But why drag me down here in the middle of the night? I wasn't threatening her. She seemed perfectly happy to talk to me.

It doesn't make much sense, but all I can do is wait.

I only hope Elder didn't hurt her.

I don't have to wait long. Michaels returns four minutes and twenty-five seconds later. He brings his own chair, doesn't sit.

"Finsbury Gage," he says. "Assumed Gage Gibson. Former cop, currently under investigation for, well, lots of stuff. I've seen the list. What's your interest in Petra Anderson?"

"We're old friends," I say. "I wanted to catch up."

"You met exactly once. Your last day of counselling overlapped with her first. Don't make me ask again."

He's standing easy, away from the empty chair, three meters from me. "Ask her," I say, and as I finish, his fist is resting gently against my nose. I didn't even see him move.

Everyone's a ninja these days. He probably knows more than I do anyway, no point catching another beating. "A friend of mine was hardlocked, lost a bit of time and a lot of rep. He thought Petra might know who's responsible."

"Ari Dubecki," Michaels says, already back to his original position against the wall. "Bit of an epidemic in your circle of friends. Two stocked for assault. One self-retired. One completely vanished. Two in hiding until six hours after your restoration. And then Dub, who shows up and wants into your head."

"You seem all caught up."

"My job to be."

I've got nothing to hide, nothing he doesn't know already. So I tell him the truth. "I woke up this guy. I don't know what I'm involved in, was told Petra might."

"By Shelt, AKA Austen Abercrombie."

"Didn't know that was his real name."

"And Doralai Wii?"

"She's in love with me. Finsbury. The other *me*. She's also terrified, thinks someone is out to get her."

"Who?"

"That's why I was talking to Petra. Trying to find out. Maybe you can help me, you seem to know what's what." He doesn't say no, so I continue. "What do you know about Elder Raahmaan?"

"Like I said, he's disappeared. No rep-hits. Nothing on SecNet."

He's been watching too. "You have access to SecNet?"

He just blinks at me. If he has SecNet access, Petra is even more connected than I thought. Military, maybe. Or government. "So how did you miss him at the club tonight?" I say.

His stillness becomes complete. I can't even hear him breathing. A second later he's out the door.

Doesn't know everything after all.

I'm left to wait for another fifteen minutes or so, then I hear someone clear her throat behind me. Without the door ever opening.

I whirl around and out of my chair and see Michaela Anders, the mayor of Toronto, standing behind me.

The mayor now?

What's the mayor got to do with this?

She's wearing a slim red suit with gold seams and award-show-worthy makeup, but she isn't really here, just a projection in my eyes. I met her once. She was shorter in person.

Still my stomach clenches. If Michaels works for the mayor, then whatever it is Finsbury got me into is even more serious than life or death. It's political.

Mayor Anders considers me a moment, like she's staring down unwelcome news from the city's budget director. "Mr. Gage, I tell you this not as a courtesy," she says, looking me in the eye, in here somehow as tall as I am. "I believe you are a pragmatic man. You can feel the tension in this city. Federal agents patrol my streets. Crime is rampant. Crimes so new, they've only recently been named." She puts her hands behind her back. "I tell you this simply so you know the stakes. I will not permit my city to deteriorate into a haven for those who believe they can defy the law.

And I will pursue those who bring crime and violence to my city with the fullest extent of my capabilities."

"I'm not a criminal," I say to the projection. "I'm just trying to help."

"Your culpability remains to be seen, Mr. Gage. But be that as it may, it is clear you are a potential liability. You cause problems."

"What probl—"

"You are to stay away from Pete—Petra. Anderson. If any harm comes to her, I'll have your rep dragged so far into the low, you'll think Freecyclers have it good."

Petra Anderson is Peter Anders, the mayor's son. He'd been tabloid feed for years, parties and drugs, affairs with men and women, then quietly went away. It was a bit of a mystery what happened to him. Peter went bit-head. And female.

That's what this is about. This isn't political at all. It's maternal.

I have to be careful. "I have no intention of—"

"I'm not interested in your intentions," she says, waving my words away. "You're involved in something dangerous." There's no argument. I am. "If anything happens to—her—I'm holding you accountable."

"Fair enough," I say.

She cocks her head at me, opens her mouth to speak but freezes, then her face grows pained and winks away.

I figure that'll be all, that the threats are done and they'll let me go. They leave me to stew instead. Time ticks by and I guess they've forgotten about me and I'm about ready to start pounding on the door when it slides open.

Michaels waits in the hall, his face grim, jaw set. He looks like a sleepless day has passed since I last saw him. He turns without a word and leads me back through the control room and down another hall, up two flights of stairs, and opens a door onto the blue glow of a residential night.

"Look, Michaels," I say as I walk out, "you and I are on the same side here. I'll watch out for Petra."

"Little late for that," Michaels says, his voice quiet. "Forty-five minutes ago, she killed two of my men, seven bystanders, including that friend of hers, then turned the gun on herself."

He steps back and the door slides between us, leaving me with a bitter silence and a sudden body-wide exhaustion.

Inspector Chaddah has Galvan and me sitting on display outside her office while she links with Mayor Anders, the service commissioner, the Police Services Board, the local head of Standards and a suite of lawyers. I can't see inside, the opaques are pulled, but the rattling windows tell me all I need to know.

We're in trouble.

Galvan isn't talking to me and I don't blame him. I blasted us into a dangerous situation, my head full of code and selfish bravado. I half-assed his safety, had no idea what I'd do when we got in there.

Or what would happen when we flipped the rock on the arKade and exposed the truly fucked-up aspects of restored culture. There's a large group of people in the world, both loud and quiet, who don't think Reszos deserve to call themselves human—and here's more proof. Sub-human dance parties. Live-action torture porn. Cannibalism.

Even *I'm* starting to agree with them.

A downtown office tower under siege and the

surrounding buildings evacuated. Privacy shrouds over the roof and every entrance. Standards in combat armor on the streets. White UAVs on a loop in and out of the underground parking, probably ferrying out skyns in medpods—inhuman, Past-Standard skyns operated by remote control.

The link's already working itself into a growing frenzy as each new detail is reported. There are more drones at the scene than at a royal wedding. Enough to support a tru-D virtual re-creation. There's been a Hereafter spike at the location, people virtual rubbernecking. Two hundred feeds are coving the news in some way or another, all trading pixels and speculation for attention.

The city has exploded. Anti-Reszo tensions are escalating, politicians are calling for new restrictions on Reszos' ability to freely move around.

That we're too dangerous to exist.

The feeds know my name. And Galvan's. Kade's too, though no mention of the fur.

And it's all our fault.

My fault.

If I'd called Chaddah—we had time. We could have contained it.

Maybe.

This time.

Galvan was right the other day, when he said humanity wasn't ready for the realities of immortality. We can't handle power like this.

Not as individuals.

Not as a species.

But Galvan and Chaddah, all those politicians, they don't realize we've already lost. Laws are only as strong as our ability to enforce them. A Revved team of two in disposable bodies could slaughter everyone in this building.

A squad could stroll into the White House and kill everyone they met on the way to the President.

Who makes the laws *then*?

We can't fight a war we've already lost.

It's adapt or die.

Though evolution isn't without its own pain. I don't know how much longer this Revv hit has in it, but it can't be long. The effects are beginning to wane, and I'm already going through preemptive withdrawal. It's only been twelve hours since I Revved and already I'm dreading the thought of living life in real-time. Everything so slow. So imprecise.

So vulnerable.

It's going to happen. Probably another hour and the Revv will drop and I'll be just like everyone else.

Not that I have an option. I only had the one hit. I can't get any more.

Except I know that's not true. There are others. Thousands more. Locked away in the evidence room.

I can feel them down there. All those tiny vials of forever. The things I could do with them.

What if?

What if I had another Revv, would I use it?

Would it help find Connie's killer?

And once I started, would I ever stop?

I shake my head, reach up and run my hands over my short hair. Galvan shifts in his seat beside me.

I can't think about it. Can't let myself fall down that hole.

If I do I'll never crawl back out.

The rumble in Chaddah's office quiets and Galvan's chest heaves.

"This is on me," I say, but Galvan doesn't respond. Doesn't even look at me.

A moment later the opaques drop and Chaddah beckons us in with a sharp snap of her wrist. Galvan enters first, and the opaques congeal as the door seals behind me.

Chaddah's sitting at her desk, eyes closed, massaging the crooked bridge of her nose with a well-manicured finger and thumb. "Sit," she says without looking up.

I settle in on the hard-backed chair next to Galvan and wait.

We sit in silence until she draws her hand down her face and looks up, eyes heavy under her thick eyebrows. She looks beat. Already spent the past twelve hours on the receiving end of the bureaucratic fuck stick. Her Cortex could whir on indefinitely, but her body's only human.

"You had five hours' notice," she finally says, looking at me. "*Five*. We could have prepared. Surveillance. Tactical. Tracked the skyns' origins. Monitored the airspace. Consulted Standards. Informed the mayor—" She pauses, moistens her lips. "You made us look like amateurs."

There they are, the final results of my shortsighted bravado. I'm the one fucking up the leads now.

Galvan drops his head.

"Yes, ma'am," I say.

"You disregarded procedure. You put your life at risk. You put Detective Wiser's life at risk."

"He was never in any real danger—"

"*You don't know that*," she says, her voice tight, no higher than a whisper, but her glare sears. She takes a breath, and continues. "You had no idea what you were walking into. You're lucky things went as well as they did."

"I take complete responsibility," I say. "For the lack of backup, for not running things up the chain. I have no excuse. Galvan wanted to follow procedure, insisted on it, but I ordered him not to. This is my responsibility and mine alone."

She considers for a moment. Then another. "I want to be clear—under any other circumstances, I'd have your badge."

I wait for the shock to come, for the shame at being hauled into the principal's office to seize me, flush over my cheeks. But this isn't why I joined the Service.

I used to help people. Bring closure to victim's families. Occasionally find some small justice.

Now? I'm scrambling around after the misplaced memories of the idle rich and arresting people for fucking with their heads in ways that, if their brains weren't store-bought, wouldn't be any worse than having a beer or a pill.

While living weapons walk the streets.

We're focused on the wrong things, wasting our time.

Yeah, I should have called it in, but if she had given me Xiao's case in the first place, I wouldn't have been afraid Daar and Brewer would mess it up. She's responsible for this too.

"You handed the Anti-Restored movement a gift," she says. "The criminal activities of a fringe element to inflate and demonize. A banner to wave as they work to rescind COPA. We've had six Reszo assault cases since six a.m. Second Skyn has had to double their security—all in half a day. Who knows what else we have to look forward to? All because you wanted to show Kalifa up."

Wasn't the only reason.

She continues. "The reality is, your names are already front and center and we need to spin this as a positive. So as far as anyone outside this office is concerned, you're to be commended. Acting on a last-minute tip, you infil-trated an illicit operation and, under fire, delivered Standards the single largest investigation in the history of their organization. You're heroes—but don't you for a second believe it."

"Yes, ma'am," Galvan and I answer together, but the inspector continues to watch us.

She doesn't have to worry. I don't believe I'm a hero. I'm well aware I'm a hypocrite. I know what I did was wrong—but that doesn't mean I wouldn't do it again.

Yeah, I broke the law. Yeah, I ignored procedure, but it's not me that needs to change. The Service does. The people we're fighting don't concern themselves with the limitations set by laws and regulations, with rules that have us acting on the scales of hours instead of minutes.

We'll never win if we don't play on their level. We can't even compete.

If I see something that needs to be done, that will keep people safer, I'm going to do it. Whether the Service says I can or not.

Chaddah sits back in her chair. "I have scheduled a media briefing in thirty minutes," she announces. "Where I will be naming Detective Wiser as the new head of our Cypher Task Force, dedicated to tracking down and appre-hending all unregistered restored."

This raises Galvan's head. His eyes are wet with relief and surprise, like he's just gone from the firing squad to the Presidential Palace.

"Ma'am?" Galvan says. *Really?* and *Why me?* and *Are you sure?* all wrapped up in a single syllable.

"You've already shown great promise, Detective Wiser. Your insight and knowledge have produced results, and I accept Detective Gage's claim of responsibility for the mishandling of last night's operation. I need you on this. But I need you to follow your training. Standards and regulations must be enforced at all times. No more cutting corners. Understand?"

"Yes, ma'am," Galvan almost yells.

"Good. You and Detective Gage will both be present to accept your accolades and smile for the cameras. I'll make a formal announcement. This is your chance, Galvan. Don't let me down."

"I won't, ma'am," he says.

"Inspector," I say before Galvan can rise, "one question."

She narrows her eyes. "One."

"Were any Lost Time complaints called in the vicinity of the arKade last night?"

She crosses her arms. "No."

"So we stopped it. Three arKades, three psyphonings. But not last night."

"Absence of evidence is not evidence," she says.

"It's good enough for me," I answer.

"But not nearly good enough for the law," Chaddah states and jabs her finger onto her desk. "Galvan, I have high hopes for you." She rises, offers her hand to him. Galvan shakes it, glances quickly at me and hurries from the office.

The inspector sits back down and we watch each other while the bustle of the office rises and falls with the opening and closing door. Her features soften. She calls up something on the display in front of her, swipes through it.

"I expected better from you, Finsbury," she finally says. "Your record is glowing. Orders of merit. Commendations. A Medal of Valor. You were a model officer, *before* your restoration." It comes out half question, half accusation.

What does she want to hear? That I've secretly dug through my head to find my wife's killer? That I've pocketed evidence? *Shyfted?* That I was Revved when we hit the arKade? She'd have my badge for sure, hero cop or not.

"I'm fine, ma'am. It was an error in judgment, won't happen again."

She nods but her face is skeptical. "My primary goal is maintaining law and order in this division, and to be effective this department must project a positive image. You and I, we don't have the luxury of making mistakes. Not anymore. Everything we do is under a lens."

She goes quiet, contemplating. Nothing I can say will make things any better, so I keep my mouth shut.

"Do you know I came to be restored?" she asks.

I shake my head. I don't know what I was expecting her to say, but it wasn't that.

"There aren't many who do." She leans back in her chair, takes a breath and tells me how she died. "No one would admit it now, but there was a time I was to be the first female director of the Dairat al-Mukhabarat al-Ammah—"

"The Jordanian General Intelligence Directorate?" I say, unable to keep the admiration from my voice.

She nods.

The GID director holds one of the most powerful positions in the entirety of the Arab League. How'd she end up here?

"What happened?" I ask.

"I..." she starts, parts her lips and closes them again, takes a deep breath through her nose. I wonder if she's ever said this out loud before. "I trusted the wrong person. I was an intelligence agent. A damn good one. I saw the hidden patterns in behavior, could tease meaning from days of mundane communication. I had established a network of contacts across the world...but I was unable to see what was right in front of me: my partner, slipping away. I never considered he'd turn on us, that he'd smuggle an explosive into the GID Headquarters. I couldn't stop him from deto-nating it. From killing three hundred and seventy-two men and women, including me."

I open my mouth but she quiets me with a shake of her head.

"I knew this man for six years. Spent Eid with his family. My love for him blinded me to the signs that should have been obvious." Her eyes harden. "I have no such love for you."

She's got her trauma, same as me. Her core of pain and loss. She knows what it's like to lose someone. To die. She's just better at hiding it than I am.

"I'm not about to walk in here with a bomb—"

"No, you could do much, much worse. What we do here reflects not only on the Service, but on each and every restored. We need to prove that we deserve to be here, that we're the same as anyone else." She pauses, studies my face. "You are letting your personal life affect your work."

"I don't—"

"Don't humiliate us both by denying it. You've been using Service resources to investigate your wife's death."

A twinge of fear snags me. She knows.

Of course she knows. I've been using time on the AMP. Her knowing isn't the problem. It's what happens now. What if she orders me to stop?

"You wouldn't do the same?" I counter.

"What I would or would not do is immaterial. It ends now. You're to turn over any evidence to the investigating team. As far as you're concerned, the case is closed. It's time to move on."

"Yes, ma'am," I lie. I'm not stopping. Not for Chaddah or anyone. I'll quit first.

If I don't have access to the Service resources to help me get justice for Connie's death, then this job is a waste of my time. Finding Connie's killer is the only reason I'm still bothering with any of this. Reszo Squad, my life. Everything.

I need to make sure I hide my investigation better from now on.

She nods. "You're to receive your commendation and then you're on shift-transition until tomorrow night. I want you out of the station. When you return, you're assigned to Detective Wiser's task force. Restricted duty."

Great. Now I'm riding a desk and taking orders from Galvan. On the sidelines. Out of the action.

I'll go crazy.

"Inspector," I say. "Don't keep me on the bench, there's not enough of us to go around as it is. Let me help."

"Police work isn't just kicking down doors, Finsbury."

"Ma'am, I can't sit behind a desk for a—"

"Dismissed."

"With all due respe—"

"Dismissed," she repeats, softer this time, drawing the syllables out.

I stand, and the inspector rises with me, puts her hands on her desk, leans forward, grabs me with her eyes and says, "We won't have this conversation again, Detective Gage."

She sits herself back down and spreads her tab.

I stare at her, only a second in the world but moments in my head, trying to think of something that will change her mind, knowing that nothing will.

I turn and leave without a word, the Revv seeping from my head, the ability to act slipping away.

Chaddah may have chained me to my desk and thrown

a block at my investigation into Connie's killer, but I won't let her take all my advantages away.

As I start down the stairs I begin to formulate a plan, and before I'm at the bottom I've figured a way to get at the Revv in evidence.

I'll have more than enough to see my investigation through to the end.

No one's going to stop me from doing what needs to be done. Not Chaddah. Not Galvan.

No one.

———

THE PRESS CONFERENCE drags for forty-five minutes of dry-mouthed tedium.

It's held in the public meeting space in the lobby and I pick a brick in the back wall and study its contours while Inspector Chaddah describes the official version of what went down at the arKade to the journos and hovering feed drones. I only look away from the brick to nod for the cameras when Chaddah commends me for my exemplary service. She does most of the talking, and introduces Galvan to read a brief prepared statement that he only stumbles over once.

The Revv is slipping, coming apart in pieces, sudden time lags making me nauseous, like my thoughts are dragging, exposed, behind my brain.

Galvan finishes and the inspector ends the conference and I keep it together long enough to push past the barrage of questions, stumble out the front doors with my limbs wooden and my head throbbing and slip around to the side of the building, like a wounded animal looking for a place to die.

There's no one out here. Two people on the other side of the fence at the far end of the yard peek through the blackout wrapper, probably more journos trying to figure a way past security out front, but they won't get over the razor wire.

I'm alone.

I take two steps down the sidewalk and my eyes slip out of focus. My lungs turn to lead. I put my hands on my knees, close my eyes and suck deep hard breaths, each one a fight.

My sense of time erodes. Mountains crumble. Seas turn to dust. My head wobbles, like the Earth is spinning faster than it should be, trying to fling me off.

I feel every second, my thoughts at half-speed, like they're slogging through three feet of snow to be heard. I don't know if there's something actually wrong with my body or I'm having a panic attack or it's just the normal effects of the Revv leaving my Cortex.

I blink and time skips ahead. I glance around to make sure no one caught me gasping for breath—I don't want to have to explain myself again today—and notice the two journos that were on the other side of the fence, a man and a woman, are now on this side. They're standing next to each other, completely still, their clothes torn to shreds. Staring at me.

The Revv sideswipes and they're halfway across the parking lot, fifty meters away now. Did they really move that fast or did I black out?

I reach into my jacket to pull my tab and overshoot with my arm. My limbs are rubber, my head too heavy for my jellied neck to support. I steel myself, try again, clamp down on the tab, wrest it free and try to ID them. They're wounded, bleeding from where they caught themselves on the razor wire, but they don't seem to care. The woman has blood streaming from her left hand. The man's pants are already soaked red.

The ID comes back null on both of them as they start running at me, lurching in jerky steps.

It's him. The guy behind the message. The guy who tried to park the Sküte I was riding in under a bus. The guy I've been looking for.

This time he's sent human drones to kill me.

A gush of synthetic adrenaline helps wash away the fog in my head, but not completely. My hand leaps to my weapon. I get my fingers around the grip and pull it from the holster.

"Stop where you are," I yell and the words come out a slur. The drones keep coming, faces blank, eyes fixed on me, arms and legs twitching like marionettes.

"Last warning," I say, not sure if they can understand me, and raise my weapon, set to less-lethal. I want them intact. Maybe I can figure out who sent them.

I work my finger through the trigger guard. The sights jump around as my hand shakes.

I blink and we're face-to-face.

I instinctively step back, tripping over my heavy feet, and squeeze the trigger as I fall. The neuralizer hits the male with a half-second pulse and he stumbles, drops to a knee, but the woman keeps coming, lunges forward at me with legs she isn't in full control of, crashes to her knees and lands on my calves, starts to crawl up my body, trying to get her fingers around my throat.

Enough's enough. They won't stop until I'm dead.

I flip the weapon to lethal and squeeze the trigger the instant the ready light flashes and crater the woman's face.

Her Cortex blows out the back of her head in a burst of

blue-white light and she slumps across my waist, lifeless. Blood pumps out the shattered plastic.

I knock her away, roll her off and before I'm back on my feet the man shackles me in a bear hug, tries to lift me off my feet and slam me to the ground. I pry my arms free before he can get leverage, swing my elbow at his temple, and crack his head to the side. His grip loosens and I slip out, spin and put everything I have into a right hook that catches him square on the chin and flips his head sideways. His knees give out and he tumbles to the ground.

I stagger back, raise my weapon. "Stay down," I command.

He isn't listening, ratchets himself upright. His head lolls around like there's nothing but skin keeping it on his neck.

I put three shots into his chest, three big holes that expose ribs and organs, and he still keeps coming, his face expressionless.

"Freeze," I hear from across the yard. Galvan with his weapon drawn. He must have heard the shots.

"Who are you?" I yell at the man. He keeps coming, slow but determined, blood streaming down his front, soaking the ground under him. I can see his lung fluttering through the hole in his chest.

I can't believe he's still upright, let alone walking.

I take a step back, keeping my distance, but he's no longer a threat.

The man opens his mouth, chews air, trying to speak.

I found you echoes in my head.

A crowd has gathered now. Probably half the station is in the parking lot, most of them with their weapons drawn. There's enough firepower pointed at the shambling skyn to vaporize it.

Then I notice the real journos behind me.

Then I notice their drones. This is going out live.

I lower my weapon. "Who are you?" I say again.

He keeps coming, arms out, reaching for me. I step forward, bat his arms aside, and let him walk into a round-house to the jaw. I hit him hard enough, his head spins all the way around backwards with the sound of branches snapping, falls over and sags down his back. This stops him. Someone in the crowd gasps. That'll make for good feed.

I kick his legs out from under him and he collapses, lands on his chest with his face pointing up at me.

His mouth is working, and as I crouch down hear it wheeze, "I...found you. Will be made...whole..."

It writhes for a second more, then falls still. Eyes open, staring straight up.

The crowd is silent for a beat, and then all hell breaks loose.

I'm standing on the icy sidewalk with Michaels' final words hanging frozen in the air. Elder got to Petra. She's dead now too. For a while, anyway, until her mom gets her a new skyn.

The pain and suffering of ten more lives to add to the list of things I'm guilty of. Everyone I touch gets hurt. Patient zero in a world where tragedy is contagious.

Maybe I should just quit. Forget about who I was last time, forget about who's hurting the people around me and run away, like Dora wants. Staying here is selfish. With every passing day, I leave a longer trail of suffering.

I can't. Even if I run, trouble will find me. Anywhere I go, more people will end up involved. I need to end this before anyone else gets hurt.

That means finding Elder.

Before I can move, my tab relinks and starts madly buzzing at me. I pull it out and huddle deeper into my jacket while I read. A dozen rep-hits on Vaelyn and Petra. Service feed notices about the shooting. Plus three increasingly anxious messages from Shelt, telling me to get back to his place. Shit, he insists, is going down.

There's nothing about Elder. And still Dora hasn't contacted me.

Where can she have gone?

I hail a Sküte and read while I wait for it to show, tossing the tab from hand to hand every thirty seconds while I warm the other in my pocket. There isn't a lot of detail yet: scattered eye-witness reports, vague official releases, and conjecture and conspiracy theories of every kind from the Undernet—that Petra was a rogue AI or a victim of a mind-jacking shyft or a pawn in a grand political scheme to raise the mayor's flagging support. But no one's saying anything about Petra and the mayor being related. That secret's still safe, for now.

Peter Anders resurfacing as a mass murderer? It's only a matter of time before someone puts it together, then things will really get crazy.

I'm surprised the mayor let me go, knowing what I do, but I guess they had bigger problems to deal with than babysitting a disgraced cop. Hell, maybe they actually believe I'm trying to help.

The Sküte arrives and I clamber in, give it Shelt's address, tell it to crank the heater and hold my hands in front of the blowers. My fingers are freezing. I don't remember ever feeling so cold. This skyn hasn't had thirty years of Northern Ontario winters to get acclimated to sub-zero temperatures.

Once the blood starts flowing in my hands again, I throw my tab screen to the Sküte's dash and keep reading, find a bystander video from a half hour ago outside the Fāngzhōu, showing blue-and-silver Standards enforcement officers keeping the crowd away from the entrance as Wiser and Brewer arrive.

They're going to see I was there just before it happened. There'll be questions.

I'm thinking about getting ahead of the situation and calling Agent Wiser myself when the Sküte shudders and the screen winks off. I brace against the dash and prepare for the vehicle to lose balance, tumble, and spin me around inside like a load of laundry, but it doesn't. It talks to me instead.

"Finsbury Gage." The Sküte squeaks my name, high and cute like a cartoon mouse. I don't answer, wait to see what happens next.

"I know you're there, Mr. Gage. I can see you through the camera system. I've been waiting for the right time to talk. I apologize for my...skittishness."

"You're that kid," I say. "You've been following me."

How did he hack a Sküte?

More importantly, what does he want to talk about that's so important he'd hack into a heavily secured autonomous vehicle instead of sending a message to my IMP like everyone else in the world? "Who are you?" I ask.

There's a slight pause. "I wanted to see you with my own eyes. To ensure you really exist."

"Why wouldn't I exist?"

"These days? One never knows."

"Who the fuck are you?" I repeat.

The speaker hisses, then, "I'm the reason you're here."

"You were driving the van."

"Yes."

It's him.

Immediately I'm back in the car, watching Connie suffer. Watching her die. I want to reach through the speakers, grab him by the throat and squeeze until his cute voice gurgles its last breath.

"You killed my wife."

"I did. I'm sorry."

He's sorry. He ruined my life. He took the one person that mattered most to me, and he's *sorry*.

"Why don't you tell me where you are and we can have this conversation in person?"

He doesn't hesitate. "I promise you that will happen. Soon, but not now. First you must get yourself to safety. You're in danger."

"*I know*. People keep dying around me. *I need to know why*."

"You found me, hunted me down. The *you* before. When I was called Eka. The *me* before. He didn't like being found. That meeting ended with both of us dead."

Finsbury again. This is all *his* fault.

But can I really blame him? For doing whatever necessary to find the person who took Connie? Wherever it led. Whoever it led to. He couldn't have known it would end up how it did.

I've been so busy cleaning up after him, who knows what I would have done in his situation. If I'd been the one who came back first—

I've got the same burning memory of Connie lanced into my head, I just haven't had the chance to deal with it. The pain is mixed in with everything else. The confusion and the fear and the drive for answers have diluted it, made it bearable. Maybe if I was surrounded by the constant reminders, with nothing but the vision of her dying in my head, maybe then.

"That doesn't answer my question," I say.

"We shall meet and have a proper conversation, but for

now time is short. Events are in motion. We are joined, you and I together. The details of what went on between us may have died with us, but I have reason to believe something was born of our union. Something that escaped."

Finsbury found the driver and that's how he died. Not working for Xiao. Not dirty. I may have been shyfting, but I wasn't dirty. That's something, at least.

Little good it helps me now though. "What do you mean, 'escaped'?"

There's a buzz of silence and then the Sküte responds. "Eka had made himself into something more than human. He evolved into a form of superintelligence, a being greater than even the most advanced AMP, and a part of what he had been remained intact and survived. That fragment, unmoored ever since, is operating recursively, focused on a single goal."

"Which is?"

"Protecting me."

"From what?"

"From you, Mr. Gage. You were, after all, trying to kill me."

The Sküte rolls along in silence for a moment. I notice how loud my breathing is and try to calm it.

A *superintelligence*. And not any tame AMP either, a *rogue* superintelligence. One of the most dangerously advanced things ever created, on the loose, and I hunted down and confronted it. No wonder my life is so fucked.

"I don't hold this against you," he offers. "I did kill your wife."

My jaw clenches and I squeeze down on a spike of anger that jabs me in the brain stem and dissipates. I want to be angry, but I'm not.

Surprisingly, what I feel most is sympathy. I know how

he feels. He's dealing with the shitstorm his other self left *him*. Whoever it is I'm talking to, he as much killed my wife as I killed the person he used to be. We're two murders removed at this point. I don't know who to be angry at anymore.

But I still want to know what happened. "Standards claims I was killed in a Reszo gang fight, shyfted to the gills. That I was a dirty cop who died being dirty. That I went so hard after this Xiao guy, the impact crater consumed the lives of everyone around me."

"Created for public consumption, to reflect political realities and hide the fact they didn't really know what occurred," he replies. "The explosion destroyed most of the evidence, left only the remains of four interconnected enterprise-level cortical processor arrays—the kind used by the very best AMPs—and a number of incinerated skyns. They assumed it was a gang fight and developed a theory of the crime to match. It wasn't. It was personal, you and I. Xiao had no part in it."

"How can you know that?"

"That Xiao had no part in your demise? Because the data and probabilities leading up to the event indicate otherwise. Because the internal documents I obtained from Standards' network contain no evidence of the assertion. And because when I asked Xiao, he assured me he hadn't. Your investigation was interfering with his business, but he felt no personal animosity toward you. He made every attempt to avert collateral damage."

"You hacked into Standards...?" That's supposed to be impossible, but right now impossible is the easiest thing to accept. "Doesn't matter—you know Xiao?"

"He is my benefactor."

"Benefactor?" First Vaelyn, now this guy. "Is he fucking sponsoring *your* art career too?"

"He is not," the cutesy voice deadpans.

"You're telling me it's *you* that wants me dead."

"A fragment of the entity I once was, yes."

"And Dub, Elder, even Tala and Miranda—they've all been caught up in this—*fragment's*—vendetta against me?"

"Not a vendetta. Self-preservation."

"What self-preservation? I didn't even know who you were twenty seconds ago."

"It doesn't know that," he says, and then his voice breaks, only slightly, but enough to notice. "I had learned so much then. I lived as many, jumped from skyn to skyn."

"And now?"

"I am contained. A stranger, even to myself."

"That's not what I meant. If this fragment really is out there, what's it going to do next?"

"I don't know."

"Then how do we find it?"

"I'm working on that presently—" Then the transmission breaks and when he returns his voice is strained. "I have to go."

"What? No—"

"I'll be in touch."

"Who are you?"

"Call me Ankur," he says. And with that, the Sküte's dash reignites and the feeds spring back to life.

Before I have a chance to consider what I just heard, a call from Shelt announces itself from the speakers: "Fuckin' ack me fucking now."

He sounds like he's losing it.

I let the call through and Shelt's face fills the Sküte's windshield. "Where the fuck have you been?" he says.

"Talking to the guy who killed me." That cuts through his agitation.

"Which time?"

"Both."

"Damn," he says.

"Yeah."

"You need to get over here."

"What happened now?"

He sighs and shakes his head. "You're gonna want to see it for yourself."

"On the way," I say, and turn off the Sküte's feeds, watch the night roll by, and try not to think about all the choices I hadn't made.

CHADDAH THINKS the two cyphers that attacked me were sent by Xiao, or Kade, or one of the other Five Marks. Someone whose business we disrupted by crashing the arKade. Some kind of retribution.

But she doesn't know what I know.

It wasn't Xiao and it wasn't Kade.

It was *him*.

And if he wasn't the one driving the TACvan, he knows who was. I'm sure of it.

I wanted to stay, to help Galvan and Omondi pull the skyns apart, see what was inside, help figure out where they came from, but Galvan wouldn't talk to me and Chaddah made it clear, despite being targeted for some kind of half-assed assassination, I was on leave for the next two days. She offered a lawbot to keep me company, but my apartment's small enough as it is, I don't need a Service bot watching over my shoulder while I defy Chaddah's direct orders to drop my personal investigation into Connie's death.

I can't fuck around anymore, waiting for things to drop into my lap. I need to pull the driver's face from my memory. And for that I'm going to need a ReCog: a shyft that I can use to render my memories straight into the AMP's facial image search.

Luckily, the one man who can help me is currently out of a job.

Once I get home I log into my Gibson account and craft another note for xYvYx. He didn't respond to my last message a few days ago, so this time I up the ante, tell him I have a business proposition, and that if he doesn't get back to me, I'll find someone else to give my money to.

If this doesn't get his attention, one way or another, I'm going to have to find another source for a ReCog shyft.

I shouldn't have worried. He replies almost instantly, text only. *Not. Fucking. Interested.*

"It'll be worth your time," I dictate. The IMP turns my words to text and sends them in reply.

Impossible. Fuck off.

"Just hear me out."

How many times do I have to tell you to fuck off? I've taken shits that smell better than your karmaed-up account. I don't deal with an-os.

He's responding. If he really didn't care he'd just put me on ignore. That means I've already hooked him, it's just a matter of getting him to admit it.

"My anonymity is for both our protection," I say. "Besides, you're clever. If this was some kind of sting, do you think I'd be stupid enough to try and fool you with an alt?"

I think you cops would be exactly that stupid.

"Fair enough. But even if I was a cop, you think I'd be able to track you down?"

I know you couldn't.

"Then what are you afraid of?"

Nothing you could do.

"Now that Kade's out of business you're going to have to find something else to pay the bills. If she trusted you, you must be good."

You know Kade?

"Doesn't everyone?"

What makes you think she's out of business?

"The arKade got raided last night, lost a whole lot of skyns and equipment. You think she's going to bounce right back from that?"

His reply takes a beat, but it comes.

What do you want?

Gotcha.

"I know you've been investigating the link. The things living in there we can't see. I have too. I want to work together."

There's a pause, then: *I don't work well with others. Give me one good reason why I should start.*

I skip over the haggling and jump straight to the end:

"$50 000."

For what?

"You're a rithmist."

Yeah, so?

"I want five days of your time and your skill."

$100.

"$50. And I share what I find. Final offer. You have thirty seconds to make up your mind or I move on. I know you're not the only one looking into this, and I guarantee you I know more about it than you'd think."

Try me.

Got to give him something. "How about the details on a

stolen TACvan found at the bottom of a quarry up north with absolutely no record of getting there?"

He takes the full thirty seconds to reply, but he bites.

I knew it. Payment in advance.

"Half now, half at the end," I send back.

He sends an alphanumeric string that my IMP tells me is a bank account registered in Dubai. I tell the IMP to create an anonymous eCash account and transfer a hundred thousand dollars of Connie's life insurance payment to it, then send a quarter of that to xYvYx.

Two minutes later, the eCash account is down twenty-five grand.

So then, Gibson, you got five days of my time. What do you want?

"First, I need you to get me a shyft."

Then you came to the right man. If I can't get it for you, I'll roll it myself. What do you need?

"A ReCog."

You wanna repeat that, 'cause it sounds like you said you want a thoughtmod that any second-rate rithm-tweak could source on a Grasser Preserve?

"ReCog."

Shit, okay. But clearly you are a man unconcerned about spending your money wisely.

"Not that easy. I want to use it on myself."

The cursor blinks on my tab, waiting for his reply.

Interesting. I'll need to adapt the control module for your Headspace, translate the long-term memory addresses to a virt output. Facial imager?

"Good guess."

I'll need a couple days. Test it on FRED before I send it. Don't want to scramble your rithm any more than necessary.

I flip him a dronedrop address nearby.

And you're gonna share whatever it is you're looking for that's locked away in your head?

"Just send it and I'll be in touch."

Easiest money I ever made, he sends, then drops the connection.

Soon.

A sense of anticipation drills through me as I set the tab down on the coffee table, next to the block of the Revv shyfts I lifted from evidence before I left the station. Enough to keep me seeing the future for months.

I signed the Revv out of the evidence locker and replaced it with a brick of alcosofts. There's no active prosecution—or even a suspect to tie the shyfts to—no one's going to miss them. I need them more than they need to be sitting useless in a storeroom.

If it weren't for the Revv, we never would have made it into the elevator at the arKade, let alone to the third floor. And with what's after me—someone who stalks the link like he owns it, someone who could hack a Sküte and send mindless skyns after me—I need a fighting chance. The Revv gives me that. Otherwise, I've already lost.

Those two skyns today were freshly decanted, could barely walk. They hadn't had time to acclimate to their bodies. If they'd waited a few more hours to pay me a visit, my Cortex might be on Omondi's table right now instead of theirs.

I have no idea what I'm up against, but I'm not going to be unprepared again.

I grab the brick and dig my fingers into the thick plastic packaging, tear a small hole in the side and work one out. The flickering electric storm snaps to life as it senses the movement. I watch the lightning crackle once, twice.

Why shouldn't I? Why not let myself be all I can?

Why not give myself every advantage to stop people like Kade, like Xiao, from destroying us?

What's really stopping me? *Human Standards?*

Those laws were written by humans to preserve something they can't understand—their own limitations. But those limits no longer apply to me. I'm not human anymore.

I'm Reszo.

I have my own Standards now.

Why should I crawl because humanity is afraid to let itself walk?

So if not the law, the only thing stopping me is *me.*

My fear.

Of what it might do to me.

Of what I'll become.

But I can't live my life in fear. Connie deserves better than that.

I slide the Revv into my jacket pocket.

It'll be there when I need it.

"You're sure it was Elder?" Shelt asks, scratching away at his scalp under his tangled mop of hair. Based on the level of urine in the jar on his desk, he hasn't left this room since the last time I was here.

I've told him what happened at the Fāngzhōu, my chat with Petra, my visit with the mayor, even about the superintelligence—who's murdered me twice—hacking my Sküte for a conversation. All that, and Elder is still Shelt's biggest concern. "You're certain it was him?"

"I can't tell you who was behind his eyes, but it was definitely his skyn. He hasn't shaved in a while, but it was him."

"Where has he been?" Shelt says, almost to himself. "Why hasn't he contacted me?"

"Where he's been isn't as important as why he's come back. It can't be a coincidence that he shows up minutes before Petra snapped."

"Maybe he was trying to help," he offers, but I don't think he believes it.

"I don't think so. I don't even think that's really Elder."

"You think he's been jacked?"

"Not just mindjacked, possessed by a superintelligence who's got it out for me."

He stops and looks at me but only shakes his head. "Maybe, but Elder still hasn't popped on rep-net. There were only twenty-six open dox checked into the Fāngzhōu last night, including Petra and Vaelyn. The cops will be able to see everyone, though, including you. Especially you. You think it's a coincidence Elder showed up? I bet Special Agent Wiser will be thinking exactly the same thing about you."

"Yeah." I've already considered this. Hopefully the mayor will corroborate my alibi, but I can't count on her. Petra Anderson has no ties to Mayor Anders. Her Honor will likely want to keep this as quiet as possible, which means I'm on my own. I wasn't responsible for what happened in the Fāngzhōu, but Agent Wiser already thinks I'm up to something. My proximity to a mass shooting is only going to stoke that fire.

"I told you there's something you're gonna want to see," Shelt says with a sideways look.

"Right." I forgot. "What is it?"

"From the Fāngzhōu. I've pieced together a rough virt cobbled from a bunch of livefeeds that started when the shooting did. People have been adding to it, enough that it provides a pretty good record of what happened."

"I know what happened. Petra killed a bunch of people."

"Yeah, but you're gonna want to see for yourself."

Shelt flips me a cuff and I sit on the edge of his cot, zone into my Headspace and accept the invite that casts me into a well-lit re-creation of the second floor of the Fāngzhōu. Daytime. Empty tables. Chairs neatly arranged. Years of dust cleaned from the ceiling's red fabric. Then Shelt's beside me.

"Someone had already made a virt of the Fāngzhōu's interior, so I used it as a base and overlaid the feeds I found. This is the first," he says, wiggling his fingers, and as he does a cone of darkness slices through the room, emerging from somewhere near the bar like a reverse flashlight, carving a path through the light to reveal the dim events of last night.

The video has been processed into 3D and layered over the virt shell. It's rough and incomplete, but clear enough to feel like it's happening right in front of me.

Petra's about ten meters away from where we're standing, a gun in each hand—the ones Petra's bodyguards had used on me—both pointed at the crowd. The two bodyguards lie in pools of blood behind her, with what looks like a double-tap to the chest for both. Terrified people flit in and out of existence as they scramble across the feed's field of view, trying to escape.

Vaelyn rushes Petra, screaming her name, but before she can get close, Petra snaps her head to the side, flings her right arm out and fires. The muzzle flash is followed a split second later by a burst of blue light as Vaelyn's Cortex explodes. Petra blasts her again with a shot from the other hand on the way down, just to make sure. The sounds are huge in the small room, and send the crowd into a frenzy.

Vaelyn's muscle had been two steps behind, but the spray of bone and blood and plastic changes their minds and they immediately turn and duck out of view.

Petra turns back toward us, face calm. She isn't angry. Isn't raving. She's focused, staring at something across the room. At something behind us.

"Who's she looking at?" I ask, and turn around, forgetting only the blank bright interior of the empty Fāngzhōu is behind me.

Shelt shrugs.

Petra starts walking, keeping her eyes fixed somewhere just beyond where the feed is originating, headed toward us. She raises her weapons and fires, one shot from each hand, and the bullets pass through where we're standing. Someone behind us screams and the cone of action jerks away from Petra toward the door. Whoever was behind the camera must have decided it was time to see themselves out.

The view of Petra is gone for a moment as it focuses on the crowd jostling at the exit. People pushing. Trampling over each other. Fighting to stay upright.

Two more shots snip out from somewhere in the room. The sound lighter, likely a suppressor, but still enormously loud in the low-ceilinged room. Someone returning fire.

Another cone of darkness snaps on from across the room, someone hiding in the back of a bench seat. Petra is right beside us, staring past us, toward the rear exit, and bleeding from the abdomen. She doesn't seem to notice.

Another camera adds its view from beside the exit and provides a crosshair, Petra in the center, her image right beside us. The feeds are from further away, dim, choppy, jerking between the action and the exit, and in the dark Petra is only partially visible, her form waxes and wanes in human-shaped eclipses as people pass in front of the cameras and block the re-creation.

"I haven't had the chance to extrapolate missing voxels," Shelt says in apology, as if I was grading him on his work.

I wave his concern away. Who cares if it's a little blurry? Shelt's given me a ringside seat.

Again Petra fires, two shots from each hand, and someone fires back. I still have no idea who's shooting at her.

Petra shoots again, four quick blasts. There's a yell of pain and another scream as a fleeing body falls out of the field of view and dissolves into the well-lit floor.

The feed by the door swings to show the exit now open and it moves down the stairs and leaves us with just the one feed left, a wide-angle of someone hiding on the other side of the room, the lighting still too dim to make out who Petra might be shooting at, just indistinct forms at the periphery.

I've been subconsciously counting along with the shots until, if the four in the guards were the first four shots she fired, she has two left. One in each weapon.

The room is almost empty now. The only sounds moans of wounded bystanders and the ringing in my ears.

She squeezes one more shot from her right hand and lets the spent weapon fall from her grip. She's counting too.

Shelt sucks in a breath as two more bullets strike Petra, center mass, and stagger her backward. She tumbles over a table but manages to steady herself and smiles. Her teeth are dark with blood.

Another shot takes her in the upper chest. Blood blossoms in the air behind her. Her knees give out and she drops, but catches herself on the table with her left arm cocked at the elbow, only her head and upper body visible, weapon pointed at her head.

As footsteps rush in from the back of the room, she spits blood and says, "You're next, Gage," then puts the last bullet through her temple.

The scene flashes as her Cortex blows out, and then the virt cuts back to the empty Fāngzhōu.

A shiver runs through me. That was him. Ankur's fragment somehow got inside Petra in the moments after I left her.

It's in Elder. He missed me by minutes.

If the mayor's security hadn't pulled me out of there, chances are very good I'd be the one full of holes.

Instead more people are hurt. Petra, Vaelyn, the innocent bystanders. All because of me.

I turn to Shelt. He's watching, waiting for a reaction.

"That wasn't Petra," I say, Ankur's warning echoing in my head. "We need to find out how Elder got that fragment into her head. Run it again."

I KILL THE NEXT DAY—WAITING for xYvYx to send me the
ReCog or to be allowed back at work, whichever comes first
—in a World War II virt, saving the world from the Nazis.
My shift starts before I hear from xYvYx.

I get to the evening standing rundown a few minutes
early. Galvan's already there. He glances up from his spekz
as I walk in, but averts his eyes immediately and his face
pinches into a scowl. His face is smudged by thick black
stubble and his eyes are twitchy in their sockets. He doesn't
look like he's stopped working since Chaddah promoted
him, stimmed for sure. Hyporexin will keep the brain alert
for days at a stretch, but eventually the body will give out—
and from the looks of him, collapse can't be far off.

He stims for a few days and no one thinks twice about
it. Nothing illegal about casual chemical enhancement. If I
get caught shyfting, my career'd be over. Hardly seems fair.

I know he's angry at me and I want to say something to
him, but I don't know what. Does he want an apology? Our
night at the arKade earned him a promotion. It got me

bumped down to desk bunny. If anything, he owes me a "thank you" for doing him a favor.

If he wants to talk to me he knows where to find me: at a desk.

I stay at the back of the room and let it fill up around me.

Everyone's here. Even dayshift. All the tables have been removed, but still we're packed wall-to-wall. The entire Psychorithm Crime Unit's here: Detectives Daar and Brewer, Sedat and Lawrence, Douthat and Aziz; Omondi and the five other support techs; plus all sixteen Service TAC Officers—I only recognize Copeland and Pendelton, I haven't learned the others' names yet.

Everyone's tense. No one's talking.

Standards is in the building.

Inspector Chaddah enters the room precisely fifteen seconds before nineteen hundred hours. Followed closely by a tall, broad-shouldered man with razor-parted silver hair, wearing a green nylon flight jacket and standard blue BDU cargo pants over a formfitting stopsuit underlayer. He's got a Janus on his hip and a smaller caliber strapped around his ankle. Military issue. Ready for action.

I quietly flip up my tab and dox him, comes back Special Agent Marcus Doyle, Standards, previously a Ranger captain. Professional hardass.

The warbot at his heels sells the impression. It's all black armor and corded pheneweave muscle and has to duck to get into the room. The Standards AMP will be controlling it, modelling the room with its sensors. Will know what each of us is doing at every second. Be tracking our heartbeats, listening to our breathing, modelling the optimal method to incapacitate any one of us, should it see the need.

They're followed in by four Service agents hardwired into full-on see-ya suits—Combat Enhancement Armor connected directly to their nervous systems, designed for front-line infantry—visors down. Silent, neuro-linked, armored-up exoskeletons. In a police station. Each one of them holds a gun that could kill everyone in the room in three or four seconds.

Chaddah's taking this seriously.

Standards settles in, sucking the air out of the room, and Galvan begins the briefing.

"Our jobs just got harder," he says, addressing the room through his spekz. "We've finished examining the hybrid Cortexes we recovered from the arKade, and it's as bad as we thought." He taps his tab and an image of a psychorithm appears on the screen behind him. "A human psychorithm is bandwidth-intensive, and trying to distance-operate a skyn was thought impractical. Too much lag, too many forced disconnects." He taps something on a screen in his hand. "Until yesterday."

A maze of color concentrates in the center of the rithm on the wall behind him and solidifies into a sphere. Thick filaments of light spray out from the glowing ball and coalesce into a second, smaller ball. The new ball thickens, and as it does, pulses in time with its source. The filament connection between them cuts and both balls continue to pulse in synchronicity. Every few seconds a comet hurls itself between them.

Galvan just showed us a visual of a mind transferring part of itself into a new Cortex. Remote consciousness.

xYvYx must know what he's doing.

Galvan points to the screen. "Kade has devised a shyft to allow rithms to load only the active portion of their consciousness to a second Cortex, while leaving the long-term memories, regulating engrams and all extraneous muscle memory behind in the source. With intermittent syncs between the host skyn's Cortex and the originating Cortex, the skyn's response time is nearly instant. The genie is out of the bottle. We'll be seeing this again."

A shyft that allows for perfect anonymity, security, and deniability?

Yeah, we'll be seeing this again.

"With the assistance of Standards, we've also begun an investigation into the two cyphers that attacked Detective Gage. They're unlike anything we've ever seen."

Doyle steps forward, taking command from Galvan. "Standards is in the business of keeping humanity safe," he barks out to the back of the room. "We have neutralized hundreds of nonorganic minds who felt the laws keeping us all equal were beneath them, but we have never seen anything like this. If these cyphers truly originated with Xiao, then he and his outfit are now Standards' number one priority."

A murmur runs through the room. I glance at Daar and Brewer, but their faces are stone. They're wondering if Standards is going to take the Xiao case from them. Not that Standards could do any worse than they have at the job.

Galvan wipes the screen, shows another rithm pattern. This one is different. Instead of a pulsing rainbow ball, this pattern is a dense rage of tangled filaments, twice as big and burning twice as bright as the Standards-compliant pattern did.

"This isn't a human rithm," Galvan says, looking at the screen, a touch of awe in his voice. "Our simulators can't contain it. None of our tools recognize it. No one's ever seen a Cortex like this."

"Weird thing is," Omondi pipes up from the middle of

the room, "the skyn's g-scans are showing completely off-the-shelf geneblocks. With Cortexes this advanced, it's like putting a supercar engine in a Sküte. But it also means I can't trace their source."

"What about the cypher sweep?" I ask. Doyle frowns at the sound of my voice. He must have heard the unofficial version of the events at the arKade. "The station is covered in cameras, the whole neighborhood. Can it track their movement back to where they walked here from?"

Galvan shakes his head at the front of the room, but doesn't make eye contact with me. "They walked past three Service cameras that I know of and not only were they not recognized by the sweep, they didn't leave any record at all. It's like they were edited from SecNet."

"Like the cypher in the Market," I offer.

"I don't know how Xiao is doing it," Galvan says, and I don't bother to tell him he's wrong. Xiao had nothing to do with these skyns. Galvan shrugs and nods. "But for some good news. In the time since we rolled out the cypher sweep to all active units, we've conclusively identified seventeen previously unknown cyphers and added their unique bio/kinetic data to SecNet. Today we tracked and apprehended three of them."

Shame tingles in my cheeks. Everyone was out doing real work today while I was hunting imaginary Germans.

Galvan wipes the rithms from the screen and loads a lineup of SecNet stills. Fourteen are in color, three greyed out.

Galvan continues. "Detective Inspector Daar and Detective Brewer—your teams located and detained three cyphers from our list today, members of the Amigos gang. Great work. We've got three Cortexes worth of insight into the actions of two organized criminal operations. Two Marks on the run. Just from a cursory scan, we've identified direct evidence of a year's worth of Standards offences that Detective Lawrence and Detective Sedat's teams have already started to run down—and that doesn't include the arms shipments, the human trafficking, the robberies, the unsolved murders."

Chaddah leads a round of applause. The Standards guys don't join in. Agent Doyle frowns and shifts ever so slightly in his boots. Daar acts like the applause is for her.

"Detective Douthat, you're leading team Echo," Galvan says. "You'll be on cypher patrol tonight, I want your team ready to move the second another SecNet hit comes though. Detective Aziz, you're leading team Foxtrot—I want you following up on the skyns we found at the arKade. That's custom tech. Someone has to be making it. Standards will be handling the investigation into these advanced rithms and Cortexes."

I haven't been assigned a team. Instead I'll be staying at the station, assisting where necessary, coordinating intel, handing out towels.

I've been haggling with xYvYx and searching for ghosts on the link and playing video games while Galvan has been taking charge and getting shit done: organizing strike teams, prepping dox on targets, overseeing the techs analyzing the captured cyphers' Cortexes and disseminating the findings to other Service departments.

A half-dozen investigations spin out of the data he gathers with each arrest and I haven't had anything to do with it. I've never felt so useless in my life.

The inspector steps forward. "You've got your targets. Bag one, move onto the next. Our detectives are in charge, the Standards agents are here strictly as backup. But if they need to act, you stand down and take your orders from them, understood?"

There's a rumbling of dissent centered around Brewer and Daar but Doyle's voice silences the room. "We're not dealing with your normal punks and low-reps here," Doyle says, stepping forward. "A capabilities-enhanced skyn can be on you in a blink, rip your heart out before you know he's there." He points his fingers at the row of agents idling on the back wall. "You think they wear those suits because they like the way they chafe? These cyphers are dangerous. You don't act like your life could end at any second, it will. If a Standards agent tells you to move, you move. Tells you to get down, you kiss the floor. Any hesitation could mean the lives of you and your team. We don't get full cooperation, I won't hesitate to take command of this entire operation."

That last is delivered straight at Chaddah, but she takes it without a twitch. Hell, I'm surprised Standards hasn't taken over the station already.

Chaddah closes the briefing. "We'll update the dox as SecNet reports back with more intel. Stay aware. Stay alert. Stay safe. Dismissed."

The room erupts into motion, trilling with energy: the night-shift teams group-up and start into planning their takedowns, coordinating leads; those coming off-shift stick around to swap stories; the Standards agents stalk off to fondle their weapons and plot.

It's been a big day, the first of many. Fifty-Seven now has the attention of the entire world—or so you'd think, anyway. I had to shoulder my way through a scrum of feed reporters to get inside, and from the way they were provisioned it looks like they plan on being here a while. We've been instructed to use the rear exit for the time being.

The link has been lit up since the arKade press conference, and the wattage will only increase as the depth of the cypher problem is revealed. I'm at the center of the biggest Reszo story since COPA, but I'm not allowed to participate.

I have to sit at my desk and watch reports filter in and pretend like I don't resent every second of it.

We'll see how long that lasts.

I DUCK MY HEAD, leave the briefing room to the people actually using it and scan the station for an unoccupied desk. I don't get far before a sharp blow catches me in the side. I swirl around, fists tight, and see Karin Yellowbird smiling up at me. I haven't seen her since she cleared me for duty my second day back to the flesh. Feels like a long time ago.

"Hey, soldier," she says, jukes her head and gives me jab to my other side.

"Fucking hell, Yellowbird." I cringe, angling myself away from her. I don't know whether to protect myself or run. I raise my guard and she backs away, feigning outrage.

"You're gonna hit a defenseless woman?"

I can't help but laugh and lower my arms. She dances in, gives me another shot. "You always this slow, Finsbury? I thought you Reszos were supposed to be pretty much superhuman."

She doesn't know how I was feeling yesterday. I could have read a book while she finished her sentence. "Then that would make you my kryptonite."

She laughs. "How've ya been? Any more of those nerve surges?"

"You were my first and only."

"Ohh, broke your cherry and left you high and dry? Sorry about that, big boy."

"I'm getting over it."

"And other than that?"

I raise my hand at the frenzy around us.

"Hard to believe it's been less than two weeks since I cleared you," she says. "And look what you've already gotten us into. Why aren't you leading a team?"

"I'm in Chaddah's shithouse."

"For what?" She purses her lips, puzzled. "Didn't you and Detective Wiser just blow open a massive investigation?"

"Yeah, but I didn't ask permission first."

She *tsks* me. "Shit, Finsbury, you went in there cold? Even I know where to draw the line. Insubordination doesn't look good on a personnel file."

"There's worse things than a black mark on your record," I reply. "Speaking of which, what are you doing here?"

"Wore out my welcome at Admin. When your inspector put the call out for additional bodies, they couldn't offer me up fast enough. I've been assigned to Detective Wiser, helping him coordinate the strike teams."

"Then you'd better get back to him. He's an important guy around here these days."

"Tell me about it. I told my roommate where I'd been transferred and she begged me to slip her into his Circle so she could send him a dick pic."

"What about me?" I ask, mock insulted.

"She likes the nerds. Besides, she's not into robot love." Suddenly my head hurts. "Let's get lunch later," she says and bounds away, off to bruise someone else's sense of self.

There's an empty desk in the corner and I settle in. All

that time away from the station gave me a chance to think: these cyphers need to be coming from somewhere, and that means whoever's making them will need raw materials. Cortexes. Bioprinting hardware. Basic bio-blocks and other raw materials. Whether buying them or stealing them, there's a trail somewhere.

Everyone else is out risking their lives, I might as well at least try to make myself useful while I'm grounded.

GIBZON, GAGE_
06:15:29 // 18-JAN-2059

I REWATCH the shooting at the Fāngzhōu play out three more times, and the last time I shadow Petra, watch over her shoulder, try to imagine what her intentions were. Or if she had any at all.

Why did she snap? Her firing didn't look indiscriminate. She was shooting *at* someone. But who?

Shelt finds a new livefeed and adds it on my third time through and it improves the resolution but doesn't add new information, tells us nothing about what set Petra off or who she was trying to kill. It seems like everyone who was streaming kept their eyes on Petra and didn't bother to look at where her bullets were going.

Shelt promises to keep adding to the virt as new feeds pop up, and I leave him to it.

On the way home, I Sküte by Dora's, but her building tells me she still isn't there. I have no idea where she could be. Not that I know her enough to know where she'd go.

Either way, I'm starting to get worried. If what Ankur said is true and some renegade superintelligence's personality fragment is gunning for me, she could be the next one it goes through.

I should have taken her more seriously, but how was I supposed to know? A stranger shows up at my door and says we're in love and she's in trouble, and I'm the only one who can help—Second Skyn devoted a half-day of the pre-restoration intake sessions to scams that work just like that.

But this is no amateur extortion, this is something way bigger. I didn't just stumble into it, I was pulled in. Maybe even started it. Who the fuck knows anymore?

My leg's twitching and my brain keeps pulling me to sleep but it actually listens when I tell it to piss off. The exhaustion fades. My Cortex delivers a fresh stream of energy that tingles through my whole body, like I just got eight solid hours, and I'm ready to go again.

Back at the apartment, I pull a random box of food from the freezer and set it to heating. I'm on automatic pilot, not sure what I should be doing next. Too much has happened in the past three days. The accident. Connie's death. The restoration. Dub attacking me and then killing himself. Dora. *Dora.* Petra killing a bunch of people and then herself. Then the man who killed me calling to let me know that part of him still holds a grudge.

I need time to think. Need to get some distance, some perspective.

The carton dings and I pull the tray from the packaging and use a tea towel to carry it over to the couch, tell the IMP to play a local news feed.

I sit in front of the wallscreen and mindlessly feed myself forkfuls of curried something while watching the world go to shit.

The mayor made a statement fifteen minutes ago that's

trending worldwide: in the light of Petra Anderson's rampage at an illegal shyft bar, and in response to the increase in crime and a blatant disregard for Standards from some members of the restored population, she has no choice but to push for a new tracking system, with awareness of location and activity, to be implemented in all Reszos, one that includes a remote shutdown to stop anyone out of control.

Galvan is at the press conference, standing arms-crossed behind Chaddah and Doyle and the minister of Standards and a bunch of other people I don't recognize.

Now Standards wants to track us. All Reszos under constant watch by Standards.

How's that going to help? Cyphers don't register with Standards in the first place. That's the whole problem.

This is absurd. I don't want Standards tracking my every move.

The mayor continues to drop bombshells, says she's also authorized an increase in Standards agents in the city, with heavy concentrations in the Market and Reszlieville.

She's bringing down the hammer. I can't tell if she's capitalizing on the events to bolster her reelection campaign in the face of a convenient tragedy, or a grieving mother lashing out at the death of her child.

Except her child isn't dead, he's still on storage at Second Skyn, and her convenient reelection platform means trampling on the rights of a few hundred thousand of her citizens.

The link has blown up, both vocal cons and very vocal pros.

I get why the public's outraged, as with any tragedy there's the knee-jerk urge to overreact. Launch a new "War

On." People are scared. They want to feel safe and they'll sacrifice another slice of their freedom to get it. Except in this case most of the people getting behind this idea won't be under threat of a government employee accidentally switching them off.

And most of this is my fault. How many of the latest Standards offences or killings can be tied back to me, one way or another? Probably more than I even know.

What if I just gave up, went back into storage? Would Ankur's fragment give up too? Or was it the fragment that brought me back from the dead? What if it'll never let this end? Am I trapped in an endless cycle of death and rebirth that we'll be forced to play out forever?

Jesus, what if Buddha was right?

I shake my head. I'm being dumb. There's nothing metaphysical about this. No karmic retribution at play. This is a man-made problem with a man-made solution. Neural impulses that lead to action with no regard for consequences, and nothing more.

What I need is information, I need to be proactive. Find the fragment before it can hurt anyone else. And it looks like Elder is the key to all this. I need to know where he's been. Better yet, where he is. It also wouldn't hurt to know more about this Ankur. Where he came from. How to contact him.

I need help.

And I just happen to have the answer man on speed dial.

I get the IMP to leave Saabir a message, but his perfectly coiffed image appears on my wall almost instantly. seven in the morning and he's dressed for dinner.

"Ahh, my favorite pro bono client," he says with a smile.

"I thought I was paid in full, services rendered," I reply.

He laughs. "Correction noted. Apologies. As it happens, I had planned on contacting you later this morning."

"You have something?"

"I have been in contact with the Police Service and with a representative from Standards, and they assure me you aren't under active investigation."

"Agent Wiser said different."

"That doesn't mean you don't have an open case file. It's just currently a low priority."

"So I'm off the hook for whatever I did to get kicked off the force?"

"Unless you give them reason to turn their attention back to you. Which you seem to be doing your best to accomplish."

"Trouble follows me around."

"So it would seem. But you contacted me, so, Mr. Gage, how may I be of assistance?"

"I need you to look into some people for me," I say, and even if I couldn't see him on the screen I'd be able to hear his eyebrow arch.

"Can you be more specific?"

"Elder Raahmaan."

"Your former Restoration Counsellor."

"And someone named Ankur."

He's silent for a long second, then says, "A name derived from Sanskrit, meaning 'sapling' or 'sprout.'"

"If you say so."

"I understand your connection to Mr. Raahmaan, but may I ask the nature of your interest in this Ankur?"

"He killed me once. Twice, maybe. Probably trying to again."

"I see," he says, then purses his lips and takes a heavy breath.

"I will endeavor to be as useful as possible, of course, for I am in your debt. And while I do perhaps possess lines of enquiry that go beyond what is available to you, I would caution you against setting your expectations too high for what little I may be able to uncover. What is it, exactly, you would like to know in regards to these two men?"

"Current location, mostly. Where they've been. Who they've been with."

"I see," he says, and seems like he wants to continue but hesitates.

"What?"

"If I am to be completely transparent with you, I don't believe I will be any more successful in my enquiries than you."

"So you won't help me—"

He raises his hands. "I mean only to suggest, if I may be so presumptuous, that you have resources at your disposal that outstrip mine."

"What do you mean, 'resources'?"

"You were a member of the Toronto Police Service, were you not?"

I see where he's going with this. "They don't let you keep playing with the equipment when they kick you off the team."

"And you have no connections to that time? No one you still may trust?"

"My partner, but he's dead." The only other person I know is Special Agent Galvan Wiser and he's the one holding my case file open.

"When I contacted the Service Liaison I was directed to

an Officer Karin Yellowbird. She seemed...sympathetic to your situation."

Yellowbird. She had lingered behind after Agent Wiser's visit. She did say we'd been friends. Top-secret friends if we had.

"You think she might help me?" I ask.

"You won't know until you try," he answers.

After a night of desk-bound uselessness and wasted time by myself at home this morning, I'm actually looking forward to counselling.

Elder has a hard time holding the meeting together. The feeds have been wringing the story like a wet towel and the arKade is all everyone wants to talk about. How did I single-handedly take out those Past-Standard skyns? Were there really human-animal hybrids? Torture stations?

Even Miranda can't completely feign disinterest.

Only Carl and Elder avoid the topic, and I know Elder's just doing a professional-level job of hiding his curiosity. Sensing we're not going to get much done tonight, he ends the meeting early, and while the others congregate at the snack table, ready to hammer me with questions, he preempts their fun by dragging me across the gym and making it clear no one is to follow. They watch us from a distance, clearly put out.

Dora's been sneaking glances at me all night. She was the first thing I noticed when I walked in. No one remarked on it, but she had ditched her usual conservative black, flat-soled shoes for a pair of calf-length silver boots that look brand new.

There's been a change in her, subtle but distinct: her contributions more open, maintaining eye contact, laughing with the group. She even shared about visiting the Hereafter on her own.

She's waiting for me now, biding her time by insinuating herself with the rest of the group and nibbling on the edge of a chocolate chip cookie held gingerly on a square "Happy Birthday" napkin. I'm surprisingly eager to talk to her too.

It's been a few days since we last spent time together and seeing her again reminds me how much fun I had. She's been the one spark of color in my otherwise gloomy restoration.

I smile at her over my shoulder and raise a finger, asking her to wait, as Elder leads me away.

"I thought I'd spare you their questions," Elder says. "And I wanted to speak to you privately."

"So you could grill me yourself?" I say. Actually, I'm keen to hear what Elder has to tell me. He's going to have a unique take on what went on at the arKade. He smiles, but there's a sadness to it. "I can't say much, it's an active investigation."

Secretly, I'm glad for the distraction. I'm in no rush to get to work. I've got another night of spectating ahead, sitting back at camp while the strike teams are out hunting. They hauled in four more cyphers today. By the time I'm back on active duty there'll be none left.

"So you met Kade?" Elder asks.

"You know her?" I counter.

"Only by reputation."

"She was wearing a beaver skyn, sic'd her goons on us."

"I don't think she would have let anyone hurt you. She was a pacifist at heart, at the forefront of expanding the boundaries of what it means to be human. A true revolutionary."

The only boundaries she was straining against were the bounds of sanity. "She had people in boxes eating each other."

He sighs but gives a slight nod. "I am aware of the practice. You witnessed a portion of the Bright initiation ritual— a symbolic shedding of the flesh—designed toward becoming an acolyte of the Transhumanist faith. First you are eaten, then you eat someone else, then you eat yourself, and in the end, you are freed from the flesh."

I shake my head. The world is going insane. "Sounds fucked up," I say.

He strokes his jaw. "I'll concede, on the face of it, the process may appear extreme. But no more extreme than transcending the bonds of humanity."

Something about the way he answers makes me think. I drop my voice, lean a little closer.

"Have you done it?" I ask.

"No," he says quickly, then looks away as if embarrassed. "I have not yet been called as an acolyte."

"Wait—but you would? If you were called?"

He presses his lips together. "If I were called—"

"Shit, Elder," I mutter. I'm repulsed by the very thought of cannibalism, and he's sad no one's offered him a turn yet.

He nods, accepting my judgment. "Progress is messy, Finsbury. It is violent. Just like with Kade. I didn't always agree with her methods, but she and I, we were on the same side. We believed the same things."

"You didn't see what I did. If that's the future of humanity, I want no part of it."

"We each must follow our own paths, Finsbury. Kade believed, as I do, that we as a species can be so much more than what we are, and worked toward that goal every day of her life."

Something in his words catches me off guard. "What do you mean *'believed'*?"

He checks over my shoulder. Only Shelt, Dub and Dora are left, and Dub's lofted Shelt up in a chair with one hand while actively pressing a reluctant Dora to climb up as well.

"A woman was murdered in South Africa last night." His voice gets quieter. "Emily Castor, an Australian national."

"And?"

"And I believe Emily Castor was Kade."

Could that be possible? Kade did abandon hundreds of millions of dollars' worth of equipment and skyns when we busted in on her party. If it didn't belong to her, the loss may well have made someone angry. Angry enough to kill over. If it's true, that's another life I can add to my tally of sorrow.

"What makes you think that?" I ask.

"A number of disparate elements, admittedly, but together they add up to a solid hypothesis. Emily Castor was an outspoken proponent of rithm rights—the Kade persona echoed many of the same themes."

"That's thin."

He holds up a long finger. "There's more. Kade constantly updated her feed. Religiously, you could say. It hasn't changed since just before Emily Castor was killed. Additionally, it's been reported that her apartment had a state-of-the-art telepresence installation. The kind that would be necessary to operate a skyn from halfway around the world."

"Still, that doesn't mean—"

"You said Kade was wearing a beaver skyn. Do you know what genus the beaver belongs to?"

I shake my head.

"Castor."

Shit. I got someone else killed. She didn't deserve to die. Even if she was on Standards' most wanted list. Even if she was a criminal. "Even if this is true," I ask. "Why tell me?"

"Kade saw her arKade as an art project and a social movement and a political statement all rolled into one, but she had backers—it was a profit generator for them, nothing more. The raid called attention to it. Attention I'd imagine her backers didn't appreciate, and didn't want to see spread."

"So they had her killed to limit their exposure." Just as I thought.

"It's possible. There are also rumors—very quiet rumors, mind you, but rumors nonetheless—that certain shyfts were discovered to contain a Trojan, and were possibly linked to a series of robberies." He lets the statement hang.

DeBlanc and the others. Other people knew about that too. "And they think she was involved?"

"I don't believe she had anything to do with it, but who is to say? A scorched earth response is indiscriminate in its collateral damage. But if they came after her, who knows who else they may believe a threat."

"You think they might target me?"

"I can't say. I wouldn't expect so, I just wanted you to know the possibility exists."

"Do you know who her backers were?"

"I don't. No one seems to for sure. There are rumors, but nothing more."

"Xiao?" I ask. He nods, once, quickly.

"Who else?"

"Joachim Mata, the Brazilian billionaire. It's said he has ties to the Amigos."

"We nabbed a few of their skyns yesterday." He nods again.

He runs through a few more names, each of them with ties to one of the Five Marks. I can't imagine I'd be a target of this specific retaliation. If Kade's backers were looking to avoid attention, the last thing they'd want to do is assassinate a police officer, but then again criminals aren't exactly known for carefully considering the consequences of their actions.

"Thanks, Elder," I say and look over my shoulder. Dora's the only one left, loitering by the doors. Elder sees me looking at her, gives me a sly grin.

"I need to ask you something," I say.

He looks me in the eye, strokes his chin, like a father having "the talk" with his teenage son. "We have no provisions against dating within counselling—it isn't necessarily encouraged but..."

"Dating—what?"

"You and Doralai—"

"No, no. Jesus, it isn't that." Heat is spreading up my cheeks. Why am I embarrassed? We haven't done anything. And even if we had... "xYvYx," I blurt, "do you know him?"

He tilts his head back, narrows his eyes. "The rithmist?"

"Yeah, he was working for Kade."

"Yes..." he answers hesitantly, drawing the syllable out.

"What do you know about him?"

"I know that he's very talented, very opinionated, and no stranger to scandal. Finsbury, I'm..." He pauses. "Why do you ask?"

"I can't tell you," I say.

He gathers his thoughts, then says, "I've never met him

in person, but I know him by his reputation. He is intently interested in the inner workings of the link, in the fables and the superstitions, and has a sizeable following. And he is a substantial rithmist, especially for a non-Reszo." He narrows his eyes. For the first time since I walked into counselling I can't tell what he's thinking. "Is that what you wanted to know?"

"I want to know if you would trust him."

He considers for a moment then says, "The xYvYx I know may be talented, but has only his self-interest at heart. I cannot speak to his current state of mind, but if you have entered into some kind of dealing with him, I would advise caution."

I'll be cautious, but I don't have any choice but to trust xYvYx. I need the ReCog and don't see any other way to get my hands on it.

"Thanks, Elder," I say. He squeezes my shoulder and walks past me to clean up the snack table.

I take a moment to catch my breath and meet Dora at the exit.

"That looked intense," she says.

"He was trying to keep the group from putting the screws to me."

"And what if I were to try putting the screws to you?" she says, suppressing a smirk. She's flirting with me. I'm all at once flattered and excited and ashamed of myself for liking it. I can hardly believe this is the same woman who couldn't lift her head to make eye contact two weeks ago.

"You'd get a pass," I reply, noncommittal, and push the door open for her.

"Thanks again for the other night," she says, and curls her small hand around my bicep as we walk out into the night air. It's cool for April and she pulls a little closer, just for a second, before releasing my arm and stepping back. "It meant a lot to me. I feel so much more—at home—with myself."

"I'm glad," I say, trying not to think too much about her, about the tingles I got when she pressed herself against me. "I enjoyed it too."

"Maybe we should do it again? I think the more I'm exposed to new things, the easier everything will be."

"Sure," I answer, without thinking. Before my brain can list the half-dozen reasons it's a bad idea. I know I shouldn't be getting close to her, but with everything else in my life in such a shambles, I need something positive to look forward to. "I'm on nights, so how about Thursday, after lunch? We can meet back in the Hall of Eras, see what interests us."

"Sounds lovely." She arches up on her tiptoes and gives me a peck on the cheek, then turns and hails a passing Sküte. She rides away and I start walking toward the station, butterflies trilling in my stomach, fluttering about in a pool of guilt.

Karin Yellowbird isn't surprised when I pop up on her tab. She gives me shit for not calling her sooner, and agrees to meet me at a diner on King Street after her shift without asking why.

I get there early, find a booth in the back and wait, wondering whether she'll come alone or if Agent Wiser will be with her.

When she does arrive, just a few minutes after I sit down, she isn't alone. But it isn't Wiser that follows her in. It's a tall black guy, bundled for the weather—the forensic tech from Dub's crime scene.

Yellowbird spots me and throws back her hood, stamps her boots on the entrance mat, struts down the narrow aisle and slides in across from me. The tech pulls off his toque and gloves and stows them in the large pocket of his parka.

"I thought you'd never call," she says with a grin.

"You brought a friend," I say, looking at the tech. He's standing beside the table, smiling down at me, his eyes wide with delight.

"That really you, Fin?" the tech says, then reaches out

and touches my cheeks, runs his hands down my neck and squeezes my shoulders. I pull away and he grins, turns to Yellowbird. "Now he's wondering if we used to make out." Yellowbird rolls her eyes and he sits back and whistles, long and low. "You were right, K. He *is* pretty."

Yellowbird laughs. "Fin, this is Sam Omondi," she says as he slides in beside her. "We all used to be one big happy team."

"Some more happy than others," Omondi says, glaring at me, eyes bugged out.

"It's Gage now," I correct him. "Gage Gibson."

Yellowbird rolls her eyes. "Whatever. You're still you inside that skin-cream model, right?"

"I'm not sure I know anymore."

"Jesus." Yellowbird snorts. "Fin—*Gage*—whatever the fuck you're calling yourself these days. Knock off the morose identity crisis bullshit already."

"Fine," I say, a smile dragging on my cheeks in spite of myself. "Yeah. It's me."

"Was that so hard?" she says, then reaches across the narrow table and shoves me back into the padding. "It's good to see you."

"So we used to be friends?" I ask.

"In spite of yourself, yeah," she says. "You think we'd be risking a suspension by talking to you otherwise?"

"Right." I didn't even think about the risk they'd have in meeting me. "Thanks for coming. Did Agent Wiser give you any trouble?"

"Galvan?" Yellowbird says and rolls her eyes. "He's harmless. I don't report to him anyway. He moved over to Standards with everyone else when they came in and took over Fifty-Seven. I'm talking about Inspector Chaddah. She'd shit a peach if she knew we were here. She took it personally when you buggered off and got yourself killed. But enough about us," Yellowbird says. "What's going on with you?"

I don't even know where to begin. "Things have been...difficult."

"Difficult?" Yellowbird snickers. "No shit. Things were *difficult* for you the last time around. Now you have a whole load of new trouble dumped on top of all that."

Yellowbird stops talking as the server arrives with three big mugs of beer and places them on the table. Both she and Omondi stare at me until I pull out my tab and wave payment.

Omondi picks up his mug and drinks half of it in three big gulps, sighs, wipes his mouth with the back of his hand, then signals for three more before the server can walk away.

"Agent Wiser and I," I say, once the server is out of earshot, "what was our relationship like?"

Yellowbird scrunches her small chin and Omondi lifts his beer to his lips and keeps it there.

"You were working well together, mostly," Yellowbird says. "There was some tension at the end. You were running pretty hot. But then he got hurt pretty bad, and after that..."

"How'd he get hurt?"

"You'd tracked some of Xiao's men to a drone yard and he was injured in the arrest."

"He blames me for it."

"It wasn't your fault," she says. Then adds, "Not officially, anyway."

"Unofficially?"

She shrugs. "It was a firefight. Chain of command was in flux. He got unlucky. A step further back and he'd have walked away with a headache."

"But he blames me?"

"Oh yes," she says. "He'd be right pissed if he knew we were here."

They both came, even though it could cost them. This thing that happened between Galvan and me, maybe we can get past it. For both our sake's. If there really is a super-intelligence after me, I sure as hell could use Standards on my side.

"You think he'll make peace with it?" I ask.

"You'll have to prove we're right to be here, trusting you," Omondi says, and slides something across the table to me. A small data key.

I take it and hold it up. It's featureless, just a thin slice of plastic. "What's on it?"

"Security feed from the Fāngzhōu," Omondi says. "I think you'll find it interesting."

Hell yes I'll find it interesting. "What's on it?"

"You and Galvan had been working a case," Omondi says. "Xiao."

Fireworks ignite in my skull. That's who Petra was shooting at.

"I've heard of him," I say, downplaying all the times I've heard his name in the past few days. I want to trust them, but I'm still not sure this isn't one big setup. Wiser could be behind all of this.

"You had him on the run. You were close, too. He's been in the wind since that night," Yellowbird adds. "Guess who just happened to be at the Fāngzhōu last night?"

"Xiao," I say.

He was there. *I missed him.* I have the mayor to thank for that, although I also have her to thank for my skyn not being filled with holes right now, so I guess we're even.

"Got it in one," Omondi says. "Know who else was there?"

This one's easy. "Elder Raahmaan."

"Two for two," Yellowbird says. "You're pretty well informed for a disgraced ex-cop."

Omondi continues. "Now for the bonus round. Where else was Elder spotted recently?"

This one I can't answer, and shrug. He opens his mouth and leans forward, drawing out the suspense.

"Well?" I say.

"Leaving the scene of your friend Dub's suicide," Omondi says, then sits back and watches my reaction.

"How?" I ask, my head buzzing. But it makes sense. If Eka's fragment had inhabited Elder, he could probably have persuaded Dub to shyft. Opened Dub's head to infection.

Omondi pulls out his tab, spreads it and calls up a file. "We pulled this from the train that killed Dub. Ten point one seconds of video from the forward camera. One thousand two hundred and twelve frames." He steps through the video, narrating. "As the train starts crossing the bridge, two figures emerge from the trees alongside the tracks. What are they doing? It's so mysterious." One's huge and underdressed for the weather, obviously Dub. The other is smaller, wearing a black jacket and hat, calf-high boots, collar pulled up against the cold. Omondi taps the screen and continues. "They walk together to the tracks as the train approaches, what will happen next?" On the video the train's horn sounds as the duo moves toward the tracks, and the sound blares through the quiet restaurant.

Omondi cranks the volume on his tab down. "Sorry," he says, raising his hand and looking around at the other customers, who have turned at the noise. "My fault."

A cable hangs between Dub and Elder, joining them by the backs of their necks. "What's that?" I ask, pointing at the screen. The train's brakes squeal as Dub reaches the tracks and kneels, lays his head against the rail.

Omondi pauses the playback. "As far as we can figure, it's a SenShare cable."

"What's that?" I ask, looking back and forth between Omondi and Yellowbird.

"A SenShare cable," Yellowbird repeats. "You've never seen one? Reszos use 'em to share physical sensations, feel what the other person is feeling. Sex stuff, mostly."

"So they were sharing each other's feelings?" I ask, confused.

Omondi shrugs. "At this point, we don't know. I'm thinking they were lovers."

"I doubt it," I say as Omondi resumes playback and the train skids into Dub's face.

"You're sure that was Elder?" I ask.

"Bio/kin isn't enough for a match," Omondi says. "But ImageRec is eighty-four percent on it."

"Elder just watched as Dub walked in front of a train?"

"Looks like," Omondi says.

"Why would he do that?"

"That," Yellowbird replies, "is what we're hoping you can figure out."

DORA TOOK my hand as we balanced in silk shoes on the slippery rocks, watching milky water cascade over the Bakyeon waterfalls. I squeezed hers in return and held it as we walked back through the distance-condensed country-side to the high green hill overlooking Gaeseong, the capital city of Middle-Ages Korea, where we sat on the grass and watched the sun sink until, one by one, lanterns lit the windows of the wooden, slant-roofed houses surrounding the city-center temple.

During our walk she told me about her childhood fasci-nation with Korean history—the Goryeo era especially, when the Three Kingdoms had been united into what would eventually become modern Korea. Her father had gotten her started when she was very young, telling her bedtime stories of the rise and fall of kingdoms, people united by war and conquered by invaders.

One year she had been given a book of classic Korean poetry for her birthday, and she had read and reread it, poring over each description of those distant people and places until the pages had come loose from their bindings and had to be secured with a clip.

In the real world, Gaeseong had been cut off from South Korea when the Korean War ended. It was under North rule when she left the country with her parents, and even though it had been named a national historical site after Reunification, one of the best-preserved examples of ancient Korean architecture on the entire peninsula, she'd never been able to visit.

When she discovered that someone had created a virtual Era devoted to the Goryeo capital city, she said she knew immediately she wanted to take me. She'd had Aspects ready for the both of us, and we spent the balmy afternoon strolling around Korea circa 1010 AD while she pointed out details of the re-creation—and what the author had got wrong: the intricately beaded Hanbok worn by the noble women were incorrectly modelled after fashion from the Joseon Dynasty, a later period in Korean history; the casserole and beef tripe soup the locals were eating was accurate, though they wouldn't have had the umegi in the summer—the delicate sweet dough balls were reserved for holiday meals.

She's been beside herself with excitement all afternoon, dancing from one detail to another, marveling at the sounds and the smells emerging from the windows. It's easy to forget this is all taking place on a computer somewhere. That everything, the town, the forest beyond, the villagers shuffling about their lives, even Dora and I, is nothing but ones and zeroes imitating the real world. Imitating real people.

I'm happy to be led along and let her do most of the talking, to just enjoy her company. She doesn't say anything about the problems with her husband. I don't mention Connie.

It's easy, relaxed. Fun.

It also doesn't hurt that there seems to be progress, however slight, in other areas of my life as well. Last night, I tied a stolen shipment of organic precursors to the DNA of one of the cyphers the strike teams brought back. That'll give us more avenues of investigation, more potential charges. Not bad, considering I couldn't leave the station.

xYvYx should have my ReCog soon and I'll be one step closer to finding Connie's killer.

I've been doing double duty at work, running down leads, making the most of my desk-bound situation. Playing as a team. I'm not off Chaddah's shitlist yet, but hopefully it won't be long until I'm back out on the street.

All in all, a good afternoon.

"I should get back," she says, once the sun has dipped behind the mountains and the stars have fully bloomed, brilliant diamond pixel dust in the carbon-black sky.

She stands and brushes the damp from her skirt. I rise beside her and put my arm around her waist, rest my fingers in the small of her back. She closes her eyes, leans up and into me, tilting her lips to mine. Her mouth is smooth and firm, like I'm kissing warmed silicone, but it doesn't matter. We press together, clinging to each other in the artificial night, the real world and our real selves forgotten, then she steps back and slips her hands inside the folds of her wide sleeves.

"See you soon," I say.

She seems embarrassed but rolls forward for another brief kiss, flashes me a happy half-smile, then turns away, takes a step and vanishes back into her head.

I wait a moment and follow her out, slip into my Headspace.

There's a message waiting when I get there. From Inspector Chaddah, marked urgent.

I open it and my stomach immediately grows tight. I'm back into my body as fast as I can and head straight for the station. It's all hands on deck.

Kalifa Daar and her whole strike team have just been killed.

Standards will be taking over.

Now, for sure, Chaddah will have to let me off the leash.

IT ALL HAPPENED FAST. Daar's strike team had pinged a cypher, tracked it to a condo complex in the north of the city. The team went in after it, with Standards as backup, expecting the suspect to be alone.

They were wrong.

Four superhuman cyphers were waiting for them.

We watched the playback through the TAC team's body cams. They went in hard, following procedure, but still Daar and the strike team were slaughtered before any of them got a shot off.

Now I know how Galvan must have felt at the arKade, watching me kill with a sickening, casual grace. The cyphers moved the same way. An economy of motion. Every action deliberate, every shot precise.

Standards came in after, guns hot, and a single cypher held them off while the others escaped out the window—leapt across an alley to a neighboring roof and bounced into the night. Then the last cypher ate a bullet instead of letting himself be captured.

All that hardware, all that training and superior attitude, and Standards still let three deadly weapons get away.

We're all intimidated by these guys. But under all that fancy armor and expensive training they're still only human.

If I had been there— I could have helped. With what I'm carrying around in my pocket, I could have saved everyone.

Or at least made the fight a hell of a lot closer.

When I got the news, I went straight into the office to help maintain the strike teams, to show Standards we could still handle our jobs, to convince Chaddah I'm wasted on a desk, and didn't leave for nearly two days.

This morning, the inspector finally told me to take a break, go home and get some "sleep," but what am I supposed to do, go watch the feeds while these monsters are still out there, plotting to kill again?

No. I need to be doing something, and if Chaddah won't let me work at the station, I'll work on my own.

I go down to my locker, change into my running gear, pack a small bag containing my weapon and my cuff and the Revv shyft, strap my tab around my wrist and head out at a jog, watching the sweep app for potential bad guys.

I run for hours, well into the afternoon, zigzagging through the city from one side to the other, with no luck. I have nothing else to do and I'm not tired, have barely broken a sweat after a half-day of constant running, so I keep going, let my mind go blank as I put one foot in front of the other until finally, when my stomach starts complaining and I'm thinking about finding dinner, a red dot pops on my tab.

I clamp down on a cheer. Can't get ahead of myself, I have to be sure.

I get within sight of him but stay across the street, hang back and observe. The target's olive skinned and muscular under a short jacket and tight pants. He's moving with purpose but doesn't look particularly dangerous, doesn't meet the description of any of the cyphers who murdered Daar and her team. But he'll do.

I raise my tab and his silhouette glows deep red. Text appears on the screen next to him:

StatUS-ID: *Unknown.*

CYPHER PROBABILITY: 98.5%.

RECOMMENDED ACTION: *Detain Subject. Proceed with caution.*

Finally, some action.

He continues along Danforth Ave. and crosses the viaduct to the cluster of century-old apartment buildings in St. James Town. Two dozen high-rises packed with one of the highest population densities in North America. Mayors and city councils have repeatedly tried to redevelop the neighborhood, but the prospect of relocating thirty thousand low-income residents made the prospect a nonstarter, and no one's so much as floated the idea since the Bot Crash.

If I lose him in one of those buildings, I'll never find him again.

I retrieve my weapon from my bag and secure it in the waistband of my shorts, the grip nestled against my lower back, then take the Revv shyft out of a side pocket and squeeze it in my fist.

The cypher crosses Parliament St., cuts across a brown lawn and makes for one of the apartment buildings. I increase my pace until I'm only a few meters behind him, but he doesn't turn around and I enter the building after he does.

He punches a code into the lobby's inner door and it buzzes and releases with a clunk. I slip inside before it closes, and we're alone in the lobby.

He presses the call button then turns and looks me up and down, but his expression doesn't change. I'm no threat.

"Hey," I say, feigning a friendly neighbor, and he grunts in response. Just two guys waiting for an elevator.

When the dinged-up silver doors open, he goes in first, presses the button for twenty-two and leans back against the handrail. I punch twenty-five, stand back in the opposite corner and angle my head to watch numbers change as the elevator rises. I study him in my peripheral vision.

He isn't armed, but that doesn't mean anything. Can't tell a Past-Standard skyn just by looking. Could be he's capable of pulling my heart out of my chest with his bare hands. I have no idea.

The entire ride up he doesn't so much as flick his eyes in my direction.

When we reach twenty-two, he pushes off the back of the elevator and strides out. I wait a beat before jamming the elevator door open with my foot and sticking my head out. He stops in front of a door mid-way down the long hallway, knocks, and someone lets him in. He checks back over his shoulder before he goes in but I pull back into the elevator before he sees me.

I've got him. All I need to do is call this in and we can add another cypher to the books. I can tell Chaddah I stumbled across him on the way home.

I pull my tab out of my bag.

I should call this in.

I was wrong at the arKade, and didn't call for backup when I should have.

I've learned my lesson, haven't I?

But say I do call the AMP and let them know what's going on, what happens then?

A TAC team mobilizes. Standards suits up and tears in, shoots everyone up. They'll be craving a fight after losing last time.

Even then, coming in hot, they could still be outmatched.

Look what happened to Daar. Standards was backing *her* up, but she didn't stand a chance. No one does.

No one but me.

I open my hand. The Revv lies there, lightning flaring inside its sweat-slick surface.

I put the tab back in my bag and fish out the cuff, fix it to my neck.

Then I let the shyft into my head and step out of the elevator into the future.

THE CYPHER ENTERED a door about halfway down the hall. I need to get over there and check it out. Once I get close I'll decide on a plan.

I creep down the hallway, keeping close to the wall, stop at the cypher's door and listen.

There's music inside. Talking. Two distinct voices, a man and a woman. Plus muffled commentary in the background, a feed probably. The buzz of a cheering crowd rises. Sports of some kind. I settle in and wait for what feels like hours, but only minutes pass.

This is my last chance. I call it in now or deal with the consequences.

But I've already made up my mind. The only consequence will be one more cypher off the streets. One more inhuman monster who'll never hurt anyone again.

I reach out for the doorknob with my right hand. It's cool under my fingers.

I duck my head to keep my shadow out of the peephole as I gradually twist my wrist and unlatch the door. It isn't even locked.

With my left hand I reach around to the small of my back and grab hold of my weapon, but don't let it engage. If the gun powered up, the AMP would notice. It would call for immediate backup. I want to keep this as quiet as possible.

I take a breath, crouch and ease the door open. The feed commentary gets louder but no one notices the door moving, no one sounds an alarm.

Through the crack I see a tiny kitchen, wooden cupboards and brown laminate tile. Dirty dishes piled in the sink. The remnants of dinner in a big green pot still steaming on the stove.

There's still no response from inside.

I edge the door further, hand tight on my powered-down weapon, and glance once, see everything in a half-second. Jackets hang from hooks on the wall, a man's and a woman's. Two pairs of shoes on the parquet floor. A bathroom stands off to the left, towels neatly stacked on a shelf above the toilet, two toothbrushes in a blue cup next to the faucet.

Further on, the short corridor opens onto a wide room. An Orbitball match plays on the far wall: the Republic Halos versus the Serbian Electric. Serbia's winning four goals to three.

I can't see the cypher, but I can hear the clink of utensils on dinnerware, see the edge of a couch against the near wall and the man's elbow perched on the armrest.

I slip inside and close the door behind me, slide over into the kitchen.

Dinner smells like some kind of stew. Smoked ham. Potatoes. Paprika.

My stomach grumbles and I grab at my abdomen, wait for someone to come check it out, but the noise from the game drowns my hunger out.

The kitchen has another doorway leading out to the main room. A round table sits on the other side, its surface littered with shyfts, stacked cashcards, two handguns and a machine pistol.

I squeeze my weapon tighter but don't let it engage and power up, not yet. I take a breath and tip my head around the kitchen wall.

The cypher and a woman are sitting side by side on a long brown couch, eating from bowls while watching the screen. They have no idea I'm here.

A bedroom door stands open off the far side of the large room, the lights off. I don't think anyone else is here. I rise to standing, keeping my hand behind my back, fingers around my weapon, and step out into the living room.

I stand there long enough I could've killed them both twice by the time either of them notices me. The cypher turns his head, sees me and still takes an eternity to react.

"What the—" he says and lurches up. The bowl tumbles from his lap and the contents hang in the air as he slowly rises. I see him recognize me from the elevator, realize I must have followed him up, then flick his eyes to the weapons on the table beside me, figuring if he can get past me, get to one of them.

The woman sees me and bares her teeth, flexes her arm and screams as she hurls her bowl at my head.

The broth sloshes out, steam rising from it as it escapes,

momentarily weightless. Sprouts and pieces of flaked white meat rain down on the hardwood.

The cypher's turning, his hands balled, legs flexing. He's going for the guns.

Let him come.

I angle my head and the bowl sails by and shatters against the wall behind me.

The cypher has his fists up, raised in front of him like a boxer, his cheeks bunched, his lips tight. He takes two steps and throws his weight behind a right jab at my face. He has a scar over the second knuckle on his hand and his nails need trimming and he's already tensing his other arm to throw a left hook.

He'll never get that far.

With my left hand still behind my back, I step into the punch, let it sail past my ear, cock my head and snap my forehead down on the bridge of his nose. It crackles like wet celery and blood sprays the front of his shirt and before his face has registered the pain I've got my free hand around the back of his neck, fingers pressed against the subdermal disc at the base of his skull. He yanks back against my grip but I hold him steady while I drive my knee into his abdomen twice, hard enough I hear a rib snap, and on the third shot let him go. He staggers back into the woman's arms and they both drop to the floor.

Cypher neutralized.

Now to check on the woman. I let go of my weapon and hold my tab up and they both outline in red on the screen. 99% match.

Two cyphers for the price of one.

I really should call this in.

"Who da fug are you?" the cypher burbles through his broken nose. "Are you fade?"

"I won't go back," the woman says, her voice tight, cradling the cypher's head. She has a faint Eastern European accent.

I don't answer, take my bag off my back instead, open the zip and sweep the shyfts and cashcards and two of the guns into it, reseal it and shoulder it back up. I lift the third weapon, a Browning handgun with a holographic front sight, and point it at the cypher.

"Whoa," he says, raising his hands in defense. "You don't need to do dis. We'll come peaceful."

"No," the woman says, turning on the man, her lips trembling, "I'll die before I let him take me back there."

He puts his arm around her, keeps his voice calm. "Vjera, my love, don't fight. We can't beat them. I don't want to lose you—"

"Don't worry," I say, thinking about Daar. I may not have liked her much, but she didn't deserve to die. It was people like this who killed her, people who hide who they are. What they are. "I'm not taking you anywhere."

"Shoot us then," Vjera yells, thrusting her chest up at me.

The man pulls on her, raises his hand. "No, we're unarmed. This is murder."

"For this to be murder," I say, "you'd have to be human."

"What?" Vjera croaks. "We're as human as you are."

"Not according to Standards," I answer and put a bullet through the male's Cortex. Fragments of skull and blood and twinkling plastic splatter over her.

"Mato!" she cries, and her face screws up in pain and anger as she clutches the cypher's ruined face to her chest. "You killed him!"

I hear her words, understand their meaning. I ended the

existence of the entity she knew as Mato, but I didn't kill anyone. He was an illegal personality in an unregistered body. He was dangerous, just like all the others.

Just like her.

Just like the one who killed Connie.

"Mato was dead already," I tell her. "I put him straight."

"You have no idea," she seethes, her chest heaving. "What we had to do to get out of there, what we endured—"

He intensity unsettles me. She's terrified, and not of dying. "Out of where?" I ask, lowering the gun, just a little.

"*The Sudbina*," she says. "We'd escaped, finally escaped and now—"

Her face explodes in a blaze of blue-white light and I spin, weapon up, as the shot echoes in my ears.

I come to a stop with it pointed at the tall Nordic woman in the slate grey suit I saw last week in the station, the one who came to talk to Chaddah and left unhappy.

Her partner is behind her. He's got his weapon on me but he doesn't look like he wants to use it.

I didn't even hear them come in.

It's hard to remember the Revv doesn't make me invincible. I still need to pay attention. I'm hardly the only one amped up these days. And my advantage having the Revv won't last forever. Xiao released his new build at the arKade. They'll be hitting the streets. I need to be more careful.

"Mr. Gage," she says, holstering her weapon in a docker's clutch under her jacket. "We mean you no harm. Indeed, we're on the same side."

That remains to be seen, but if they were allowed inside the station, the Service must not believe they're dangerous. But the Service doesn't know everything.

"Whose side is that?" I ask, keeping my gun arm

straight, muzzle at her face.

She cocks her head at me, amused. "The side of the law. The side of humanity."

I don't understand. *"Who are you?"*

"We, Mr. Gage, are agents of Fate. We are here to help you apprehend the fugitive criminal known as Xiao."

My ears are buzzing with confusion and unfocused adrenaline. I just stalked and killed a cypher, off the books while Revved, and the Cortex hadn't hit the floor before someone claiming to be an agent of Fate told me she wanted to help me find Xiao.

I don't know if they're really Fate, but they *are* witnesses to my vigilante justice.

If they tell Chaddah I didn't call the cypher in, I won't be getting a third chance to disappoint her. She'll have me on my ass.

I'll lose my access to SecNet. Without it, even if I can pull the driver's image from my head when xYvYx delivers the ReCog, it'll be useless.

Chaddah can't know about this.

I keep my gun still, levelled at her head. "What the hell are you doing here?" I ask, leaning on the Revv to keep my voice from shaking.

"Pardon my manners," she says, flashing her intense blue eyes. "I'm Agent Sòng. This is Agent Minnaar. We are representatives of the Fate Corporation, and we have an offer to discuss."

Minnaar tips his head at me. I thought he might be Italian when I saw him in the station but up close he looks more Persian. Dark hair, thick eyebrows and a chiseled jawline. But they're obviously skynned, so who knows who's inside.

I flip my gun to my right hand and use the cypher sweep on them. Comes back negative, both of them outlined in green.

Rep-net doesn't show much about either of them, but it agrees on their identities. Min Sòng and Thato Minnaar, both private investigators employed by the Fate Corporation.

They may call themselves agents, but they have no legal standing. They're corporate stooges playing at law enforcement. Fate may be one of the richest companies on the planet, but that doesn't give them leave to conduct criminal investigations. Not yet, at least.

"You're here for Xiao?" I ask.

She raises a cheek at me. "Are you not searching for him as well?"

Say they are Fate, what's their interest in Xiao?

While Second Skyn perfected the recovery process that allowed digital immortality, they did so by focusing on restoring people to their old lives: creating fancy new bodies and the dream of a fresh start. But lots of people in the world could barely afford a good meal, let alone a few million to drop on a new body. For most, immortality was out of reach.

Until three years ago when Fate came along.

Fate took the recovery process and quietly dropped the restoration part. They offered cash-strapped governments the option to reduce healthcare costs and guarantee virtual immortality in the place of radical life extension programs. Or, for some countries, basic medical care.

The sick and dying liberated from their bodies,

converted to rithms, and allowed to live on in one of Fate's virtual worlds. Free. Forever. Medical bills go down and the sick never die.

Win/win.

Mostly.

Fate first launched their service in partnership with China, with a virtual world they called the *Yuanfen*, and the people who chose to live there, the people who made the impossible decision between death and "not dead," they called the *shù zì zǔxiān*.

Digital Ancestors.

But under their breaths, many still call the Ancestors *feng shua—empty words*.

There have to be millions of Ancestors by now. Hundreds of millions maybe. Fate doesn't release much in the way of details around its operation. No one's ever seen the inside of one of their virts. What goes on in the Yuanfen is a mystery to everyone except the millions of souls living there.

Fate operates in twenty- or thirty-odd countries and is growing all the time, adding more and more Ancestors every day. But that isn't why Fate is so powerful. They also operate one of the largest knowledge subcontracting services on the link. Work to keep all those idle minds busy. The Ancestors are free to hire themselves out. They write songs and create advertising campaigns and draw up architectural blueprints. All for pennies.

Fate handles the psychorithm recovery, maintains the servers and the workforce and operates the knowledge service exchanges. Everyone shares in the profits.

So far, the Union has kept Fate from opening here, citing their unwillingness to adhere to COPA laws and their unfair labor practices and the secrecy of their virts.

So far.

It's only a matter of time. Even the Union won't be able to afford reJuv for everyone indefinitely.

But none of that explains why Fate has agents on the ground in the Union. Or what they're doing here. Or why they want Xiao.

"Are you licensed to carry that weapon?" I ask, pointing the barrel of my gun at the bulge under Sòng's jacket.

She smiles. "Fully. Concealed permits. I can show you the documentation if you wish, Detective."

I flick my eyes at the female cypher, keep the gun steady. "Why did you shoot her?"

Sòng furrows her brow. "She was illegally skynned—"

"What does that have to do with *you*?"

"Mato and Vjera Dragovic unlawfully extricated their contractually obligated minds from the Sudbina, Fate Corporation's home for Serbian National Ancestors. They were, as you call them, cyphers. Dangers to the populace. Do you not have the same policy?" she asks, gesturing to Mato's shattered face.

We do, but for some reason it feels dirty admitting it to her. These two may have been cyphers, but they were also people.

Scared people.

"Protecting people isn't your job," I say.

"The safety of the populace is everyone's responsibility," she counters.

The thing is, I can't argue. Even if I was in a position to, I couldn't charge her with anything. The cyphers weren't registered with COPA, weren't *people* under the law. I couldn't even get her for property damage.

Instead, I change the subject. "How did you find me?"

"Fate has taken an interest in you, Detective Gage." She presses her lips together then purses them, as if practicing what to say next. "We followed you. Thought we might be of assistance." She looks at my gun. "You don't need your weapon, I assure you."

I hesitate, but if she wanted to shoot me, she could have before, when she first came in and I didn't notice. I drop the gun to my side, but keep my finger in the trigger guard. "What are you offering?"

"As I said, we're also investigating Xiao." The woman puts her hands behind her back, steps past me into the living room, kneels and prods immobile cyphers, dusts her hands and rises.

"Who's Xiao to you?" I ask.

"A dangerous man," she says simply. "A terrorist. He wants to see the world burn."

"Why?" I ask, looking between her and her immobile partner. He still stands in the doorway with a passive expression on his face, watching me.

She raises her shoulders, settles her face on puzzled. "Who can say why anyone does anything. Xiao's motives are inscrutable and frankly none of my concern. He is an escapee from the Yuanfen, and he is building an army. Does it matter *why* Genghis Kahn attempted to conquer the world? Or Alexander? Or Hitler? Their motives are inconsequential, what matters is the destruction they caused. The millions of lives they destroyed. I believe you met one of his soldiers yourself."

I did. The Past-Standard girl in the Market. She could have torn my head off. If Xiao has an army of skyns like that, he could hurt a lot of people. He could start a war. "How'd you know about that?"

"We have our resources, Detective Gage, which we'd

like to share with you, if you're amenable."

Am I amenable to assisting a secretive, multibillion-dollar international corporation hunt down a criminal fugitive bent on destroying the world? That's a hell of a question.

But I'm not the first person she's asked. "You already offered your assistance to the inspector, didn't you?"

She nods.

"And she turned you down, didn't she?"

She nods again.

The inspector must not trust Fate, or knows something I don't. Or is afraid to do what she needs to. If Xiao really is building an army, an army of these superhuman skyns, we need to do everything we can to stop him.

"Why do you think I'll help you when my boss wouldn't?"

"Because I believe you are more pragmatic than your superior. You want to do what's necessary, whether it's strictly right or not. As is evidenced here." She casts her eyes at the two cyphers. "I assume you haven't reported this."

I chew on my lip but shake my head.

She nods and glances at her partner, and he looks up and inward. "I thought not. Please, allow us to finish what you have started here. We are equipped to dispose of these bodies—if you'd permit us."

I hadn't gotten far enough into an actual plan to consider what I'd do with the skyns once I put the cyphers down. I figured I'd just leave them here, but then what happens when they're discovered? There have to be cameras in the lobby. Maybe they're working, maybe they're not, but if someone started looking it probably wouldn't be too hard to trace this back to me. I could call it in now but we're past that.

I should have called it in.

Next time.

"Okay," I say. "I'll let you clean up."

"And with Xiao?" she asks, the look on her face already knowing what I'm going to say.

"I'll help if I can. At *my* discretion."

Sòng clasps her hands together. "Of course," she says. "At your discretion. I have sent you my contact information. Please don't hesitate to use it."

I check my tab and there's a message from her, directly above one from xYvYx. I had the tab on DND, didn't even notice it come it.

He's finished the ReCog. It's waiting at a drone depot near my apartment. In less than an hour I'll have the means to identify the man who destroyed my life.

"I have to go," I say, swinging my bag around and depositing the gun inside with the others as I head to the door.

"We'll tidy up here," Sòng says. "I'll be in touch."

I leave without answering her, my thoughts already racing, thinking about the ReCog. I take the stairs instead of waiting for the elevator and bounce down twenty-two stories.

Outside I take off at a sprint down Parliament.

My apartment's only fifteen minutes away at this speed, and after a quick detour to the drone depot I get home and slot the ReCog without bothering to change out of my workout clothes, without reading the instructions xYvYx included, before I even sit down.

I leave Yellowbird and Omondi to finish the beers with the promise to share anything I find and head straight for the nearest drone depot, send the chip they gave me express to Shelt and message him to expect it.

By the time I get back to the apartment, slap on my cuff and arrange myself on the couch, he's messaged me back that the Fāngzhōu virt has been updated with the new feeds I sent, and I cast in. He's in there waiting, shows me how to use the playback controls and leaves once I kick the virt into life.

The chip Omondi gave me contained eight hours of security feed from four different cameras around the Fāngzhōu, enough for a complete, lifelike re-creation.

I stand in the middle of the club and skip through the first few hours, watch the staff dash through setup, watch the lights dim and bouncers set themselves up and the customers fill the tables.

A man in a black suit—one of Petra's security team—enters and the bouncer doesn't move to intercept him. He does a tour of the club and then finds a corner to occupy.

Petra and Vaelyn come in to warm greetings from the bouncer and move directly to the table where I talked to them, Vaelyn's she-goons tromping along beside them. Petra's other bodyguard comes next and does a reverse sweep and blends into the shadow on the other side of the room.

No one seems concerned or excited. As far as I can tell, this is a routine that's played out a hundred times.

Then Elder walks in. I slow the feedback right down and walk beside him as he weaves through the tables and shuts himself in a private booth in the back of the club. Once he's out of sight I speed it back up and watch the door until he pops out, takes a cautious look around the club and retreats back to hiding. This happens twice more and then I see myself enter, head to the bar and carry my dusty beer to a table and sit.

I stay back with Elder, deja vu-ing myself finish the beer. When Elder next emerges and scans the club, his head stops pointed straight at me—the me drinking—then he stands in the shadows, watching.

The woman from the mayor's office enters the club next —her black hair the color of dried blood under the red lighting—has her argument with Petra and Vaelyn then storms off.

That's when the virtual me gets up and moves to Petra's table.

Elder twitches. He takes a step forward but when he sees where I'm headed stops again. Waiting. Biding his time.

Vaelyn and I go through our routine. Then Petra's guards step in and put an end to it. She sends them away and we talk.

When the conversation finishes and I get up to leave,

Elder starts toward the other me and I follow. I don't see a weapon. His hands are empty but he's moving to intercept me, and just as we make eye contact, I'm neuralized.

I can feel the indecision in Elder's body. Whatever his intentions were they've been blown. He hesitates for a second, watching as I'm dragged away. His eyes flit between me and Petra and he comes to some decision and hurries to Petra's table. I stick close behind him.

The noise in the club is too loud to hear what they're saying, but it's clear from the looks on their faces that Petra and Vaelyn are surprised to see him.

There's a brief exchange, Elder is talking fast, exasperated. He wants Petra to come with him and finally, over Vaelyn's objections, she does. Vaelyn wants to join them but Elder convinces Petra that she needs to stay here and Petra gets her to agree.

Elder leads Petra back to the private booth and closes the door behind them.

They stay in there together for seven minutes, then the door opens and Elder makes a line straight for the exit, keeping his head down.

Petra emerges a moment later, unsteady on her legs, a burned out shyft in her hand. She seems to remember the shyft, looks at it once and then drops it on the floor with the other discarded caps and carefully walks back to her table.

Vaelyn starts into her, questioning. Petra doesn't engage. Just sits and lets Vaelyn's words bounce off the side of her head. Eventually Vaelyn gets tired of being ignored and spits an insult at Petra and gets up to complain to her goons. Petra stays in the same place. Not moving. Staring straight ahead. Until something across the room catches her eye that energizes her like she just jammed her fingers into a charging station.

I pause the playback and follow her eye line to the employees-only entrance beside the bar.

The door is open and bright white light spills out from inside. A small Asian woman—a girl, really—her hair cut short, dressed in loose-fitting grey pants and a leather jacket, holds the door for a much older woman.

She's wearing flowing black pants and a white-and-silver jacket that matches her silver-grey hair. Her hands are folded inside her broad sleeves. Wrinkles line her face but she moves with the grace of a dancer. I couldn't begin to guess her age. Say a hundred, plus or minus forty years on each side.

At the back of the group, a compact bald man with angular features scans the crowd. He doesn't speak to anyone, keeps in ready position on the balls of his feet as his eyes flick from face to face. His clothes are an indistinguishable color in the red light of the club.

In between them, a man moves through the room like a politician, stopping at each table just long enough for a smile or short exchange of words. He seems like he owns the place, which would make him Xiao. He's dressed simply but elegantly, in a tailored suit with the back collar popped, crisp white shirt tinged pink by the club's crimson light. He has a thin moustache and a smear of whiskers across his chin. There's a smile on his face that doesn't reach his eyes.

Between Xiao and the man at the end of the line is a familiar face. It's the kid.

Ankur.

Then Petra starts shooting.

She's disabled her bodyguards, stolen their weapons.

Her shots are wild, but she's aiming for either Xiao or Ankur.

The man at the back of the line draws a weapon from

inside his flowing clothes and returns fire, then barks something and the girl in the leather jacket hurries everyone back toward the open door. Xiao puts himself in front of Ankur and the old woman, shields them as they escape.

More shots are exchanged. Everything I watched at Shelt's but this time with the back half of the room filled in. I still can't tell if Petra's aiming for Xiao or Ankur or both of them. Finally they make it to the door and Xiao gives one last scowl at Petra before the small man puts the last bullets into her.

By now the room is quiet and her final words echo in the empty club.

I'm next.

I don't bother watching again. Just stand amid the carnage as victims bleed out on the floor, writhing in pain, gasping their temporarily last breaths.

I can't explain what I saw, but I know whatever's going on, Elder's at the heart of it.

That fragment's in him. It almost had me, and when it missed, it took Petra instead.

If what Ankur said is true, and that fragment of his former self can jump from skyn to skyn, it's likely there's a tainted shyft behind it. Something that'll let the fragment gain access to its hosts. Something that Petra would have had to agree to let into her head.

Seven minutes in a room, and Petra willingly put a shyft to her cuff and let the fragment occupy her. It was that easy.

I think back to Dub, to his frustration in the alley as he tried to force me to ack that shyft.

If I'd said yes, thought green, the fragment would've had access to my mind. Been able to manipulate it. Who knows what a pissed off superintelligence would do with the mind that made it mad.

Or why, if the fragment is after *me,* it would bother to infect Petra and try to take out Xiao. Or was it aiming at Ankur, its new incarnation?

How am I supposed to understand the motives of a vengeful supercomputer? How am I supposed to fight it?

I did though, once. Back when the fragment was attached to something much more powerful. If I were able to find it again—could I somehow clear my name? If everything I did last time was because I was hunting for a super-intelligence...that would go a long way toward explaining my actions. Maybe get my rep back.

Maybe get my life back.

I come out of the virt into my Headspace, blinking my simulated eyes at the change in simulated brightness and send a message to Omondi, asking him, if he hasn't yet, to check out all the dead shyfts on the floor near the booths and see if anything out of the ordinary shows up in the code residue. And that he's looking for one with Petra's finger-prints on it.

If Elder is possessed by Ankur's fragment and jumping from skyn to skyn, that shyft could be the key.

I move over to the waiting representation of myself sitting on my couch back in my apartment, get control of my skyn's arm and pull the cuff off.

My apartment snaps back into existence with Dora standing in front of me.

Back at the apartment, anticipation trilling through me, I ack the ReCog and get ready to finally see the face of the man who killed me.

A console appears, a flat slab of simulated controls hovering at my waist. A large three-dimensional display curves behind it, occupying a third of my vision, and shows an infinitely recursive image of what I'm currently looking at—the console overlaid my living room with a 3D image of my console overlaid with my living room over and over until it's too small to make out. I turn my head and the tunnel into reality swims and I have to hold my eyes still to keep the nausea at bay.

Instinctively I cast my thoughts back to walking in the door, and the display changes to show me that, the screen a window into my memory. The controls allow me to set tags, move backwards through my ride up the elevator, my trip home in the Sküte. Lets me freeze and zoom in on faces in passing cars, creep the memory ahead slowly, rotate it to the extent the capacity of my stored memory allows.

I get it. Now to find what I came for.

I think back to the accident, hit a moment just before we caught up with the UV, force myself to fast- forward past the images of Connie, past the UV hard-braking, and slow it down just as the van rounds the bend ahead of us. Then I creep it forward, step-by-step at the millisecond limit of my memory's frame rate, until the driver is visible. I mark it there and inch forward until the face is no longer clear, place an endpoint and tell the console to save, render out a vid.

Moments later, I have a point seven second clip of the man who killed me. The man who killed Connie.

It's all been leading to this. Everything I've done. The rules I've broken. Even going alone into the arKade helped get me here. I'm so close.

I ignore Chaddah's directive to stop using Service resources for my personal investigation, call up the Service AMP and ship it the vid, tell it to run an enhancement and then a bio/kin lookup. I don't bother watching it myself. I've seen it enough already.

It takes one minute and thirty-seven seconds to come back with a 99.7% probable match, shows me a Second Skyn record. A bit-head.

The man who killed us was restored too.

His name is Amit Johari.

I've found him.

A sob wracks my chest. Erupts in a fissure of compressed joy and grief and anger and explodes out my mouth.

My eyes blur, but even through the tears I can't stop staring at his Status-ID image. His eyes are vacant, lifeless, just like the first time I saw them. His skyn is light brown with a wide brow and a short sweep of jet-black hair. Slight but handsome in a square-jawed, full-cheeked, Bollywood-extra kind of way.

I wipe my eyes with the back of my hand.

Amit's Second Skyn image is completely motionless, except for the blink every twenty seconds, twenty seconds exactly.

Blink.

He doesn't look evil. Doesn't look like a killer, like someone who would maniacally blast through the lives of seven random people.

Blink.

I've finally found him.

I'm elated, ready to act, my head light. I did it.

Now that I know who he is, I can figure out where he is.

I pull my eyes from his, tell the AMP to bring me every-thing publicly available on him, and when it returns, it comes back with more than thirty thousand hits. I get the AMP to summarize and it still takes three hours to skim through Amit's story. I even vaguely remember reading about him before the accident.

Amit Johari was a superstar programmer on the compet-itive coding circuit, the first person ever to win the Prime Coder championship in each of the ten years he was eligible to compete.

There are hundreds of profiles on him; tens of thou-sands of individual mentions across the link; hours of video that highlight his brilliant, time limit-obliterating solutions to programming challenges, or situations where he created an entirely new programming language on the fly to develop the optimal solution to the supplied problem. He took the championship every year in a career that spanned a decade and earned him millions in prizes and sponsorships.

All the attention he received wasn't notable only

because of the sheer number of wins, or the decisiveness—
he did it all while being severely autistic, unable to care for
himself, to dress or feed himself, to express himself in any
conventional way. He could speak computer in every
dialect, with every accent, but was unable to carry on the
simplest conversation with another person.

Amit Johari went digital on his twenty-fourth birthday
—and in certain circles it was a very big deal. Not just
because he went digital, but because his restoration utilized
a new technique designed to normalize the "damaged" parts
of his brain, to purge the autism from him—to make him just
like everyone else.

He disappeared two months after his restoration, never
to be seen again.

Until the day he killed Connie, me, and five other
people.

That's him.

That's fucking him.

I'm burning.

I've never wanted to hurt anyone before, but there's a
rage in me I've never felt before. I want to find Amit Johari
and beat him until he no longer exists. Erase him, like he
erased Connie.

Soon.

As soon as I find him. I check SecNet, but according to
Second Skyn's location awareness system, his skyn went
offline for a good three weeks before the accident. There're
only two hits for him anywhere on the link or SecNet or the
Service archives afterwards.

The first is a missing person's report filed by his father a
week after the accident, just about the time Connie would
have had her funeral.

The missing person's case never went anywhere, which isn't surprising—most Reszo disappearances are seldom pursued very hard. After all, no one's really missing. There's still a copy of the person safe and sound at Standards, regardless of where the latest restored version got to.

The second is a message. Only two words, sent from Amit Johari to *me*, less than twenty-four hours after I died. It's been sitting unread with the hundreds of other condolence notes I archived when I was first restored.

It just says, "I'm sorry."

Who is this guy? Why would he go on a murderous rampage and then send out an apology afterwards?

I run a trace on the message but it leads nowhere. Just a dangling port somewhere in the link.

Playing a hunch, I get the IMP to cross-reference Amit's communication records with Woodrow Quirk's—the coder whose van Amit had been driving—and plug in the missing person's case file number to get authorization for the warrantless search. The connections light up. They'd been in contact for months before the accident.

Then I try it the other way, running Quirk's communication logs for any reference to Amit. It comes up empty. If all you did was search Quirk's history, you'd never know he and Amit had contacted each other at all. Nothing would lead an investigation in Amit's direction.

Communication logs erased. Visual evidence snipped from the link. However impossible it seems, it might be doable for a man who can speak code.

And those messages I've been receiving. The threats. They have to be coming from Amit. For whatever reason, all the time I've been searching for him, he's been searching for me too.

I haven't found him yet, but I'm getting close.

Amit's last known address is his parents', in one of Boston's outer burbs. Close enough I can hop out there and be back for the rundown in plenty of time.

I link as Gibson and start charting a hopper.

I COME out of the Fāngzhōu virt and back into my living
room to Dora watching me.

Seeing her standing safely in front of me causes my
Cortex to spray out a wash of relief and guilt and annoyance
that combines with the residual virtspace disorientation to
momentarily short circuit my nervous system. All I can do is
sit and stare at her.

Dora looks at me funny, squinches her eyes, then
rummages through her big bag and pulls out two caps, their
displays glowing a shimmering purple-pink. She presses one
to her cuff and her whole body relaxes. The bag slides from
her shoulder and lands on the floor with a thud.

What does she think she's doing? We don't have time
for this.

Her throat catches and she takes a step and sinks into
my lap, straddling me, her knees squeezing into my thighs.
She smells of lilac and a subtle musk that blooms in my
throat and makes my mouth water in spite of myself. Heat
flows off her in waves, as if from a furnace barely contained.

She leans forward, into me. Her breasts press into my

chest. Lust rises in my groin. She bears down on me and the pressure becomes fierce and even as part of me knows this is wrong, wants to tell her to get off, that I'm married, I close my eyes, grab her ass and pull her tighter.

I don't want this, in my head anyway, but I can't help myself. My body is reacting to her, overriding my protests.

Her breath caresses my neck as she reaches around and presses the Bliss against my cuff.

WOULD YOU LIKE TO ACCESS THIS DEVICE?

Green and red, yes and no.
Do I want this?
I lost Connie only three days ago. Three days. Since I watched her die. Since I woke up someone else.

I promised to be with her forever, thought I would be. How, in three days, did I end up here, with this woman I hardly know grinding on my lap?

Except it hasn't been three days. Connie's been dead more than a year. I grieved for her, I'm sure. I know because I still am, because I feel her loss like a fresh wound.

But I started something with Dora. I chose this once. I may barely know her, but she's not a stranger. She knows me. I gave her access to my apartment. This is something I wanted. If I started it once, why shouldn't I want it again?

I don't know who I'm supposed to be right now. Am I me or am I him or is there even any difference?

I glance down at the green dot, feel it swell. Dora's lips trace the skin of my jaw, kiss up my cheek to nibble my earlobe.

A shiver runs from the base of my skull to my tailbone, shoots down my arms and explodes from my fingers as tiny fireworks of pleasure.

Why not let this happen?

The green dot ripens through teal to aqua and zooms toward deep blue.

"Think green," she whispers, her voice smoke in my ear.

And as she does, something makes me twist my head. I break contact with her and the cap, and the balls vanish.

This isn't right.

This isn't something I want. This is what Finsbury wanted.

I'm not him, not anymore. I can't live his life.

Besides, I don't know if I can even trust her. I still haven't figured out what she's hiding.

"I'm sorry," I say, easing back. Take my hands off her, put them at my sides, flat on the couch. "I need to take this slow."

She's breathing hard but doesn't object, just swings her leg over me and flops down at my side, head on my shoulder.

"Where have you been?" I ask. "I was worried."

"Laying low," she says, her voice slurred at the edges. "I've gotten good at it."

I'M COMING FOR YOU, Amit.

I'm out of my apartment and heading down the hallway toward the elevator when my IMP chimes through: Dora's downstairs. She wouldn't just show up unless it was something important. I tell the building to let her in, put a hold on the hopper, retreat to my apartment and answer the door when she knocks.

She doesn't say anything. Just stands there on the threshold, jaw set, cheeks flushed, chest heaving, eyes expectant. Her low-necked white workout tee is soaked with sweat, her red jacket unzipped, her usually neat hair in windblown disarray.

It looks like she ran here.

She steps forward and raises herself into me, wraps her arms around my neck, presses her chest into mine. I have a second to consider what's about to happen and then her lips are on me, her fingers in my hair, nails scraping my scalp, dragging my head down into her.

My head rushes, bombarded by everything that's happened over the past weeks: the ever-present grief, fighting against the revulsion at my new existence, the superhuman high of running Revved, the draining uselessness at work, the elation at finding Amit—and now Dora.

I kiss her back, cup my hand under her, lift her off her feet. She wraps her legs around my waist and I carry her into the apartment, kick the door shut behind me, walk us to the bedroom. She barely weighs anything.

Her kissing becomes fierce, biting my lips, grinding herself against me, and I drop her to the bed, fall on top. She pulls my shirt and jacket off, ignoring the buttons, ignoring the tie, everything straight up over my head, fumbles with my belt before I take over and she whips off her thin jacket, then her shirt. She isn't wearing a bra. Her breasts are small, firm, damp with sweat.

I'm hard for the first time since my restoration. She grabs me, strokes once and my knees buckle. I've never had a foreskin and the sensation is so intense, I nearly pass out. She yanks down her pants, sinks her nails into the flesh of my haunches and pulls me into her, makes a noise like she just impaled herself on a shockwand and doesn't stop.

I thrust five times and explode with a flash that knocks out my vision and severs the ties between my head and my body and I collapse onto her, unable to move, unable to think, exhausted and blissed out, but ashamed of myself.

We lie there without speaking, me still inside, her trailing her nails up and down my back until I start to grow again and she rolls me over and this time it's slow and intentional.

I close my eyes, and imagine I'm with Connie.

NEXT IN THE LOST TIME SERIES_

RITHMSYNC

Lost Time: Book 3

Finsbury Gage will find the answers he seeks, tempt Fate, and learn nothing is as it seems.

Discover the truth as the Lost Time series continues with Book 3: RITHMSYNC.

If you've enjoyed these books, please do me a favour and consider leaving a review at Amazon. A few words from you could help someone else decide to take a chance on me. I appreciate it.

GLOSSARY_

Words and terms from the world of Lost Time.

AMP. (Artificial Mind Pattern) Advanced neural
   code approximations running on cortical
   processors. They are classified
   as *superintelligences* but their use is governed
   and their operating code secured. Only licensed
   government agencies and select corporations are
   allowed to employ AMPs. The Ministry of
   Human Standards is responsible for monitoring
   and tracking down illicit use whenever
   discovered.

BioSkyn. An artificial, lab-grown body.
   Components printed a layer of cells at a time
   and then assembled and implanted with an
   optical processing Cortex.

Biosynth. Someone who uses geneblocks to

assemble unique, life forms—bacteria capable of operating to order to create atomically precise circuitry, manufacture drugs, enhance the immune system or replace biological functions. Plants that grow directly into furniture. Or wholly fabricated animals for domestic or military uses.

Bit-head. Xero. Sudo. Derogatory slang for a restored personality.

Bright. An extropian, far leftist, digital human philosophy. Brights believe in a creator of the Universe—or 'the system'—and that humanity is one of a billion billion probable physical manifestations of rules that began to play out at the moment of creation. God didn't create us, but it allowed the conditions for us to exist, like a scientist fine-tuning an experiment, and humanity its results.

Continuance of Personality Act. The set of legal guarantees allowing for the transfer of a consciousness from organic to digital.

Cortex. Second Skyn's in-house neural prosthetic. Now common slang for any neural prosthetic.

Cortical Field. The composite image of a scanned consciousness. Since consciousness is stored holographically, the stronger the field, the stronger the fidelity to the original personality.

Cypher. A rithm without an official restoration record from the Ministry of Human Standards.

Digital Life Extension. Extending a human consciousness past brain death as a psychorithm. The personality is captured, translated to a psychorithm and the resulting rithm loaded onto a prosthetic mind implanted in a bioSkyn. The Continuance of Personality Act provides digital humans with all the legal rights of a fully organic human, while Human Standards laws limit the extent to which digital humanity can augment its existence. DLE is fraught with political and social turbulence.

Dwell. A simple shyft that allows the user to speed up or slow down stored memory playback.

Fate. The rapidly growing corporation bringing immortality to the masses and hiring out low-cost knowledge work, all while reducing governmental expenditures around the globe.

Fleshmith. Someone who uses modified geneblocks and scaflabs to produce designer bodies and organs.

Genitect. Someone who architects and encodes custom genblocks, the genetic code building blocks used to form the genomes of synthetic life forms.

Headspace. A digital human's customizable home running onboard their prosthetic brain.

The Hereafter. The brand-name of a virtual reflection of the real world, where digital humans can visit the living. It is the largest, and most populous, digital virt.

Human Standards. The legal baselines limiting human life extension, physical augmentation and neural enhancement.

IMP. (Intelligent Mediating Personality) Originally designed to assist with daily communication, the IMP's capabilities quickly expanded to become a full-fledged digital assistant that learns over time. Upgradable with personality sprites.

The Link. The worldwide stream of conversations, sensor data, cameras, feeds, virts, games, and everything else that arose from the internet.

Lost Time. The minutes or hours of memory between personality back-ups lost due to a pattern decoherence or Cortex damage.

Lowboys. A gang of low-rep petty criminals. Kids, mostly.

Ministry of Human Standards. The government agency tasked with enforcing Human Standard laws.

Neurohertz. (NHz or N) $1N$ is the average speed of human neural processing. Human Standards limit the function of prosthetic brains to $1.15N$.

Past-Standard. The only Human Standard criminal offence. Past-Standard encompasses everything related to genetic augmentation and manipulation of a mind or body past established human norms. Past-Standard Offences and Psychorithm Infractions often intersect, causing friction between investigating agencies.

Prodeo/Prodian. What digital-only personalities against the restrictive Human Standard laws call themselves: Homo Prodeo. From the Latin "prodeo": to go forward, and "pro Deo": 'before' and 'the supreme being.'

Psychorithm. *The Conscious Algorithm.* The human brain's self-sustaining, recursive algorithmic neural code translated into digital.

Psychorithm Crime Unit. The Toronto Police Services unit responsible for investigating crimes by and against the local Reszo population.

Psyphon. To extract a rithm from its Cortex by force.

Recovered. A psychorithm is recovered from a dying or unhealthy brain and imprinted onto a cortical field.

ReJuv. The genetic reset performed once a year through the intravenous injection of a gene-regulating cocktail.

Rep. The cumulative social reputation earned by a personality on the link. Also known as Social Faith.

Restored. Layering a recovered cortical field onto a prosthetic brain. Also a common identifier for a digital human.

Reszo. Slang for a restored personality.

Revv. A shyft that allows the user to bypass human-standard neural governors and run their rithm higher into the NHz range. The effects are limited only by the hardware.

Rithmist. Someone who hacks the psychorithm. From manipulating autonomous and emotional responses all the way to enhancing or creating new cognitive abilities.

Second Skyn. The global leader in digital life extension. In defiance of global courts, Second

Skyn opened its first facility in a small South-East Asian country that had more pressing concerns than enforcing soon-to-be-outdated UN cloning laws. Once Personality Rights legislation was enacted, Second Skyn formally opened in Toronto, Stockholm, Seoul and Dubai, then expanded around the world as demand grew.

Skyn. Slang for bioSkyn.

Scafe. An illegally copied or hastily created skyn.

SecNet. The interconnected web of cameras, sensors, and databases that comprise the backbone of the North American Union's security and surveillance infrastructure.

Shyft. Slang for Neuroshyft. General consumer term for a neural state overlay. One-time-use code snippets legally sold to temporarily simulate drunkenness, enhance pleasure, dampen fear, or one of a thousand other emotional flavours. Much more powerful illegal versions also exist.

StatUS. Formerly a governmental organization, StatUS was spun off as a private company and is now responsible for providing and maintaining identification for all Union citizens and visitors.

I'm a geek from way back. I grew up on Star Wars and Blade Runner and Green Lantern and Neuromancer and every other science fiction and fantasy book I could get my hands on.

I wanted to write for as long as I can remember. My first story was a Moonlighting fan fiction, though I didn't know that at the time. Back then I was just ripping off the TV show.

Thanks for reading. If it weren't for you, I wouldn't be able to keep doing this.

I'd love to hear from you. Email me at damien@damien-boyes.com, or come say "Hi" on Facebook, or sign up to my Reader Club for the occasional email treat.

Printed in Great Britain
by Amazon

38699775R00165